PAST PRAISE FOR THE AUTHOR

For *Song of Isabel*

"The setting and political intrigue are unusual and appealing...
Readers looking for a change from Regency and Victorian
romance may find this a worthwhile diversion."

—*Publishers Weekly*

"Set against the backdrop of the Frankish Empire, Curtis, with
her captivating storytelling, brings to life a world filled with
heroic battles, distinctive characters and high-stakes tension
that will keep readers turning the pages."

—*RT Book Reviews*

"Set against the historical backdrop of France in 825, Curtis' novel
is a classic tale of high drama and romance ... an easy-reading
traditional love story with a romantic, nostalgic setting."

—*Booklist*

"In this romance, a spirited young woman meets her match in
a stalwart soldier during the turbulent times after the death of
Charlemagne ... An old-fashioned love story in an unusual
historical milieu."

—*Kirkus Reviews*

THE NUN'S BETROTHAL

THE NUN'S BETROTHAL

A NOVEL

IDA CURTIS

SHE WRITES PRESS

Published 2020
Printed in the United States of America
ISBN: 978-1-63152-685-5
ISBN: 978-1-63152-686-2
Library of Congress Control Number: 2020900198

For information, address:
She Writes Press
1569 Solano Ave #546
Berkeley, CA 94707

Interior design by Tabitha Lahr

She Writes Press is a division of SparkPoint Studio, LLC.

All company and/or product names may be trade names, logos, trademarks, and/or registered trademarks and are the property of their respective owners.

This is a work of fiction. Names, characters, places, and incidents either are the product of the author's imagination or are used fictitiously. Any resemblance to actual persons, living or dead, is entirely coincidental.

At the beginning of the ninth century, the Frankish Empire included territory that is now France, Belgium, the Netherlands, Germany, Switzerland, Austria, and half of Italy. King Charles, or Charlemagne, as he became known, ruled this vast empire. He had been crowned Emperor of the Holy Roman Empire by Pope Leo III, making him both king and emperor.

In 814 Charlemagne died, and his son Louis took his place. Unlike his father, Charlemagne, who encouraged his daughters to have children out of wedlock, Louis was committed to the Christian view of marriage. He became known as Louis the Pious, and by 827 his influence on marriage was felt throughout the empire.

PROLOGUE

Aquis, 827

"Justin, what are you doing here?" Isabel's exclamation caused Gilda to whip around to stare at the familiar figure.

"I had a long ride. I wanted to cool off in the pond," Justin answered his sister as he stared back at her companion. He had seen Gilda without her nun's habit only once, and he remembered the way the tops of her rounded breasts had been revealed by a low-cut bodice. But her golden hair had always been under a head covering. Now it hung over her shoulders and almost concealed the shape of her breasts under the shift that was still wet from her recent swim.

"We didn't expect you until tomorrow," Isabel said as she hurried to stand in front of him and block his view of her friend. She lowered her voice to whisper, "Stop staring at the poor woman!"

"Poor woman? She's a nun and should know better than to cavort around in her shift." He grinned at his sister, who was doing little to repair her own state of undress. "At least she seems to be more modest than you are."

Because he didn't bother to whisper his reply, Gilda heard every word. She pulled her plain brown gown over her shift and quickly wrapped her hair in a head covering. Justin had a talent for irritating her, and today he was doing an even better job than usual.

Once presentable, Gilda stood up to him as effectively as possible, considering the fact that the top of her head barely reached his shoulder. "Nuns have been known to enjoy a swim from time to time, Justin. A gallant lord would withdraw when he came upon such a scene."

Ignoring the implication in her words, his eyes roamed over her dark clothing with distaste. "So, you're still a nun. Taken your final vows yet, Sister Gilda?"

Without answering him, Gilda spoke to Isabel. "I'm going to go ahead and change my clothes. I'll meet you in the great hall."

Once Gilda was out of sight, Isabel turned on her brother. "Why are you always so rude to her? I suspect you care for Gilda more than you're willing to admit."

Justin shook his head back and forth. "You're misguided, Isabel. Ever since Gilda and I met a year ago in Aachen, you've plotted to bring us together. This latest ploy of naming me god-father and her godmother for your firstborn is your most obvious attempt. You are wasting your time. Gilda and I are completely unsuited in every way, and we're smart enough to know it."

"Is that why you can't take your eyes off her?"

He was disconcerted to realize she spoke the truth. "A man can feel a completely inappropriate attraction to a woman. Don't read too much into it. And don't forget your friend is a nun."

"As you've guessed, she hasn't taken her final vows," Isabel replied, her eyes sparkling with humor. "I wonder why that's the first thing you asked her?"

⸺∘◌◯◌∘⸺

As Gilda hurried toward the manor, she thought about Justin's question. She hadn't taken her final vows, but she didn't wish to give him the satisfaction of hearing her admit it. He had implied more than once that she wasn't serious about her vocation.

Being a nun gave her a degree of freedom that other women only dreamed of. There was no husband or father to obey, no children to take care of, and no manor house to supervise. She had no intention of giving up that freedom.

During the last year, she had been too busy to think about her vows. Helping the women who came to the convent for refuge took all her time and energy. The Abbess of Saint Ives, who encouraged her work, had not pressured her to finalize her pledge to God. But she did plan to do so soon. In any case, what business was it of Justin's?

Gilda suspected the reason he brought it up each time he saw her was because they had recently been on different sides of a domestic dispute. Justin had defended the right of a nobleman to put aside his errant wife, and she had worked on behalf of the woman. The last time they'd met, he had accused her of using her vocation to influence the bishop they were reporting to. She grinned as she remembered the case and admitted to herself that his accusation was true.

The next afternoon, Gilda stood beside Justin as they became the godparents for the daughter of Isabel and Che-twynd, Gilda's brother. She stared at the chubby infant who seemed to stare back with large, solemn eyes, and something stirred inside her. At the convent Gilda often helped mothers with their children. At no time had she experienced anything resembling the pull she felt toward little Natalie as she became the child's godmother. She imagined the strength of her emotion had to do with the fact that she loved both her brother and his wife very much.

When she felt Justin's elbow jab her shoulder, she glared up at him, then realized that Father Ivo had been speaking to her. She was familiar with the ceremony and nodded her head to show she was aware of her responsibility as godmother. Isabel placed Natalie in her arms. Charmed by the soft warmth of the little bundle, Gilda smiled at the babe who looked up at her with an expression of complete trust.

Justin followed Gilda when she left the church. He thought she looked a little dazed. "Want to go for a walk?" he asked.

She nodded before realizing he must have caught her in a weak moment. The last thing she desired was to be alone with Justin, but she had agreed, and she didn't want to make a fool of herself by changing her mind. Instead she said, "You didn't have to poke me so hard. Your elbow is a dangerous weapon."

"I thought nuns were supposed to pay attention when a priest is speaking."

"You seem to think you know a lot about nuns. For your information, we're not that different from other people. We swim in ponds and lose track of what's going on, just like other women."

Justin thought about how she had looked soaking wet with the sun shining on her hair and her shift clinging to her body. She was wrong about one thing; she had looked very different from any woman he had ever seen. He shook his head to dislodge the disturbing picture that kept pushing into his thoughts.

"Where are we going, Justin?" she asked, not bothering to disguise her impatience.

He wasn't sure. His only thought was to get her as far away from the other celebrants as possible, although he couldn't have said why. When he realized he had headed toward the pond, the scene of the vision he couldn't shake, he decided it was best to walk elsewhere.

"To the vineyard." He changed direction as he answered and asked, "Have you always wanted to be a nun?"

The man was obsessed! "No, of course not. I was eight when my father sent me to the Convent at Saint Ives to be educated. When I was twelve, he found me a husband and proposed a match. I pleaded to stay at Saint Ives another two years. The count he wished me to marry had children almost as old as I was, and I didn't look forward to becoming his wife. Fortunately, my father did not force me to marry.

"By the time I was fourteen, when another match was proposed, I had decided I wished to stay at the convent. I enjoyed my life there. My father, who thought it might be to his advantage to have someone praying for him, agreed."

They had reached the edge of the valley and stood looking down the hill. Rows of grapevines extended as far as they could see. It seemed natural to stop and view the long, straight lines of green foliage. Gilda dropped gracefully to the ground, pulling her skirt around her raised knees. After a moment's hesitation, Justin sat beside her.

"Speaking of marriage, what about you, Justin? Have you and Lady Lilith decided to marry?" Gilda knew from Isabel that they had been lovers for some years. She could see from his darkening eyes that he didn't like personal questions.

"We never had plans to marry. The lady is a widow with two sons who wishes to protect their inheritance by remaining a widow. The arrangement suits us both, since I have no need of a wife and no intention of taking one."

"Most of the king's ministers are married. I've heard he prefers it that way. A very proper king, which is why we call him Louis the Pious."

"The king has done a great deal to support the Christian view of marriage, as you well know. That doesn't mean I have to adhere to his wishes in my own personal life."

Gilda turned away to hide her grin. "You seem a little sensitive. You were asking me personal questions. I didn't think you'd mind answering a few yourself."

"Lady Lilith and I have an understanding. There are advantages to having a friendship with a woman. As a nun, you probably wouldn't understand, Gilda."

Justin leaned back on his elbows, knowing he sounded defensive and not wishing to meet her eyes. From his position behind Gilda, he could see a lock of her golden hair that had come loose from her head covering. Without giving his action much thought, he reached up and pulled her head covering off.

Gilda whipped around and gave him a shove that sent him onto his back. He could see surprise in her blue eyes, but he also thought he saw something that looked like curiosity. He reached up, wrapped her hair around his hand, and pulled her on top of him. He could see it now. Definitely curiosity. He pulled her face closer and kissed the lips that were about to open in protest.

The firm lips under hers moved in a seductive manner that Gilda found enticing. She had always wondered what a kiss would be like, but she hadn't imagined it could send intriguing flutters to other parts of her body. She moved her lips against his, and the feeling increased. She heard a soft moan and wasn't sure whether it was in her throat or his. When Justin's lips became more demanding, Gilda forced herself to pull back.

Justin saw the startled look in her eyes and released her immediately. "Did you find the answer you were looking for?" he asked as she pushed herself to a sitting position.

"I don't know what you mean," she replied as she concentrated on pushing her hair under her head covering.

"Come, Gilda. Nuns don't lie," he said, his words reminding him who she was. "You were curious. I wondered what you thought."

"It was a pleasant kiss." Gilda told herself that an understatement wasn't a lie. "I guess I can understand at least one of the advantages of the friendship between you and Lady Lilith."

"Pleasant." Justin repeated the one-word description before laughing. He stood up and offered her his hand. "I'm more than happy to assist with your secular education, Sister Gilda."

Gilda ignored his mocking tone and his offered hand. An innate sense told her it was best not to touch him again so soon. She had learned that touching Justin had a disturbing effect on her.

"I don't think I'll be in need of any further education from you," she managed to say as she struggled to her feet.

"You'd better take your vows soon, Gilda," he warned.

CHAPTER ONE

Convent at St. Ives, 828

Striking the dry earth with her hoe, Sister Gilda continued the tedious chore of self-imposed penance that she had begun several hours earlier at daybreak. Since Gilda was a well-liked and respected member of the community, her toil raised some eyebrows, but no questions were asked. That didn't mean that the reason for her penance wasn't a source of speculation by more than a few who watched the young nun turning soil in the convent garden.

The Convent of Saint Ives was located south of Aachen, the location of King Louis's favorite palace. It was a teaching convent run by the sisters of the Holy Cross. Young girls came to the convent to study, some staying to become nuns and others returning home to marry. Although Gilda was well past the age when the decision was usually made, she had not taken her final vows. She had chosen to stay at the convent and become a teacher. Her capability had led to other assignments that gave her a chance to travel beyond Saint Ives.

When a nun approached Gilda to tell her she'd been summoned by the abbess, she was only too happy to lay down her hoe and clap the dirt from her aching hands. She was still brushing dust from her dark habit as she hurried into Abbess Ermguerrd's workroom. But her step slowed when she saw the familiar figure standing to the right of Mother Superior. Gilda had hoped and prayed she'd never lay eyes on Lord Justin again.

There wasn't a hair of his abundant brown locks out of place, a fact that reminded Gilda that she had pushed her head covering out of the way while she was working and hadn't bothered to readjust it. His doublet was a fine blue cloth perfectly tailored to his tall, well-formed body. Before Gilda looked away, she saw a hint of a smile twitching at the corners of his mouth as he took in her rumpled appearance. After one last vigorous brush at her habit that left the brown material swirling around her legs, Gilda lifted her chin and looked to the abbess for an explanation of Justin's presence.

"I believe you know Lord Justin, Gilda."

Finding her throat dry from the dust, Gilda nodded.

When they first met in Aachen, she had been dressed in an elegant gown to disguise the fact that she was a nun. It was a strategy she had used a few times when she needed to blend into the court scene to gather information to help one of the women she was representing. At the time, she couldn't help but enjoy the admiration she had seen in his eyes. But later, when Justin learned she was a nun, he had made his displeasure at her deception clear. She remembered the words he'd spoken to her brother Chetwynd: "Your sister should get herself back to the nunnery." And although the hostility between them had lessened when they next met, they remained uneasy in each other's company.

The abbess ignored the young nun's cool reaction toward their visitor and said, "King Louis has requested your assistance,

Sister Gilda. No doubt he remembers the last time you mediated a dispute."

Gilda stole a glance at Justin and waited for Ermguerrd to continue.

"The case concerns Lady Mariel, the young woman who came to us a month ago for a religious retreat. When it was time for her to return home, she told us that she feared for her life. We gave her shelter. It seems her husband, Count Cedric, has applied for a divorce. The king is reluctant to see the marriage of one of his counts dissolved. He has requested that you assist Lord Justin in mediating the matter."

The end of a marriage between two noble houses often had far-reaching political implications. It was not unusual for the king to enlist someone from a religious community, as well as a secular representative, to make inquiries. King Louis was determined that his subjects adhere to the Christian practice of marrying for life. But even he recognized that sometimes there were extenuating circumstances. In such cases a bishop or archbishop could annul a marriage.

"I don't know Lady Mariel well," Gilda pointed out. "Perhaps you should find someone to take my place, Mother Ermguerrd."

Clearly surprised by her words, the abbess stared at Gilda for a minute before saying, "The king asked for you by name, Gilda. I suspect he is pleased with the way in which you represented the church in the past. Besides, there is no one else as well equipped for the task. I'm sure Countess Mariel will be comfortable with you."

Although flattered by Ermguerrd's words, Gilda felt reluctant to be involved with Justin again. "Isn't the Bishop of Mainz the most appropriate person to examine the matter?"

"Of course. But the bishop has close ties to Count Cedric. They rule Mainz together. The king believes that any findings from you and Lord Justin will be free of prejudice. You will report to Archbishop Humbert of Reims, who will make the final decision. That way Bishop Gunthar does not need to be involved."

Justin, who had been silent since Gilda entered the room, spoke directly to her, forcing her to look at him. "I told the king you might be reluctant. But he insisted that I try to persuade you. Perhaps you can suggest an alternative from Saint Ives to take your place. I will make up an excuse for you and give it to the king."

His reasonable tone and offer to speak to the king on her behalf annoyed her. Just like him to try and take charge. She had a blistering reply on the tip of her tongue but suddenly became aware of Ermguerrd watching her. "There is no need for you to speak for me, Lord Justin. You may tell the king I will accept the assignment."

Lord Justin frowned. "Investigating this matter will require that we journey to Mainz." He took a step closer to Gilda, and she had to fight the urge to step back. His voice lowered as he asked, "Are you sure you wish to do that?"

Refusing to be intimidated by his nearness, she replied, "Yes, I'm sure." Her words sounded weak in her own ears, so she added in a stronger voice, "I look forward to seeing Mainz."

Ermguerrd cleared her throat and brought their attention back to her. "Perhaps I should speak to Sister Gilda alone for a few minutes, Lord Justin. You know the way to the dining hall. You will find a refreshing drink there."

When he was gone, Ermguerrd gestured for Gilda to sit and then seated herself behind her worktable. She glanced at a piece of parchment before her, giving them both a minute to think, and said, "Clearly there are strong feelings between you and Lord Justin. Do you wish to tell me why that is?"

"Justin and I clashed often during the recent domestic dispute you referred to, Reverend Mother. It's only natural that there be some tension between us."

When Gilda realized that Ermguerrd was waiting for her to continue, she added, "We seem to have completely different outlooks. Lord Justin, an advisor to the king, is one of his most powerful ministers. He looks at everything from a political point of view. My own sympathies are more directed to mending emotional problems than worrying about avoiding a political crisis. I suppose it's natural our views are different."

"And yet you held your own in your last assignment. The solution to the affair seems to have pleased the king. Perhaps it's a mix that makes for a fair outcome."

"Yes, in the end a compromise was reached," Gilda admitted.

Ermguerrd nodded. "Your different outlooks account for some of the tension I observed. It might also account for why the king wishes to pair you. He will receive a well-rounded report."

Ermguerrd paused, and Gilda knew the observant abbess wasn't finished. The nuns often jested about the fact that Mother Superior could read their very soul. "Your brother is married to Lord Justin's sister. I remember Lord Chetwynd and Lady Isabel well from the time they spent at Saint Ives. Their marriage gives you a more personal relationship to Lord Justin, does it not?"

"Yes. You could say that."

"You recently visited your brother's manor for the christening of their first child. Was Lord Justin there?"

Gilda closed her eyes for a minute, remembering the christening of little Natalie, the sweetest little babe she'd ever seen. It was an emotional event that had filled her with wonder. "Yes, he was there."

"Did you and Lord Justin have a disagreement?"

Gilda sighed, eager to confess and be done with it. "Yes, and it was mainly my doing. I have often been outspoken, something you know I have been struggling to control."

Concealing any surprise she might have felt, Ermguerrd said, "I know you have had problems in the past. But I thought you were doing well. What happened?"

Isabel shook her head, wondering if she could make Ermguerrd understand the situation. "The atmosphere at Aquis is different from anything I've experienced. Isabel and Chetwynd are extremely fond of each other. It's evident to everyone. They touch each other all the time. And when they aren't touching, they look at each other in a certain way. It's been that way from the first time I saw them together."

"Yes, I think I understand what you're saying. Go on."

"Justin and I went for a walk after becoming godparents to little Natalie. Isabel fancies herself a matchmaker. I'm sure she's the one who arranged for me to be the godmother and Justin the godfather. I was feeling very moved by the christening, and I believe Justin was also touched by the experience. There seemed to be a bond between us, and we kissed." Isabel paused, wondering again at her action. "It didn't last long."

"How did you feel about the kiss?"

"I didn't like it."

"Really. You were repulsed?"

"No." Gilda wondered if she could put her feelings into words. Ermguerrd had a reputation for helping her charges. Now that she had started, Gilda was eager to be as truthful as possible in hope of some insight on the matter. "What I didn't like was the loss of control. There was a melting inside me. I forgot everything but my desire to continue the kiss. I wanted to get closer, but Justin pulled away."

Ermguerrd looked toward heaven for a few minutes as though searching for help. Facing the young nun again, she replied, "You are the most honest person I've ever known, Gilda."

"Is it natural for a kiss to have that power? I felt like I was losing myself."

"Yes, sometimes it is. Usually it's not thought of as a problem. But I can understand how in this case you might see it as such."

"Of course it's a problem. I'm a nun."

Ermguerrd nodded her head and smiled. "I know that."

Gilda was puzzled by her amusement. "I haven't seen Lord Justin alone since the kiss. Can you find a reason to withdraw me from the assignment? I was goaded into accepting when he offered to make my excuse to the king."

"I'm not sure that's the wisest plan . . ."

Gilda jumped to her feet. "But Mother Ermguerrd . . . I'm sorry. I shouldn't have interrupted."

Ermguerrd smiled. "Gilda, you've been with us since you were eight years old. You found a place for yourself quickly. I remember how upset you were when your father wanted you to marry. I supported you when your father wished you to marry when you turned twelve and again at fourteen. I know you enjoy the freedom you found here. But I think you have to experience a little more of the outside world before you make your final commitment to be a nun."

Disappointed, Gilda moved to look out the window into the courtyard. "I thought you were happy with my work here. I love teaching the children."

Ermguerrd came up behind her and put her hands on her shoulders to turn her around. "I've been most happy with your teaching. But you have other gifts as well. I think it's too soon for you to make a decision. Many of the women who take holy orders have lived in the secular world. Some have even been married. From what you have told me, I believe you need more experience in order to know you are making the right choice."

Gilda pondered her words. It was common knowledge that Ermguerrd had been married and borne two children. When her husband and children died of a fever, she'd entered the convent. Gilda had heard that she had served happily for many years before being named abbess. She believed Ermguerrd was the wisest woman she'd ever known.

"You look concerned, Gilda. What's bothering you?"

"It's that kiss. Maybe if it happens again, I won't have the same feelings. Maybe I was reacting to the christening. Do you think that's possible?"

Ermguerrd paused before replying, taking time to choose her words carefully. "I suspect it's something you are destined to find out. I know you like to be in control, Gilda. But sometimes things happen that are beyond our control. I will send Freda along as your companion."

"Freda? Is she the best person to send?" Gilda was reluctant to point out that Sister Freda seemed rather old to be of much help.

"Don't be fooled by her age or fierce manner. Sister Freda is most rigorous, and I think you will find her a useful companion."

When Justin was called to rejoin the abbess and Gilda, he was startled to hear that Gilda would be accompanying him to Mainz. He tried to hide his surprise from the abbess, especially when he saw that her eyes were studying him in a new way. Before he could figure out what that meant, he was introduced to Sister Freda, a nun twice Gilda's size and perhaps three times her age.

"Sister Freda will accompany Gilda. As I'm sure you know, Lord Justin, nuns always travel in pairs to ensure their safety," the abbess said.

Justin suspected she was referring not only to assuring their physical safety but also to safeguarding their reputation. The deep lines on Sister Freda's face attested to her age, but her posture was upright and her eyes penetrating. Justin judged she would be a reliable chaperone.

Later, following Gilda along the garden path to the chapel for vespers, Justin finally had a chance to speak to her alone. "I thought you'd convince the abbess not to send you with me. I'm sure you tried. What did you tell her?" he asked, remembering how Abbess Ermguerrd studied him.

"I told her about the kiss," Gilda said, not bothering to lower her voice.

His shock made her smile, but her expression quickly sobered when he grabbed her arm and pulled her into a small alcove in the garden. "Are you mad?" he asked, barely controlling his anger. "If you told her that, why is the abbess allowing you to go with me?"

Shaking off his hand, Gilda replied, "She thinks I need more experience in the secular world before I take my final vows."

"And I'm the one who's supposed to give you experience."

"Believe it or not, this has nothing to do with you. I told her about the kiss because I wanted her to know why I hesitated to accept the king's assignment. That's what we do here. We're honest with each other."

He ignored the implication that it wasn't true of his calling. "What kind of nun are you? You should be saying prayers and helping the poor. Instead you're at court, dressed in a low-cut gown. Or getting involved in arguing the very personal details of a marriage dispute before the bishop." He kept his voice low but didn't try to hide his anger.

When Justin saw that Gilda was staring at him, her mouth hanging open, he couldn't believe his own lack of control. He was a diplomat with a reputation for keeping his temper and being careful with his words. It was not a good sign that Gilda was able to make him lose control. He pulled her down to sit beside him on a bench.

"You caught me off guard," he said, as calmly as he could manage. "I can't believe you told the abbess I kissed you. You told her that, and she's still letting you go with me?"

"Yes. You don't have to worry about your reputation. I explained that the kiss was my fault."

He watched her face flush to a becoming shade of pink. "It was your fault? What makes you think that?" he asked.

"You knew I was curious. Otherwise it wouldn't have happened."

"I wouldn't be too sure of that, Gilda. I have an urge to repeat the kiss so that you'd remember it more clearly. You better think about that. Then persuade the abbess to send someone else. Otherwise you are taking a chance that I might lose control of myself."

He narrowed his eyes and tried his best to intimidate her with his frown, but she only shrugged her shoulders and said, "You're making that up to frighten me off."

"No, I'm not. You should be frightened. Right now, there are nuns everywhere." He looked around. "And we are just outside the chapel. That won't be the case on the road to Mainz."

"Sister Freda will be along," she answered, but he suspected she was beginning to lose her confidence.

Before Justin could reply, Freda appeared before them. Gilda grinned, clearly satisfied that her sudden appearance was a sign of her vigilance. But Freda's words made it clear she wasn't searching for them to protect Gilda. "Lady Mariel has disappeared. There was much chatter about the arrival of Lord Justin. One of the sisters thinks that Mariel may be frightened, perhaps believing he has come to carry her back to her husband."

Already on his feet, Justin addressed Freda. "Do you have any idea where she could have gone?"

"Ermguerrd thought Gilda might know."

"I doubt Mariel has explored much of the convent on her own," Gilda said. "But I took her to the herb garden just yesterday. She seemed interested in the place. Asked a lot of questions." She turned to Justin. "There is a small shed where we hang herbs to dry. I'll see if she's there."

"I'll go with you," Justin said. "Sister Freda, why don't you tell the abbess where we're headed."

Gilda shook her head. "Perhaps I should go on my own. Mariel might be afraid if she sees you, Justin."

"I know enough to stay back until you've talked to her. If she's as desperate as she seems, it's best that we put her at ease. The sooner we do that, the sooner we can leave for Mainz. We need to interview her to learn why she refuses to return to her husband. I'm sure you are as eager as I am to complete this assignment."

Gilda didn't argue with that and agreed to his company. The herb garden was located at the edge of the convent's property, and it was getting dark by the time they approached the shed. They had traveled by foot so as not to alarm Mariel. Gilda was relieved to see a light in the building.

"It must be Mariel. All the nuns and visitors are at chapel. You stay here until I signal you to come," Gilda told Justin.

But as Gilda approached the shed, she felt uneasy. Mariel had asked her whether there were any poisons in the many jars stored in the shed. Although Gilda had been reluctant to give detailed information, she had warned her about certain herbs. She pushed the door open and her heart stopped. Mariel was stretched out on a pallet surrounded by candles. Gilda quickly knelt beside the young woman and was relieved to discover she was breathing. Gently she shook Mariel's shoulder, but although her eyes opened for a second, they quickly closed again. Gilda picked up a container resting beside the sleeping woman.

"Justin!" Gilda called out without rising from her knees. Again, Mariel's eyes opened, and this time she moved restlessly for a few seconds, then she was quiet again.

Justin found Gilda beside a young woman he assumed was Mariel. "What happened?" he asked as he dropped down beside her and felt for the woman's pulse on her wrist.

"She seems to have taken a sleeping potion. It's nothing that will harm her, but she'll probably sleep through the night. Even when she tries to awaken, she is unable to do so. She should be all right in the morning."

"Her pulse is slow. Are you sure there isn't something we should do?"

"It's probably best to let her rest. I doubt she meant to do herself harm."

"Then why would she take the potion?"

"Mariel asked me a lot of questions when we were here the other day. I was a little suspicious at the time, so I didn't give her much information. It's a little unusual for someone to inquire about poisons. I had come to fetch a preparation for Sister Georgette, who has trouble sleeping. Mariel must have observed which container I took it from. I found it here beside her."

"If she was afraid that I'd come to abduct her, why would she risk going to sleep? It doesn't make sense. What good would that do?"

"I don't know. It's only an assumption by one of the sisters that it's you she is afraid of. Perhaps she just wanted a good night's sleep. I'll try to find out more in the morning. Until then, I'll stay here with her. I think it's best not to move her until she is fully awake. You should go back. Inform the abbess that we found Mariel."

"I'll do that." Justin was almost through the door when he added, "I'll bring you something to eat when I return."

"That's not necessary," Gilda said, but he didn't bother to answer her. Before she could suggest that he send Sister Freda back instead of returning himself, he was gone.

An hour later Gilda's stomach was groaning. She wondered if Justin had taken her at her word not to bring her something to eat. She cursed herself for saying such a thing, and him for taking her literally. Gilda had a healthy appetite, and religious fasts had always been a problem for her. She surveyed the pots of herbs on a shelf near the window and gathered a few mint leaves to chew on, but they only increased her hunger.

Returning to sit beside Mariel, she studied the young woman. Even under Mariel's heavy gown, Gilda could see that her limbs were shapely. Her fair face, delicately formed with well-proportioned features, made her a most becoming woman.

When Gilda heard some rustling outside the shed, she ran to the door and flung it open. "Get back inside," Justin whispered in an urgent tone of voice.

She quickly closed the door, before asking, "Did you bring some food?"

"Here." He practically tossed her the bread. "Blow out all but one candle," he said as he peered out the small window.

"Whatever for? We're out in the woods." Then she realized from his expression that something was wrong and did as he requested. "What happened?"

"I discovered that two of Cedric's men had arrived at the convent while we were talking with the abbess. One of the nuns, when she learned that Lady Mariel was missing, told me she had seen Lady Mariel speaking to the men. We assumed she was frightened of me, but maybe it was the new arrivals she feared. I don't think we should take any chances. Mariel believes her husband wishes her harm. No doubt it's his men she is fleeing from."

"Surely they won't attempt to harm her here. The abbey is a sanctuary." She bit into the hard bread and hoped her chewing didn't sound as loud to Justin's ears as it did to her own.

Justin sat beside her. "I thought you didn't want anything to eat."

"I just said it wasn't necessary. Did you bring anything else besides bread?"

He grinned and pulled open a bag hanging from his belt. "Here's some cheese and a skin of wine. It's fortunate Freda told me you're always hungry."

Gilda bit into the soft, fragrant cheese. "I'm not always hungry," she said with a satisfied smile.

"You could save some for me."

"Shhhhhh."

"I'm the one who brought it."

"No. Not that. I hear something."

Then he, too, heard the sound of a horse approaching the shed. "I'm going to hide Mariel behind these sacks," he whispered. "Then you and I will distract our visitors."

Justin spoke quickly while pulling the pallet on which Mariel was sleeping. As soon as Mariel was out of sight, he turned to Gilda. Before she could ask how they were going to cause a distraction, he embraced her. When the door opened, Justin's arms were wrapped around Gilda. He had lifted her off the floor to make sure she had to cling to him.

Almost as fast as he grabbed her, he let her go, and she struggled to recover her footing as well as her dignity. Gilda saw two men crowding the doorway, and the light they were carrying illuminated the shocked expressions on their faces.

They were both well dressed, and one was old enough to be the father of the second, much younger man.

"I trust you'll be discreet about this," Justin said in a low, forceful tone.

The older man was staring at Gilda as she adjusted her head covering. He answered Justin with a nod. The younger man had turned away to peer around the shed.

"Was there something you wanted?" Justin asked.

The older man was clearly at a loss for words, but the younger one spoke up. "We saw you leave the dining hall. I hoped for a word with you. One of the nuns told us you are Lord Justin."

Although he wanted to question them, Justin felt he had to get rid of them in case Mariel woke up and called out. "I'll be glad to oblige you. But not tonight. I'll see you after mass in the morning."

The men took one last look around and retreated quickly. As Justin watched their departure, he wondered at their lack of persistence. If they had indeed come to talk to him, at least one of them should have been reluctant to rush away.

Justin shut the door and watched Gilda sink to her knees. "Who were those men, and what did they want? Why didn't you find out?"

"I was afraid they'd discover Mariel. She might have cried out, and I wanted to get rid of them as soon as possible. Perhaps they are the messengers from Count Cedric. What I can't figure out is how they found this shed. I would have heard them if they had been following me, as they said. Perhaps one of the nuns told them where we were."

"I doubt that. There must be another explanation."

Justin saw that Gilda was absentmindedly rubbing her arms. "I had to do something to distract attention from Lady Mariel. Did I hurt you?"

"You compromised my reputation. Couldn't you think of another way to distract them?"

"It's not easy to come up with something quickly. What would you have suggested?" he asked.

"You could have pretended to have come here for a sleeping potion."

"Yes, I could. But I didn't think of it. I never have trouble sleeping, so it didn't occur to me."

"But hauling me up in your arms did occur to you."

Justin thought it best not to answer that one. "I wanted to get rid of them quickly. Next time I'll let you think of something."

"There isn't going to be a next time. I can't go to Mainz with you now. Those men are likely to tell tales. I don't think that the fact you asked them to be discreet will deter them. How can I do any good if my reputation is compromised?"

"I'm sorry, Gilda. We don't know for sure they are from Mainz," he added lamely.

Justin thought he saw some moisture in her eyes, and it made his stomach turn queasy with guilt. He should have thought of something else to throw the men off. It was quite possible that his desire to hold her had clouded his judgment. Perhaps it was best that she didn't come with him.

Gilda sighed. Now that she wasn't going to Mainz, she wanted to. Nothing was ever straightforward in her dealings with Justin. "Why do you think they followed you?"

"I don't think they did, in spite of what they said. In any case, there is a good chance that Mariel is in danger. The count wants to end his marriage. If he can't do it one way, he might seek another."

When they heard a low whimper from behind the sacks, they both jumped and rushed to Mariel. "She looks like she's still asleep," Gilda whispered. "Let's move her back into the open where it's less dusty."

Gently they moved the sleeping woman by dragging her pallet, one on either side of her. "She looks like a child," Justin said. He hadn't paid much attention before, but now he noticed the dark shadows under her eyes.

"I think she has fourteen years," Gilda said. She studied Mariel and wondered again why she had taken the sleeping potion. If she were afraid of being abducted, she would have wanted to stay alert.

"I'm going with you to Mainz, Justin."

"You're changing your mind again?"

"Yes, and don't say another word about it. There is some mystery here, and I'd like to discover what it is."

Justin was surprised at the relief he felt at her words. "What about your reputation?"

Gilda looked again at the sleeping woman. "As you said, the men may not be from Mainz." She knew she was grasping at straws. "The king wants someone from a religious community to help you, and I'm the best nun for the task."

Justin nodded, accepting the truth of what she said. "We'll talk to Lady Mariel in the morning. You can arrange with the abbess for her to be sent somewhere safe. If those two men are from Count Cedric, I'll make sure they hold their tongues about seeing us together. I'll be speaking to them in the morning. Once all that is done, you and I can be off to Mainz."

"With Sister Freda," Gilda added, and felt her spirits lift as they always did when she had an intriguing task to perform. "Now we need to get some rest."

CHAPTER TWO

Gilda and Justin had settled themselves, one on either side of Lady Mariel's pallet, where they dozed fitfully. At first light Gilda awoke and sat up to look over at Mariel. Justin's back was turned, but she could tell by his deep breathing that he was asleep. As she watched Mariel, the young woman struggled to focus her eyes and hold them open. When Mariel turned her head, she saw Justin sleeping with his back to her. Before Gilda could explain his presence, Mariel did a surprising thing. She reached out and tugged at Justin's sleeve until he turned toward her.

Whatever Mariel was expecting to see, it was not Lord Justin. "Oh no," she cried, falling back with her hands over her face.

Startled awake, Justin jumped to his feet and in his haste bumped his head on a low beam supporting the shed. Gilda's eyes widened as he mumbled a stream of curses. The usually tidy advisor to the king appeared rather savage with his sleep-tangled hair and rumpled clothes. Gilda might have laughed if Mariel wasn't staring at him, her eyes wide with fright.

"Lord Justin is a friend. There is nothing to worry about, Mariel." With soft words and reassuring pats, Gilda sought to calm the young woman. "He seems a bit cranky, but he means you no harm."

Afraid the fierce expression on Justin's face as he straightened his clothes might give Mariel other ideas about his harmlessness, Gilda tried to distract the young woman. "Come, see if you can stand up. Lord Justin will fetch you a drink of water."

Rubbing his sore head, Justin scowled at Gilda, and for a minute she wasn't sure he'd do as she wished. But he poured some water from a nearby jug and handed it to Gilda before heading for the door. "I'll go to the abbey and send someone back with horses. There is no reason for you to walk that far," he said, regaining some of his poise.

"What was he doing here?" Mariel whispered after he left.

"We couldn't wake you. Lord Justin stayed to make sure we were both safe." Gilda didn't want to upset Mariel by mentioning the two men who had burst in on them. "He'll send help."

Later at the abbey, Gilda told Ermguerrd about Mariel's unfortunate introduction to Lord Justin. She gleefully described his rude awakening and rumpled appearance. "You should have seen him, Holy Mother. The expression on his face would have frightened the bravest warrior."

Ermguerrd grinned. "It was good of him to be so protective and stay the night. But perhaps it would be best to question Mariel without Lord Justin present."

Even without Justin, the interview proved difficult. Lady Mariel had freshened up, but her youthful face bore the expression of a sullen child.

"We worried about you, Lady Mariel. It was fortunate that Gilda remembered that you had visited the garden shed with her. Tell us. What made you go there?" Ermguerrd asked.

"I was frightened. Count Cedric wishes me dead, Holy Mother," Mariel whispered, a tremor in her voice. Seated on a bench, she hung her head and clasped her hands on her lap. The fact that she wouldn't meet their eyes led Gilda to suspect she was hiding something, although she did seem genuinely frightened.

Ermguerrd sat beside Mariel. Loosening her clasped hands, she held one of them. "Don't be frightened. Saint Ives is your sanctuary for as long as you need it. No one can harm you here," she said. "But we need to know how best to help you, Mariel. Why did you take the sleeping potion?"

"I couldn't sleep. I remembered the potion Sister Gilda fetched for the other sister. I didn't realize it would be so strong." She looked up at Gilda in an accusatory manner.

"It's very important you take the right amount, Mariel," Gilda replied. "I wish you had come to me. I would have given you something to help."

"I couldn't find you. You can't imagine what it's like to fear for your life." Mariel lowered her head again and began to sob quietly.

Gilda wondered if she had indeed looked for her. None of the nuns had mentioned that. "I'm sorry you couldn't find me. Was it your intention to sleep in the shed?"

Pulling away from Ermguerrd, Mariel began moving restlessly on the bench, and instead of answering the question she said, "I was betrayed. Why don't you listen? Count Cedric plans to kill me."

With each word she spoke, Lady Mariel became more agitated. Gilda and Ermguerrd watched helplessly as the young woman jumped to her feet and began beating her own stomach.

"There is no baby. There is no baby!" she shouted between gasping sobs.

Gilda tried to hold her shoulders, but Mariel was strong enough to push her away. Her agitation seemed to increase as she pulled off her head covering and began to tear at her hair. It took both Gilda and Ermguerrd, one on either side, to capture her hands and subdue her.

To further calm Mariel, Ermguerrd cupped her face in her hands and forced her to listen. "You are safe here. I promise. No more questions. We're not going to ask you any more questions."

The abbess had clearly said the magic words because Mariel immediately relaxed her body and stopped sobbing. Gilda, surprised, looked at Ermguerrd with a questioning expression, but the abbess just shrugged her shoulders.

After one of the nuns had been asked to help Lady Mariel to her room, Justin was summoned. Gilda was still puzzling over their interview with Mariel when he arrived, but she couldn't help but notice that Justin was once more neatly groomed. She, on the other hand, was still in her rumpled clothing. There seemed to be a pattern here, and she grimaced at the thought.

Ermguerrd explained what had happened in their interview with Lady Mariel. "She became hysterical, Lord Justin. There was no point in calling you to see her. Your presence wouldn't have helped. I suspect she'll sleep through the day. It seems she took a strong potion."

He nodded, reluctantly accepting her explanation for not calling him. "Why the potion? Did she tell you that?"

"She claims she hasn't been sleeping well. When we asked her why she didn't speak to Gilda, she said she was unable to find her. What do you think of that, Gilda?" Ermguerrd asked.

"I doubt it's the truth. No one mentioned her looking for me," Gilda added. "She's hiding something."

Ermguerrd nodded. "Lady Mariel seemed extremely nervous right from the start of the interview, Lord Justin. She kept saying she'd been betrayed and was frightened. Could she have overheard you talking to the men who came to the shed?" Ermguerrd asked.

"I doubt that," Gilda replied. "Even if she did hear them, I doubt she'd remember them being there when she finally awoke. I'm puzzled. It was clear she didn't want to answer our questions."

Justin paced the floor in front of the two nuns. "I learned something when I asked about the two men who came to the shed," he said. "One of the sisters who gave me some ale this morning saw something. Lady Mariel was talking to the men. The sister, who was certain they were the ones who claimed to have been sent by Cedric, said that Mariel did not appear to be frightened."

Gilda's eyes widened. "I forgot about the two intruders. Perhaps we can learn something from them. Did you speak to them, Justin?" Gilda asked, remembering his promise to silence them about the fact that he had embraced her.

"No. I had planned to question them, but they had already disappeared. The porter tells me they rode away early this morning. No one even remembers them giving their names. Just that they said they were sent by Count Cedric."

"That's strange. Perhaps they arranged with Lady Mariel to meet them at the shed. Once they had her alone, they could murder her. When they couldn't find her, they returned to Mainz," Gilda suggested.

Justin stopped his pacing and glared at her. "That's a rash assumption. We only have Lady Mariel's word that her husband wishes her harm. It's best not to leap to conclusions."

"I'm not leaping to conclusions." Gilda's voice was sharp. "I'm just suggesting one possibility. You didn't see how terribly upset and frightened Lady Mariel was this morning."

"No, because I wasn't here, was I?"

"Feel free to suggest your own explanation about why those men came to Saint Ives, Lord Justin."

"I don't make suggestions until I have all the facts, Sister Gilda."

The abbess watched Justin cross his arms over his chest and Gilda place her hands on her hips as they engaged in this heated exchange. She shook her head and finally interrupted them. "Each of you has your own way of seeking answers. Gilda, you do sometimes jump to conclusions before all the facts are apparent. I don't know you well, Lord Justin, but waiting for all the facts before making suggestions can sometimes slow progress. Perhaps you will find that your approaches complement each other," she said, clearly hoping this was the case.

Justin was the first to reply. "I'll try to remember your words, Reverend Mother." His tone of voice suggested it was going to be a difficult task, and Gilda thought Ermguerrd looked doubtful of his sincerity. Afraid she might come to believe they couldn't work together, Gilda remembered something they had agreed upon. "Lord Justin and I thought it would be best that Mariel be sheltered somewhere else for the time being for her own safety. But she may be reluctant to leave Saint Ives."

Ermguerrd nodded her satisfaction at this suggestion. "Leave it to me to work out the details," she answered. "There are a few hiding places nearby that we've used in the past. We have become adept at protecting those who seek sanctuary at our abbey. I don't think there is much point in trying to question Mariel further. Perhaps when you reach Mainz, you will learn more about the two messengers—if that is what they were."

At her words, Gilda remembered the scene the strangers had observed when they arrived at the garden shed. Justin had promised to silence them this morning, but he had found them gone. When she turned to him, he must have understood her anxiety.

"I'll take care of it," he promised.

"That's what you said last night."

"I didn't know they'd be gone this morning, did I?"

At the same moment, they both became aware of Ermguerrd watching them. "I don't think I want to know what this is about," she said. "I'll pray to God that your mission for the king will be successful."

Later that morning the abbess blessed their journey more formally and waved them off. Gilda, mounted on a gentle horse she was familiar with, rode beside Freda. Their party also included Leonardo, a soldier from the palace guards who often acted as Justin's assistant on his travels, and a servant named Matthew who led the packhorse. Both women had met Leonardo before, and although they weren't introduced to Matthew, they had nodded a greeting.

The two men talked together as they rode, and Gilda couldn't help but notice that they were a striking pair. Leonardo, fair of hair and skin, had the blue eyes of an angel and a smile full of mischief. In contrast, Justin was much more serious, but his dark, moody appearance had its own appeal.

Gilda smiled as she remembered Ermguerrd's last words to her. "If you can manage to avoid coming to blows, I suspect you and Justin will work quite well together."

Sister Freda must have noticed her expression. "You seem in good humor," she commented in an accusing tone as she twisted in her saddle, hoping to find a more comfortable position. The nun was tall and strong but without much padding to help her sit comfortably in the small saddle she straddled.

"I enjoy traveling. I've been north to Aachen many times. I was born in Bordeaux, but I've never been across the mountains to Mainz."

"And did you join the convent to travel the country?" Still cranky, Freda spoke in a chiding voice that carried easily.

"No, of course not," Gilda answered. She could tell by the grin on Justin's face as he turned toward her that he had overheard Freda's words. "I just think that if we need to travel to do God's work, we might as well enjoy the country he created."

Gilda's answer was directed at Justin as much as Freda. They seemed to share the view that she didn't take her vocation seriously.

Freda shrugged. "In my day, there would be no need for this journey," she said. "The entire matter would have been handled differently. Charlemagne was a much wiser ruler than his son Louis. He understood human nature. He wasn't a slave to the dictates of Rome."

Gilda knew that Freda was referring to the ease with which marriages had been ended twenty years earlier. Charles was King of the Franks before he became the Holy Roman Emperor and earned the nickname Charlemagne. The Franks often had more than one wife, and Charles didn't press them to change their ways, even after Pope Leo III crowned him Holy Roman Emperor. But his son Louis was determined to be a truly Christian emperor and uphold the laws of the church, including the sanctity of marriage. As far as he was concerned, when a man and woman married, they became one for life.

Freda's view was not uncommon among older nuns, although few voiced their opinion openly. The king and bishops insisted there were only a few cases where a marriage could be annulled. But many Franks, while desiring to be good Christians, were reluctant to accept the church's dictates on ending marriages.

"I believe the abbess would advise you to speak carefully, Sister Freda," Gilda warned in a low voice. She didn't wish to be disrespectful to the older nun, but they were about to become involved in delicate investigations. It occurred to her that the outspoken Freda might not be the best companion for this task.

Freda seemed to understand her concern. "Don't worry about me, Sister Gilda. I hold my tongue," Freda muttered. "But I speak honestly when I can."

Gilda nodded. She felt the same way and was glad to hear anything Freda had to offer on the subject as long as she was discreet. "Have you had any experience with Gunthar, the Bishop of Mainz?"

Freda checked to see that there was a distance between themselves and Lord Justin before answering in a low voice. "I met him once when I visited my nephew. He's a monk at a monastery near Mainz. I don't trust Gunthar. He looks like a toad and acts like a snake."

Gilda burst into laughter, then covered her mouth with her hand when Justin turned around to peer back at her. She was still chuckling when he slowed his horse so she'd catch up to him. Freda lifted one eyebrow but didn't comment.

"I'm glad to see you're enjoying yourself, Sister Gilda," Justin said. Actually, he had found her peal of laughter enchanting.

"Don't look so surprised, Justin. Nuns do laugh from time to time. Between saying prayers and helping the poor."

He grimaced, remembering his words about the duties appropriate for a nun. He had acted like a pompous fool.

When Gilda saw his expression, she relented. "When are we stopping to eat? I'm starving. I just told Freda that I was hungry enough to eat toads."

The stern Freda didn't exactly laugh, but her lips did turn up slightly.

Justin wondered how they could find such an expression amusing. "We'll stop soon. Then tomorrow we'll cross the mountains," he replied. "It's best to do that early in the morning when we've more energy. It's a beautiful ride. There are many long vistas, but it can be tiring for both riders and horses."

Gilda could see the tall mountains ahead and felt exhilarated at the prospect of climbing them. There were small, thin clouds that veiled the highest peaks. It wouldn't be long before the sun would disappear behind them.

By the time they stopped for the night it was dark, and everyone was tired. Their meager meal was eaten in silence. Gilda and Freda set their blanket rolls side by side, and the men settled down a short distance away.

By the next morning the weather had changed, and the mountains had vanished under heavy cloud. The women had gone into the bush to refresh themselves while Justin and Leonardo discussed whether it was wise to try crossing in the cloud cover.

"The weather can be unpredictable this time of year," Leonardo offered.

"We aren't in any hurry, but on the other hand we don't have provisions for a long delay," Justin replied, remembering how disappointed Gilda had been with the dried meat and cheese. She did like her food.

"The main problem is visibility. If it wasn't for the nuns, I'd say give it a try," Leonardo said.

Both men looked up to see Gilda and Freda approaching them. Leonardo flushed, wondering if his words had been overheard.

Freda made it clear they had heard him by saying, "I think we should give it a try. We aren't going to be harmed by a bit of rain."

"It's not just a matter of wet clothing," Justin answered. "The trail can become treacherous when wet."

"If you can do it, so can we," Freda replied. "I was riding a horse before you were born." The last comment was aimed at Leonardo.

With a grin that was meant to charm, Leonardo said, "I did notice how well you sit a horse."

Freda grinned back, knowing he must have observed how uncomfortable she had been on the thin saddle. "You have a smooth tongue, Leonardo."

"You have found him out, Sister Freda," Justin said. "If we're going over the mountain today, we should start immediately." He saw Gilda staring at the food he had been wrapping. "If it hadn't taken you so long to dress, or pray, or whatever you were doing, you'd have had time to eat breakfast."

At the expression of alarm on her face, Justin grinned. "Don't worry, Gilda, you can eat something while we saddle the horses."

Surprised that the sober Justin was displaying a bit of humor, Gilda almost forgot to be thankful that her hunger would at least be somewhat satisfied. She and Freda ate quickly while the men saddled and packed the horses.

They hadn't gone far up the steep path when a light rain began to fall. It didn't do much more than dampen their clothes, and as they continued, the visibility actually improved. Justin was hopeful their luck would hold, but by the time they reached the summit he knew it wasn't to be. A sudden heavy downpour made the path slippery and forced them to stop for a rest.

"We'll have to continue on foot. I'm afraid the horses might slip and be injured." Justin spoke loudly to be heard over the rain as they began their descent. "Leonardo, Matthew, and I will lead the horses and you can follow," he said to the women. "Just go slow and be careful."

The normally hard-packed trail was slick. As the women tried to follow Justin's instructions, Gilda saw that Freda was a bit unsteady on her feet. Not for the first time in her life Gilda wished she were taller. She did her best to steady Freda with her hand on her elbow, but it was hard to really help the tall woman, and they soon fell behind the men.

At a sharp turn in the trail Gilda let go of her hold on Freda, then watched in dismay as the nun lost her footing and began sliding off the slick trail.

"Wait, wait!" Gilda shouted, as though Freda had any choice. In her rush to catch up, she also lost her footing and slid right past Freda. She didn't stop sliding until she collided with a tree.

Freda wasn't far behind, and Gilda grabbed hold of her arm before she slipped by. Holding Freda pulled Gilda off-balance, and both nuns ended up on the ground against the tree, with Gilda on the bottom of the heap.

Justin had rushed back up the trail when he heard Gilda shout to Freda. "Damnation," he muttered when he saw the two women lying entwined against the tree. With all the black clothing, it was hard to tell where one body ended and the other started. "What can I do?" he asked.

"Help me off Gilda," Freda said as she lifted her arm toward him.

"Are you hurt?" he asked, pulling her upright.

"Just my dignity. Gilda softened my landing."

Once Freda was standing, Justin pulled Gilda to her feet, almost dropping her when she groaned. "What's the matter?" he asked.

"I'm fine now," she said, trying to pull away from him.

Justin's grasp tightened. "You're not fine. Just relax, Gilda. If either one of you is hurt, you'll delay our journey," he pointed out impatiently.

"I'm not hurt," she muttered. "Just a bit sore where I hit the tree."

Leonardo had come to help Freda, and they carefully worked their way up the slope to where Leonardo had tied the horses.

Although there were no more accidents, they descended the mountain slowly, stopping often to rest. It was dark by the time they reached level ground where the men could put up a shelter. Since the rain gave no sign of letting up, they made up their pallets under cover. Gilda thought of asking for something to eat, but for once she was too tired to make the effort and was soon asleep.

When Gilda awoke, she found herself face-to-face with a sleeping Justin. She couldn't remember settling so close beside him, but then she had been the first person to fall asleep. She thought about moving but didn't want to disturb him. At such close range, she couldn't help but notice that his dark eyelashes were exceptionally long. She marveled at them for a while, until she was distracted by the gentle purr of his lips. Remembering the feel of his kiss, she became alarmed. What was she doing? When she tried to wiggle herself away, she felt Freda wedged behind her.

Determined to sit up, Gilda's hand bumped Justin's arm, and it came tumbling down on top of her sore hip. She yelped at the sharp pain.

Justin's eyes flew open and he stared into her face. He must have noticed the tears in her eyes as she struggled to lift his arm from her hip.

"Lord, I'm sorry," he whispered, looking at where his arm had landed. "That's your sore leg."

"I've got to get up," she whispered back.

They were wedged in the middle of Freda and Leonardo, but Justin managed to put his hands to her back and push her up far enough so she could crawl out of the shelter. He followed her and was happy to find the sun shining. When he saw that Gilda had disappeared, Justin wondered how badly she was hurt.

He gave Gilda a few minutes on her own before heading for a small stream they had discovered the night before. He found her struggling to brush mud from the damp skirt of her habit. Gilda had taken her head covering off to sleep, and the sun shone on her golden hair. The beautiful sight stopped him in his tracks, and he wondered at the fact that she hadn't cut her locks.

Although Gilda didn't look at him directly, she must have felt his presence. She turned toward the water and pulled on her head covering, pushing her hair out of sight. When all her hair had disappeared, Justin moved toward her again.

"You'd better let me have a look at your leg, Gilda. I've had experience with injuries." When she shook her head, he added, "Everyone else is still asleep. At least let me put some cold water on it. You'd let a physician tend it, wouldn't you?"

"You're not a physician, and it's my hip, not my leg. I've put a cold cloth on it."

Since examining her hip didn't seem a good idea, Justin let the subject drop. To distract himself he pulled an apple out of his pocket. When he held it out to her, Gilda accepted his gift with a smile. He had been worried about her injury and was pleased she could smile.

"We'll arrive at Mainz today," he remarked. It couldn't happen soon enough to suit him.

Gilda nodded and sat to eat her apple. He noticed she was taking small bites, no doubt to make it last longer.

Justin turned away from her and washed his face in the stream. "We have to be careful how we approach Count Cedric. I don't believe it would be wise to tell him that Lady Mariel has accused him of trying to kill her. He'll point out that she is being hysterical."

"Of course. Whenever a woman fears her husband, she is being hysterical. I've heard that many times before."

"I'm not agreeing that's the case, Gilda," he reminded her. "He may be expecting us to bring his wife home with us. It might be best if we have a reason why Mariel has remained at the abbey."

"We can say Mariel is unwell. Continuing her spiritual retreat will put her at ease. Improve her health." She tossed away the few seeds that were left of the apple and grinned at him.

Justin's eyebrows rose as he watched the apple seeds disappear. "I think he'll have to accept that. I didn't know nuns were so good at lying."

"I prefer to think of it as stretching the truth. Lady Mariel is on a retreat of sorts. Plus, I didn't think she looked particularly well. What I want to know is how you are going to handle those messengers."

"That really depends on who they are and why they were at the convent. They may not wish it known that we saw them. That will give me some leverage. Leave the matter to me."

"Just make sure you deal with it quickly. I don't care to have my reputation in ruins."

"No, we can't have that," he commented, sounding as though he didn't care an apple pip about her reputation. When Gilda scowled at him, he extended his hand to help her up, and this time she accepted it.

Later that day the five travelers rode over the bridge and through the portal at Mainz. The walled city was bursting with activity as they made their way through the crowded bailey in the direction they had been given to find Count Cedric. While Leonardo, Matthew, and Freda sought refreshment in the great hall, Justin and Gilda climbed the stone steps that led to the count's quarters. They were ushered into a private chamber to meet Cedric.

"I bring greetings from King Louis," Justin said to establish his authority. "May I present Sister Gilda from the Convent of Saint Ives. She joins me in my commission from the king to review your request for an annulment of your marriage, Count Cedric."

The count, a handsome man with white hair and an easy smile, rose to meet them. "Welcome to Mainz," he said, including both Justin and Gilda in his greeting. "I hope your journey was a pleasant one."

While Justin and Cedric exchanged pleasantries, Gilda surveyed the elegant chamber. The dark tables and chairs had a high polish, and the tapestries, most of them depicting hunting scenes, were richly colored. Glittering gold candlesticks lit the room with a warm glow. Mariel wasn't running away to escape cold and dreary living quarters, Gilda decided. As for the count, although he was much older than his wife, he was still a comely man.

"I am disappointed that you have not returned Lady Mariel to Mainz, Lord Justin. She should be here. We need to settle this matter," Cedric said.

Justin replied as he and Gilda had agreed. The count accepted the explanation that Mariel was on an extended retreat and made no further enquiry about her health.

"I have set aside an apartment of rooms for your party, Lord Justin. You will be shown where they are. Refresh yourselves. It is almost time for vespers and supper. We'll delay our interview until tomorrow morning. I hope you'll find your quarters satisfactory."

When the count turned to ask a servant to direct them, Gilda whispered to Justin, "Ask him if he sent messengers to the abbey."

"Not now," Justin mouthed.

"Why not?" Gilda whispered.

"You heard him. He doesn't want to talk until morning."

Turning back to them, Cedric scowled as he asked, "What's the nun whispering about?"

Justin answered before Gilda had a chance to say anything. "We were just wondering about the rest of our party. Could you have someone find them and direct them to our chambers, Lord Cedric?"

"Of course." Cedric dismissed them by saying, "I will see you at supper, Lord Justin."

To ensure that Gilda would follow him, Justin took her arm in a tight grasp. As the servant led them up a winding set of stairs, Gilda pulled her arm free and tried not to limp. She was about to complain about his treatment when she spotted a familiar-looking young man coming down the steps. When he caught her eye, he veered off to the right, following a corridor that led away from their path.

Gilda spoke to the servant who was leading them. "Who lives on this floor?" she asked, pointing to where the young man had disappeared.

"This is not your level," he answered. "Your chambers are one floor up."

Gilda was about to say that wasn't what she asked when she caught Justin's frown. Once in their own suite, she waited until the door closed behind them to turn on him.

"Are you going to ignore every suggestion or question I have? We are supposed to be working together."

"You're a nun. Nuns are expected to show some reticence. Especially in the company of men. You saw how the count reacted to your whispering."

"So, we're back to how a nun should act. What makes you think you're an authority on nuns, Lord Justin?"

He knew he'd made a mistake and quickly changed the subject. "Why did you ask about the lad on the stairs?"

Remembering her excitement at seeing the young man, Gilda let her question go. "Didn't you notice? The man on the steps was one of the messengers who came to Saint Ives. If you had asked Count Cedric about them as I suggested, we'd have some idea what he was doing in the private quarters."

"Are you sure it was one of the messengers?"

"Yes, and he took off down the hall to avoid us. I'm sure of it. Did you see the look on his face? He was hoping we didn't recognize him."

"I didn't see his face. Maybe he was being discreet because he remembered our embrace in the shed."

Gilda sat down and put her head in her hands. "I forgot about that. Do you think he'll tell anyone? My position here will be compromised if he does."

Justin sat on the bench beside her. "You're tired," he said. He was tempted to put his arm around her to give comfort, but he thought better of it. "I said I'd take care of it, and I will."

Glancing around, Justin observed the two rooms leading from the small main chamber. "Why didn't the count arrange for you and Freda to stay with the priest? Isn't that the usual arrangement?"

"Priests are reluctant to have their retreat invaded by women, even if they are nuns." As she, too, noticed the intimacy of the apartment, Gilda hesitated. "Perhaps we should see if there is a convent nearby that will house Freda and me."

"It will be harder and take more time to do our work if you are outside the city walls. You are observant, but you can't see things from a distance."

His words surprised her. "You gave me a compliment," she said with a grin.

Instead of acknowledging her comment, Justin looked away. Gilda studied the way his shoulder-length hair curled on his neck. They were sitting close enough so that she could feel the heat of his body. Her fingers moved slightly as though responding to her desire to see whether his hair felt as soft as it appeared.

Finally, he spoke. "Just because I don't think you should speak out in front of Count Cedric doesn't mean I don't appreciate your skills. We need to work together if we hope to find out what's going on here."

"Right, I knew that's what you meant," she said. Suddenly feeling uncomfortable at being so close to him, Gilda rose to her feet. "Let's go see if we can find out where that young man slipped off to."

He grabbed her arm and then let it go almost as quickly. "We aren't going anywhere. The others will be here soon. At supper, see if you spot the man you saw on the stairs. Be discreet and point him out to me. Please leave it to me."

Justin was still sitting, and she stared down at him. Even seated, his head was almost level with her shoulder, and without thinking she lifted her hand to touch his hair.

"It's so soft," she murmured as her fingers sunk into the curls at his neck.

"Gilda, don't." His voice sounded hoarse, but he didn't move away from her hand. "You don't realize what your touch does to me."

She wondered if his reaction was the same as hers. "Does it make your stomach flutter in a strange way?"

Before Justin could reply, the door opened, and Gilda's hand fell away. A servant, followed by Freda and Leonardo, entered the chamber.

"This should do nicely," Freda said, ignoring the fact that Justin had sprung to his feet and Gilda was looking flushed.

"I'm going to the chapel," Justin said. He was out the door before anyone else could say a word.

"My, the man seems very eager to say his prayers," Freda remarked.

CHAPTER THREE

During vespers, Gilda glanced around the crowded chapel looking for Justin. She had told Freda what had happened just before her arrival in the chamber, and they'd had a long discussion about the incident. Gilda thought about Freda's reaction and the story she'd told.

Freda had been amazed at Gilda's ignorance. "It's not appropriate to touch a man's hair."

"I know that, Freda. It just happened. We were alone in this lovely chamber, discussing things, and I became very aware of him. It was the first time we were together like that. Before I knew it, I had reached out."

"Gilda, you are a practical, honest woman. But you have little experience with men. Justin is a worldly man. You're fortunate he hasn't taken advantage of your innocence."

"I wonder why he hasn't."

Freda shook her head and rolled her eyes. "Just be happy that's the case."

"Maybe it's because we're related by marriage. His sister is married to my brother. Chetwynd and Justin trained as pages with Count Jonas and grew up like brothers."

"Listen to me, Gilda. His relationship to your brother is no protection. Men cannot be relied upon to curb their desires."

"I've heard that's true. Just as I didn't curb my desire to touch his hair. I should apologize to him."

Freda sighed. "Never mind that. You'd best forget about it. Just be aware of what you're doing next time. The abbess told me you might need some guidance. At the time, I wasn't sure what she was referring to."

They were in the small bedroom they would share, and Freda was unpacking a bundle of personal items as she spoke. Gilda watched for a minute, thinking about why the abbess might have chosen the older nun to accompany her. "Have you had experience with men, Freda?"

The older woman finished her unpacking and sat on a bench beside Gilda. "You aren't going to drop this subject, are you? I was in love once. A very long time ago. It was the most glorious and painful two years of my life."

Freda went silent, perhaps recalling those years. "What happened?" Gilda urged.

"He was married, and although he hadn't lived with his wife for several years, there were children. I would have been happy just to be with him when I could." She paused a few seconds before continuing. "He feared I would become pregnant and be ruined. So, he spoke with my father. They arranged to send me to court as a lady-in-waiting to the queen. My father hoped I would make a suitable marriage. At court, I became friends with Ermguerrd, and when she chose the monastery, I followed."

"Did you ever see the man again?"

"No. I heard he was wounded in battle and died soon afterwards. He was a reckless man in many ways, but he was protective of me."

Sitting in the chapel, Gilda pondered Freda's tale as she continued to watch for Justin. She wondered if he was being protective. It was certainly in his nature to be careful, unlike the reckless soldier Freda had loved. If Justin experienced any impulsive tendencies, he kept them under control. She knew she must learn to do the same. Being a nun was important to her, and she was aware that she had much more freedom than other women, whether married or living with their family. She also valued the work she did. She couldn't let anything jeopardize her position.

It wasn't until Gilda was leaving the chapel that she spotted Justin. When she caught his eye, it appeared for a minute he might hurry away, but he must have changed his mind as he paused and waited for her to catch up with him. They followed the rest of the worshippers to the great hall.

"May I speak with you alone, Lord Justin?" Gilda asked.

"Not now," he grumbled.

His abrupt answer made Gilda stop. There was no reason for him to be rude, she thought.

When Justin realized Gilda had disappeared from his side, he turned back. He found her seated on a small bench near the open market. The merchants had put away their wares, and the stalls appeared barren without the usual colorful display.

Rather than sit beside her, Justin remained standing, hoping to prevent a long discussion. "What is it?" he asked, impatience obvious in his tone.

Gilda remembered that Freda had discouraged her from apologizing, but she couldn't think of another way to start the discussion she wished to have with Justin. "I'm sorry I touched your hair. I shouldn't have done it."

"You don't need to apologize. Nothing happened, Gilda. Please forget it," he said. "Let's go to supper."

Gilda didn't move. "No, nothing happened. You don't have to worry about my embarrassing you in the future." Rushing ahead with her words before he moved away, she added, "I just wanted you to know that I intend to curb any desires I might feel."

Her words made him sigh. Reluctantly sitting down beside her, Justin leaned his head against the wall behind them. "I'm sure you mean well, Gilda. But saying things like that just makes it worse. I realize you have no experience in these matters. I try to be patient, I do. But my patience is wearing thin."

Gilda grinned. "I thought patience in difficult situations was supposed to be one of your strengths."

His nod was weary. "Usually that's true. For some reason, dealing with you seems to be an exception, Gilda."

"I realize my ignorance in certain areas. I just wanted you to know that. It's important that we keep our relationship on an impersonal level. Sister Freda is giving me guidance. I plan to do better."

Startled, Justin turned to search her face. The woman was serious. "You discussed this with Sister Freda?"

Gilda nodded. She'd had the best intentions when she started to speak with him, but for some reason it was hard not to provoke him. Lord Justin took everything so seriously.

"I suppose Sister Freda has a vast knowledge in this area?" he asked.

"As a matter of fact, she does. A long time ago she had a lover. It's a sad tale, but she shared it with me."

Justin jumped to his feet, afraid she might give him details of the sad tale. Gilda's ability to catch him off guard was exhausting. "It's been a long day. Let's join the others at supper," he said.

When they arrived in the great hall, it was crowded, and the meal was already underway. Count Cedric spotted Justin and waved him to a place at the head table. Gilda was about to leave him to join Freda when she noticed the young man seated beside Cedric. She grabbed Justin's arm before he could leave her side.

"You're touching me," he pointed out brusquely.

"Look there, Justin. The man beside Cedric. He's one of the men who came to Saint Ives looking for Mariel."

The young man she was nodding toward spotted Gilda. His expression was one of shock when he saw she was speaking to Justin. He leaned over and spoke to Count Cedric.

"You're right. Is he the same one you saw on the stairs this afternoon?" When Gilda nodded, he added, "I'll find out who he is and why he was at Saint Ives."

From her seat beside Freda, Gilda kept her attention on Justin as he spoke with the count. For once she took little notice of the food being passed along the table.

It appeared to Gilda that introductions were being made, and then an intense discussion ensued. She could imagine Justin enquiring as to why the young man had been at Saint Ives, and especially why he had disappeared the next morning without an explanation. The young man stood up; then Cedric spoke to him, and he sat down again. Even from a distance, Gilda could tell the young man was upset. A handsome youth, she judged him to be only a few years older than Mariel. His eyes appeared frantic as he looked toward Gilda again.

"You haven't even touched your food," Freda whispered. "Why are you staring at the high table?"

"The young man beside Count Cedric. He looks a bit like the count, don't you think?"

As Gilda asked the question, both she and Freda saw the object of their study point his finger over to Gilda. Both Count Cedric and Justin glanced in her direction and then leaned their heads toward each other. Their intense discussion continued.

"It appears they are discussing you, Gilda," Freda pointed out. "Why would that be?"

At her question, Gilda pushed her food away. She remembered the scene in the garden shed and being swept up in Justin's arms. She prayed the young man wasn't telling the count that he had found them together, but she felt sure that's what he was doing. When Justin glanced at her again, there was a strange look on his face. It seemed to hold an expression of concern that Gilda hadn't seen before.

"I need to talk to you, Freda," Gilda said, rising from her seat.

"But you haven't touched your meal. Aren't you feeling well?"

Freda saw the color drain from Gilda's face as she glanced one last time at the high table. Without another word, the older woman stood, following Gilda from the hall. By the time they reached their rooms, Freda was out of breath from rushing up the stairs to keep up with Gilda. The older nun lowered herself to a bench and watched Gilda pace the floor of the common area.

Gilda forgot about Freda as she tried to imagine what had taken place at the high table. There seemed little doubt that the young man had made an accusation about her association with Justin. What would Justin tell the count? Why did he have that strange look on his face?

She remembered that Justin hadn't wanted her along in the first place. Perhaps to explain the situation, he was telling some story about her trying to seduce him. She dismissed the idea at once. Justin was an honorable man. She knew that. He said he would take care of it, and she believed him. But how was he going to explain what had happened in the shed without giving away the fact that they were hiding Lady Mariel? She hoped he wouldn't need to do that.

Gilda was flushed with embarrassment as she remembered the scene. At the time, she hadn't minded the heady experience of being lifted in Justin's arms. But now she realized that her reputation could be severely damaged by their embrace. It would mean the end of her opportunities to work outside the convent. No one would seek her help. Because she was burning up, she pulled off her head covering and shook out her hair.

"Gilda, stop pacing. You're making me light-headed. You said you wanted to speak to me, so speak."

Reminded of Freda's presence, Gilda rushed to sit beside her and took her hands. "Justin embraced me in the shed at Saint Ives. The young man at the head table was surely telling the count about it."

The puzzled look on Freda's face told Gilda she was making a muddle of her explanation. "Remember the night we found Lady Mariel asleep in the garden shed? Two men arrived on horseback. We feared they were looking for Mariel, and Justin hid her. Then he embraced me as the men opened the door of the shed. The embrace was meant to be a distraction. One of those men, the younger one, was at the head table tonight. The one sitting beside the count."

"Was that the only distraction Lord Justin could think of?"

"That's what I asked him!"

Freda's puzzled expression had disappeared, and she seemed to consider what Gilda had told her. "I understand your concern. But Lord Justin is used to dealing with the most powerful men in the land, including the king. His reputation for solving problems and negotiating between enemies is legend. He's sure to think of a way out of this predicament," she assured Gilda.

Gilda nodded, but her eyes were full of doubt. She couldn't help but feel she carried a lot of the blame for Justin's choice of a distraction. It was that disastrous kiss at her brother's manor that had begun the whole thing.

When the door opened, Gilda jumped to her feet. She saw that Justin was holding his mouth in a tight, narrow line. She was sure he had bad news to relate.

"What happened?" she asked, before he could say a word.

"Maybe you should sit down, Gilda."

"Justin, just answer my question," she replied, refusing his suggestion to sit.

"All right. It's just that you appear a little distraught."

Actually, Justin thought she looked beautiful. Her cheeks were rosy, and her golden hair was a flowing cascade against the black background of her habit. There was an edgy excitement to her as she faced him in a challenging manner. He wondered how she would look when she knew what he had done. He had to make her understand and go along with the story he had made up to defuse the situation.

"The young man beside Count Cedric at supper is his much younger brother, Philip. His half brother, actually."

Gilda gasped, but Justin rushed on. "When I asked him why he had been at the Abbey of Saint Ives, he became upset. It was clear that Cedric didn't know anything about his brother's journey. At first Philip refused to talk about the incident. Then he suddenly changed his mind and told the count about finding us together." Justin stopped speaking and looked over to Freda.

"I told her about what happened in the shed," Gilda assured him.

"Good. That will make things easier. I think Philip brought up the subject to detract attention from himself and keep from explaining his own presence. He said he happened upon me having carnal relations with a nun and pointed at you."

Gilda blinked at the words, as they sounded even worse than she'd expected. "It was an embrace! What did the count say?"

"He asked for an explanation."

"You didn't tell him about Lady Mariel, did you?" she asked.

"No. But I'm glad to hear you wouldn't approve of that explanation."

Freda spoke for the first time. "Maybe you better tell us how you did explain the situation."

Justin glanced from one woman to the other. He folded his arms across his chest as though to protect himself. "I told him I innocently embraced Gilda because we had just become secretly betrothed."

Gilda's first thought was that he was jesting. When he attempted an encouraging smile, she realized he was serious. "Are you mad?" she asked.

"Quite possibly," he replied. "I think we should become betrothed in case someone makes inquiries. I'm sure your brother will give his permission in place of your father. Lord Chetwynd owes me a favor."

Moving forward quickly, Gilda grabbed the front of Justin's doublet with both hands, forming fists in the soft material. "I'm a nun. What makes you think I'd become betrothed to you? Who would believe that? You are mad."

He smiled down at her. "You're touching me again."

Gilda immediately pushed him away and turned to Freda for help. "What can I do? This man is ruining my life. I won't marry him."

Justin's voice cut into her plea. "I didn't say anything about marriage. We'll become betrothed for a while. Then, when we've finished this assignment and things return to normal, we'll find a reason to break it off."

Gilda could tell he thought his words should appease her. In fact, they made her even more angry. "I'm a nun," she repeated. "If you can't think about my position, think about your own. What will Lady Lilith think about our betrothal? From what I've heard, you and she are lovers."

"I don't think I wish to hear this," Freda said. "I'll go to my room."

"I need you here, Freda," Gilda pleaded, and the older nun sat down again.

Justin answered her question. "The rumors you've heard are very old. The lady remarried several months ago."

The cold tone of his voice extinguished Gilda's anger. There had been much speculation about Justin and the beautiful widow. She had two sons, and it was said that she feared to marry and jeopardize their inheritance. Clearly the lady had found a husband who was wealthy enough so that it didn't matter. Gilda wondered if Justin's cold words were meant to cover up his hurt.

"I'm sorry," she offered.

"There is no need to be sorry," he replied. "We haven't been involved for a long time. You have old news.

"I know a betrothal sounds mad, Gilda. But I really couldn't think of what else to do. It's my fault that your reputation is threatened. I want to make things right, and I think my plan can work."

Gilda sighed, finally accepting that he had done the best he could. But she still worried about how the plan would succeed. "How did you explain the fact that I'm still a nun if I'm betrothed to you?"

"You haven't taken your final vows. You grew up in the convent, and your father's manor is far away. It's a safe place for you to stay until we're married. The match is still being finalized."

Her eyes widened. "You make it sound so reasonable."

"I believe we should think of the betrothal as real." He glanced over to Freda, remembering that Gilda had discussed the situation with the nun. "There is an attraction between us, as we've already discussed. It's probably one of the reasons we are in this tangle. When the attraction fades, it will be easier to break off the betrothal."

Gilda sat beside Freda. "What do you think of Justin's plan?"

"It could work." Her words surprised both Justin and Gilda. "But what about the fact that you are supposed to be looking into Cedric's desire for an annulment of his marriage? How would your betrothal affect that task, Justin?"

"We were appointed by the king. In addition, I doubt Cedric would object unless it appeared he wouldn't get his way. So far neither party has shown any desire to continue the marriage," Justin replied.

Freda nodded. "I have one suggestion. You should think of a reason why you are delaying the marriage. I will leave you to discuss the matter. Come to bed soon, Gilda."

Justin sat down on the opposite side of the small room from Gilda. Because she avoided looking at him, he was able to study her small figure. He struggled with the urge to sit beside her and put his arm around her. Then he smiled when he remembered her lack of restraint in touching him.

"Is it so terrible, the thought of being betrothed to me?" he asked.

She looked up then. "It's a deception, Justin."

"What if it wasn't? What if we made it real?"

Gilda searched his face. "You mean until the attraction dies?" she whispered.

He stood up and walked across the room to sit beside her. "Marriages are seldom contracted on the basis of attraction," he reminded her. "Can we agree that we'll enter into a real betrothal? Neither of us had thought of marrying, I know, but it has its advantages. Having children is one of them," he said, thinking of the baby for whom they had become godparents.

Gilda's mouth dropped open at his last words, and Justin grinned. "I'm thinking this through as I speak, a method I don't usually consider advisable." He paused, wondering if he was mad, as she suggested. "Perhaps we could have a trial betrothal and get to know each other. Then we can decide whether we wish to go further. We can keep the plan to ourselves, as no one is likely to understand."

It was a novel idea. But it appealed to Gilda for several reasons. They wouldn't be lying, and their relationship would be settled. They could concentrate on why they had come to Mainz.

Gilda nodded. "It seems a reasonable plan. Our relationship has already caused too much distraction. By pointing out our connection, the count's brother has clouded the issue of why he was at Saint Ives. That's what we should be thinking about. Philip clearly went in search of Mariel, and he didn't tell his brother."

Although Justin was relieved Gilda had agreed to his suggestion, he couldn't help being disappointed that she switched subjects so quickly. "You're right, Gilda. Let's go to our rooms, meet in the morning, and work on that problem."

Freda had been awake when Gilda entered their room, but as soon as she saw Gilda, she rolled over and went to sleep. Gilda was unable to do the same. She found it hard to stop her mind from thinking about all that had happened since Justin had offered her an apple for breakfast. The gesture beside the stream now seemed a symbol of the temptation he was turning out to be.

The betrothal was as good as accomplished. Gilda knew her brother would not object to the match. Isabel had been promoting it since she had first seen Justin and Gilda together. Although Gilda hoped it would settle matters between them to have a trial betrothal, she suspected Justin might have second thoughts in the morning. She certainly had them already.

In order to banish the subject from her mind, she turned her thoughts to Lady Mariel and why Philip might have traveled to Saint Ives without his brother's knowledge. It puzzled her that Mariel had taken the sleeping potion. Her explanation seemed false. Even if Mariel had been having trouble sleeping, why would she have taken the potion at the shed? When they found her, she had been lying on the pallet, peacefully laid out and elegantly attired.

Gilda sprang up in bed and threw off the cover. Pausing only to grab a wrap to put around her shoulders, she rushed out of her room and across the outer chamber, and knocked on Justin's door. When there was no reply, she pushed the door open and called, "Justin, wake up."

There was a candle burning by an empty bed, and she wondered where Justin could be. Then she heard a muffled curse from another bed in the far corner. She thought she recognized Justin's voice, but instead of answering her he pulled a blanket over his head.

Tripping over a pair of boots as she made her way to his bed, Gilda mumbled the same curse she heard him use. Impatient with his lack of response, Gilda yanked the blanket off his head.

"Justin, I have something to tell you. Wake up."

"This had better be good," Justin said as he sat up.

When his blanket fell away, Gilda could see his bare chest covered with curly brown hair and framed by white shoulders that seemed very broad. She suddenly doubted the wisdom of her actions and stepped back, only to trip over the same boots she had stumbled on earlier.

As she sat on the floor staring up at him, Gilda said, "You

should put your boots under the bed." Then as he started to rise from his bed, she almost shouted, "No, no, don't get up."

Justin paid no attention to her plea. Gilda was so relieved to see he was wearing tights that she accepted the hand he extended to her. He pulled her up against him, and her cheek touched his hard chest before she could move away.

"Have you come to seal our betrothal with a kiss, Gilda?" he whispered.

One of Justin's hands went into her hair and the other behind her back. He leaned down until his lips found hers. His movements were so slow she could have moved away at any point. But she was mesmerized, unwilling to give up the opportunity to feel his arms around her once more. The kiss was tender. It made her knees weak, and she leaned into him. When his lips applied more pressure, she welcomed that, too, and wrapped her arms around his waist, unable to get close enough.

When Justin's lips left hers, Gilda moaned her disappointment. Then he leaned down again and picked her up in his arms. When he turned to lay her gently on his bed, Gilda realized his intent, and reason returned. She scrambled away to the other side of the bed and almost fell to the floor.

Justin saw the alarm on her face and kept his distance. "You didn't come to seal our betrothal with a kiss, did you, Gilda?"

His voice was so hoarse she hardly recognized it. Afraid to speak, she shook her head.

Justin could feel his heart pounding. He moved away from the bed and pulled on a shirt to give himself time to regain control of his emotions. Then he sat on the other bed.

"Why are you here, Gilda?"

She thought about saying she had lost her mind, but Justin's narrowed eyes told her he was in no mood for jesting. "I remembered something," she said. "I was thinking about the sleeping potion that Mariel took. She had a difficult time waking up, remember? When she did, she saw you sleeping at her side and did a curious thing. She grabbed your arm and turned you over. Remember how shocked she was to see you?"

He nodded, trying to ignore the picture she presented on his bed. She was calmer now and leaned toward him with excitement in her eyes. He tried to concentrate on what she was saying.

"Justin, I think she was expecting to see Philip. He didn't follow you to the shed. She had arranged to meet him there and took the sleeping potion to calm her nerves. I had mentioned that it was also used for that purpose. She must have taken too much."

Instead of answering her, Justin rubbed his face with both hands.

"What do you think?" she urged.

"It's hard for me to think right now, Gilda. You may be right, and it could explain why Philip was so agitated. We'll talk more about this in the morning."

Gilda nodded, feeling foolish that she had rushed to his room in the middle of the night. Being careful to stay as far away from him as possible, she slipped off the end of his bed. "Where's Leonardo?" she asked as she passed the empty bed on her way to the door.

"Out enjoying himself in someone else's bed, no doubt. Leonardo makes friends easily. Fortunate man," Justin muttered.

Gilda couldn't help glancing back to Justin's bed. Then she turned away and opened the chamber door. Justin moved quickly, and his hand touched her shoulder. "Don't come into my room again, unless you're prepared to join me in bed."

Before Gilda could respond, he pushed her through the door and closed it firmly behind her.

CHAPTER FOUR

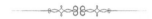

Gilda and Justin hurried along a narrow hallway. Since awakening, they had avoided each other as much as was possible. Before they'd had a chance to overcome their awkwardness and discuss how they would handle the interview with Cedric, a messenger arrived to summon them to the count's chambers.

When Justin's sleeve brushed hers, Gilda stole a glance at his brooding expression. She still remembered the feel of Justin's hand on her back as he pushed her from his room last night. The memory made it difficult for her to concentrate on the task before them. She wondered if it was as clear to Justin as it was to her that their personal feelings threatened their ability to work together efficiently.

"Don't say anything about Philip's appearance at the abbey," Justin said in a low voice. "Let me handle it."

"Of course," Gilda conceded. Then she couldn't help but add, "Try to discover the connection between Philip and Lady Mariel."

Justin was still frowning when Count Cedric greeted him. "Thank you for coming right away, Lord Justin. I wish to apologize for the scene at the table last night. My brother was a bit distraught."

Count Cedric turned his attention to Gilda. She had hung back, waiting for her presence to be acknowledged. Justin couldn't help but wonder how she managed to look so appealing in a dark habit that covered her from head to toe. The black head covering framed her face so that her delicately formed features resembled an ivory cameo.

It was clear that Count Cedric was unsure how to address her. "Lord Justin has told me you and he are betrothed, my lady. I must say the situation is confusing."

"That's understandable, my lord. I was educated at the Convent of Saint Ives, and it has been my home for many years. The prospect of marriage occurred suddenly." That was certainly the truth, and she hoped she could leave it at that.

But their host was clearly not satisfied with her answer. "King Louis has appointed the two of you to investigate my request for an annulment. I had assumed you were the religious envoy."

"I'm still a nun and part of the religious community until I take my leave or marry." She looked at Justin, hoping he would help her out.

He read and answered the silent plea in her eyes. "You can rest assured that Sister Gilda is qualified for this task. At court she is well known for her work with women who have taken refuge at the convent. In addition, she has a special understanding of the religious procedures necessary to annul a marriage."

Gilda was both pleased and surprised by Justin's words. She tried to suppress the smile that tugged at her mouth.

"Is the king aware of your betrothal?" Cedric directed his question to Justin.

"No. Although we have known each other for some time, as Gilda's brother is married to my sister, our betrothal happened rather suddenly, as Gilda said. We are keeping the betrothal a secret until her father can give final approval. In the meantime, Sister Gilda wishes to finish the task assigned her by the king."

His explanation had Gilda clasping her hands together under her long black sleeves. Justin's reply was stretching the truth more than she liked. As she watched for Count Cedric's reaction, Gilda realized how much she wanted to fulfill the role she had been given. It was not often that King Louis chose a woman to be his religious emissary, and she wished to be worthy of the honor.

When Cedric nodded and said, "Let's proceed with the reason you are both here," Gilda breathed a sigh of relief.

Cedric waved them to a bench, then took his chair behind a writing table. "If Charlemagne were still alive there would be no need for this interview. Louis goes too far," he mumbled as he made himself comfortable.

Gilda remembered Freda's words on the subject. Clearly Cedric agreed with Freda that the king was overzealous in his desire to enforce strict adherence to the papal restrictions on dissolving a marriage. Although the Franks prided themselves on being Christian, in the past their marriage customs differed from those imposed by Rome. She imagined both Freda and Cedric considered themselves good Christians in spite of their opposition to the changes sought by Louis.

Having made his complaint clear, Cedric explained his own situation. "My wife has fled, deserting me and her responsibilities. She joined a religious retreat, then refused to return home. The marriage was a mistake, and I have asked for an annulment from the Bishop of Mainz. That should be the end of it."

"As I'm sure the bishop has informed you, staying overlong at a religious retreat is not grounds for an annulment, my lord. On what grounds do you seek an annulment?"

Before answering Justin's question, Cedric glanced toward Gilda. Her head was bowed in what she hoped was an attitude to encourage frank discussion. She could have assured the count that there were no intimate details of marriage that she hadn't heard about during her work with women at the convent. But she knew that wouldn't be wise. Instead she tried to be as invisible as possible. She would leave the questioning to Justin and hope he covered the areas that were important.

The count seemed to have decided to be frank. "Our marriage was never consummated. Lady Mariel claimed the marriage was made under false pretenses, and she refused to honor her vows."

Cedric's words gave Justin pause. If what the count said was true, there should be little trouble in obtaining an annulment. But there seemed to be more to the case. "Are you saying that Lady Mariel felt deceived in some way?" he asked.

"That's what she said. She would have nothing to do with me and kept her bedroom door barred against me."

"What reason did she give for her behavior?"

It was clear they were approaching a subject with which Cedric felt uncomfortable as he turned to look out the window before continuing. Finally, he said, "Lady Mariel is from Bordeaux, where she lived with her father. His wife died some years ago, and he kept Mariel at home rather than sending her away to be educated. Until she was married, she never left her father's manor. She is an unworldly creature. Sometimes I wonder if she isn't demented. Perhaps that's why her father kept her at home."

The count seemed to be wandering in his explanation and Justin wondered why. "Do you honestly believe there is something wrong with Lady Mariel's mind?" he asked.

"No, no. I'm just frustrated by her wild antics. She is young, fourteen years, but my first wife was only twelve." He pushed his fingers through his gray hair. "My marriage to Mariel was arranged between her father and myself at Aachen during the Spring Assembly. Because I was unable to travel to Bordeaux, which is quite a distance from here, I sent my brother Philip in my place for the marriage ceremony."

Gilda had to fight to keep her eyes lowered. No wonder the count was reluctant to tell them the full story. Such a practice was common at one time but had fallen out of favor. It certainly explained the beginning of the connection between Mariel and Philip.

The count shook his head before continuing. "Lady Mariel claimed she was led to believe she was marrying Philip. Which is ridiculous, as Philip will tell you. He is much younger than I am, of course, the son of my father's second wife. Perhaps Mariel believed I would be younger, but there can be no way she could have believed she was marrying Philip. It was just an excuse to keep me from our marriage bed."

Justin was sure that Cedric was well aware that such errors and excuses were the reason the practice of using a surrogate in a marriage ceremony had been discontinued. "Did Lady Mariel make this claim as soon as she arrived in Mainz or after she had been here a while?"

"She was confused and tired when she first arrived. I left her alone for some weeks." His eyes darted over to Gilda, then back to Justin. "It was only when I attempted to make her my wife that she came up with her wild story."

Because Cedric was becoming more and more uncomfortable, Justin decided to change the subject from the marriage bed. "Did Philip explain to you why he went to the Abbey of Saint Ives without your knowledge?"

"Yes, he did. He said he hoped to speak to Lady Mariel and convince her to return to Mainz and honor her marriage vows. He didn't tell me about it because she avoided speaking with him. He felt as though he had failed in his mission. He is a bit impulsive, and I apologize again for the way he attacked your reputation at the table." Cedric glanced toward Gilda again. "I believe he was extremely distressed by the confusion Mariel felt about the marriage."

Justin paused before his next question. He wondered how Gilda would proceed, but he couldn't ask for her comments. He knew the best strategy was for her to remain silent and share her observations with him later.

"Count Cedric, you have petitioned the bishop for an annulment. You have not been married long, and your brother has tried to speak to Mariel on your behalf. From what you have told me about Philip standing in for you during the marriage ceremony, there was certainly room for misunderstanding. The king will want to know why you do not give your marriage more time to work out."

The count stood up and walked to the window, giving himself a moment before answering. He kept his back turned as he spoke. "I have come to believe the marriage was ill-conceived. I know the king is determined that we honor our marriage vows. But what if I persist in taking Mariel to bed, and the marriage proves to be a mistake? According to the church doctrine, I will be bound to her for life."

When the count turned back to face them, his expression was determined. "I wish an end to this marriage. That is all I have to say. Now I have another appointment. We can continue with this discussion later in the day if you wish."

Justin was puzzled by the fact that Cedric would already be thinking that his marriage was a mistake. From his experience it was often the case that it took a while for a young wife to adjust to a marriage. Cedric must know this. "Thank you,

Count Cedric. I have just one last question. Is there someone else you wish to marry?"

Cedric's face turned red and his eyes flashed with anger, but he managed to keep his words civil. "I suppose you've heard rumors. Lady Mariel has not been a wife to me. I suggest you concentrate on that fact."

Struggling to avoid looking at Gilda to see how she was reacting to the count's words, Justin stood. "We will definitely need to talk later, Lord Cedric. In the meantime, I would like to speak with your brother. Will you arrange a meeting for us?"

"I will," he replied tersely.

Once outside the count's chamber, instead of heading for their apartment, Justin led Gilda outside. Their living quarters already held too many memories of their personal relationship, and they needed to concentrate on the interview with Cedric.

He could see that Gilda was bursting with the need to speak about what they had learned, but Justin put her off. "We need to find somewhere quiet to talk," he said.

As they descended the steps into the bailey, people heading for the marketplace surrounded them. Justin was afraid he'd lose Gilda in the crowd, so he took hold of her sleeve. "Let's walk over toward the gardens."

It didn't take long for them to leave the main courtyard behind. Justin walked quickly, and Gilda had to run to keep up with him. She was relieved when they reached the gardens and Justin slowed his pace. There was a maze of shrubbery to the left of a garden of root vegetables, and Justin didn't stop until he reached a secluded bench inside the maze. Although they were still within the walls of Mainz, the greenery gave them some privacy.

Gilda sat on the bench and looked at him expectantly. "Before we talk about the interview, I have something of a personal nature to say," Justin said.

But instead of speaking, Justin paced silently in front of her. Already suspecting he was going to say something about her entering his bedchamber, and dreading the discussion, Gilda lost her patience. "Pray speak, what is it?"

He sat beside her and spoke quickly to keep her from interrupting. "I sent Leonardo to your brother's manor to ask Chetwynd to approve our betrothal. I wrote a letter explaining the situation. The trip is not a long one, and I'm hoping Chetwynd will send back a reply with Leonardo either tonight or early tomorrow."

Gilda gasped. "You go too far, Justin."

"Hear me out. Last night we agreed on a trial betrothal. Chetwynd is like a brother to me, and I don't want him to hear about this from someone else."

Gilda sat on her hands and stared down at her feet under the bench. Nearby, one of Justin's large boots was sprawled out in front of him, the other tucked under the bench. She couldn't help but remember stumbling over the boots in his bedchamber.

"You had no right to do that without speaking to me, Justin. You're making things worse by involving my brother."

"Maybe I should have told you. But after what happened in my chamber, I felt an urgent need to do something. You were in my bed last night, Gilda. Nothing happened, but it could have. You have no idea how close I came to joining you there."

Gilda flushed. "As you say, nothing happened. But there is a difference between having an understanding between us and involving my brother."

"His approval will make our betrothal more believable."

For some reason his words only served to make Gilda angrier. "We can seek Chetwynd's approval, and we can pretend the betrothal is real. But remember this, I'm still a nun. I have a task to complete, and I can't do it unless I'm a part of a religious community. That's why the king appointed me. Our betrothal is not real, and it's unlikely to last beyond our assignment."

Justin wanted to point out that if they ended up in bed together, she might change her mind about desiring a marriage. But he thought better of it and held his tongue.

"I wonder what my brother is going to think when he receives your message. I doubt others will understand what is happening here." She could have added, "I know I don't." Justin tempted her and made her feel things she'd never felt before, but she didn't want to be married. If there was anything she'd learned during her years helping women, it was that nuns had a lot more freedom than married women. Their husbands ruled their lives. Justin was already causing havoc in her life, and they weren't even married.

Gilda changed the subject. "I want to talk about what happened this morning."

Justin was relieved to drop the subject of their betrothal. "I'm eager to hear your opinion on what we learned from Cedric," he said.

Gilda relaxed her shoulders, putting her personal problems away and recalling how Justin had conducted the interview with the count. "I think you did a brilliant job of uncovering several important facts. That Philip stood in for Cedric in the marriage ceremony was most interesting. Philip and Mariel could have formed an attachment."

Justin interrupted, "Let's not leap to conclusions about an attachment."

"For heaven's sake, open your eyes. Remember the incident in the garden shed I spoke to you about last night? Mariel was expecting Philip. They could have arranged to meet there, then Mariel took the sleeping potion to give him a scare. Perhaps she was afraid that he'd take her back to his brother."

"You start off with facts, then spin a fairy tale. Now you've invented a reason for why she took the sleeping potion. Before, you thought she took it to treat her nerves. Can't you stick to what we know for sure?"

"And what about you? The fact is I was in your bed last night. The fairy tale is that something could have happened."

Justin's eyes widened, and Gilda cursed herself for getting off the subject. No matter how hard she tried, her relationship with Justin intruded on her thoughts. "Sorry, that wasn't a good example," she said softly.

Justin shook his head and began to chuckle. It was clear Gilda was having as hard a time forgetting last night as he was. It was a relief for him to realize that, and he threw his head back and laughed.

More relaxed than he had felt all morning, he saw that Gilda was also smiling. "No, it wasn't a good example, Gilda. Go on. What else did I do that was brilliant?"

Her eyes sparkled as she spoke. "The question you asked about whether he wished to marry another was a stroke of genius. His reaction proved that this is a much more complicated matter than we expected. Whatever made you ask that question?"

"Cedric must know that it sometimes takes a while for a young wife to adjust to marriage. Mariel is only fourteen. I assumed there must be some other reason why he thought the marriage had been a mistake. It was a fortunate guess. Do you have a theory about that?" he asked in a teasing manner.

"Now that you asked, consider this. The count may be using Philip, either with or without his knowledge, to rid himself of an unwanted wife. I think Cedric may have consummated the marriage before he found a more advantageous alliance. He persuades Philip to declare his love for Mariel, and they plan to run away together. Then Cedric pretends he hasn't consummated the marriage and asks for an annulment, so he is free to marry someone else."

Smiling, Justin shook his head back and forth. "You're amazing. Why do you believe Cedric succeeded in bedding his wife?"

"Simple deductive reasoning. Cedric said he left Mariel alone for some weeks after she arrived. If you were married to a beautiful woman, would you wait several weeks to take her to bed?"

As soon as the words were out, Gilda remembered the hard pressure of Justin's arms as he lifted her and carried her to his bed. He was staring at her, and she knew he was remembering the same thing.

"I don't think you really want me to answer that, do you, Gilda?" he asked.

She shook her head vigorously.

"For the sake of argument, let's say Cedric was telling the truth and didn't consummate the marriage," Justin suggested. "Perhaps Mariel ran away to avoid his bed, as simple as that."

Gilda paused for a minute. "There's another reason I think the marriage was consummated. When Mariel was hysterical, she shouted, 'There is no baby.' She may have been afraid she was pregnant, then discovered she wasn't. If that's what she feared, she had intimate relations with someone."

Justin had been absorbed in listening to her theories, but he frowned at her words. "You never mentioned this before, Gilda."

"She was hysterical, Justin. Her ravings didn't seem important until now. I forgot about them."

Justin wished he had been present at the interview with Mariel. "Is there anything else you neglected to tell me?" he asked.

"No. I didn't withhold the information on purpose. I suppose I thought it was rather intimate and not important. I never thought the count was going to claim the marriage had not been consummated."

"From now on, we share all information, no matter how seemingly unimportant. Understood?" When Gilda nodded, he continued. "Perhaps we can learn more from Philip. Mariel may have confided in him."

"We should also find out what Bishop Gunthar knows about the marriage. The bishop may have suggested that Philip stand in for Cedric in the marriage ceremony. If so, he gave poor advice."

"We'll talk to him after Philip. I'll be interested to see what story you can weave about the good bishop."

"Be careful, Justin. You may become addicted to my theories."

He thought he might become addicted to more than her theories. She was a pleasure to talk to, and her smile made his heart twist in a way that was becoming all too familiar.

A messenger sought them out as they were leaving the garden. Justin was summoned to the family's quarters for the second time that day. When he arrived with Gilda, Philip seemed surprised and embarrassed by her presence.

"I assumed you'd come alone, Lord Justin. We are discussing a delicate matter."

"Your brother has been most frank, and I assume you will be the same. Sister Gilda represents the religious community in these discussions, and she is experienced in dealing with delicate matters."

Philip addressed Gilda. "I understand you are betrothed. I didn't realize a nun could be betrothed. I hope I didn't cause you any embarrassment," he said, making clear why he felt uneasy.

Since he appeared sincerely apologetic, Gilda smiled to reassure him. "I can understand your surprise."

He returned her smile with a charming grin. "You gave me a bit of a start when I saw the two of you together in that garden shed." There was a hint of sparkle in his eye.

"It was a surprising evening for us all, Philip. But you should remember that I'm a representative of the king. My betrothal is not being investigated. We have some questions for you about your appearance at the convent."

Justin suppressed his own grin as he watched Gilda set the young man straight. He approved the tactic as he suspected Philip was trying to charm her with his apology and easy smiles.

A chastened Philip motioned for them to sit down. Gilda could see that he was even younger than she had supposed. In spite of his unruly brown hair and freckled face, he was a handsome lad. She could understand how Mariel might prefer him to his older brother.

Justin began the interview. "Your brother has told us that you stood in for him at the marriage ceremony with Lady Mariel. At that time, did she give you any reason to believe that she thought she was marrying you?"

"No," he answered quickly. Then, as though remembering the scene, he added, "Her father took care of everything. I didn't speak with her until we exchanged vows on the porch of the chapel."

"And after the ceremony?" Justin asked.

"It was a long journey, and we started back to Mainz that very day."

Hoping to shock Philip into an admission, Justin decided to be blunt. "As you say, it was a long journey back to Mainz. Did you at any time share Lady Mariel's bed?"

"No, of course not." Although Philip spoke with conviction, his eyes shifted away. Whether because of embarrassment or guilt, Justin couldn't be sure. "Nothing like that happened," Philip added, looking back at Justin.

In the interview with Count Cedric, Gilda had let Justin ask the questions, but she didn't hold back with the younger man. "A long journey is often an opportunity for people to become well acquainted. Did you and Lady Mariel talk much during the journey?"

Philip stared at her for a minute, then nodded.

Following Gilda's lead, Justin asked, "Would you say you became friends?"

"Yes, I suppose that's true. Mariel had never been away from home, and I felt sorry for her. She needed someone to talk to. She is very young, my lord."

"Surely not any younger than most brides," Justin replied.

Philip just shrugged.

"Why did you travel to the Convent at Saint Ives, Philip?" Justin asked.

Philip twisted in his chair as though seeking a more comfortable position. "I was worried about Lady Mariel. I wanted to see if she was all right and convince her to return to her husband."

"Did Lady Mariel know you were at the convent?"

"Yes, she did," he admitted. "I saw her when I first arrived, but we were unable to talk privately. We arranged to meet in the garden shed that night. It was her suggestion."

Justin paused, remembering that night and how they had found Mariel. "And you say you went to the convent to persuade her to return to your brother?"

Philip nodded eagerly. "Cedric said Mariel told him she thought she was married to me. I didn't believe him at first, but then I began to wonder if she could have gotten the wrong impression. I stood in for him at the ceremony, and we did talk a great deal on the journey. I went to the convent because I wanted to talk to her."

"Your brother told you Lady Mariel thought she was married to you?" Justin asked.

"That's what he told me. But I didn't bed Mariel. You have to believe me," he pleaded. "I can't help what she thought."

Gilda tried to calm the now-nervous young man. "It's understandable that you would be concerned about the situation, Philip. You and Lady Mariel are friends."

Eager to be understood, Philip appealed to Gilda. "That's right, Sister. Mariel fled from Mainz because she was afraid. When she wasn't in the shed, I thought she was afraid of me too. I came back to Mainz to try and find out why she was so scared. My brother said he never laid a hand on her, but I know she was frightened of him."

"And did you find out why she was afraid of your brother?" Justin asked.

Philip shook his head no, but before he could say more, he was interrupted by a loud noise that startled them all. Bishop Gunthar, carrying a large walking stick that pounded the floor with each step he took, entered the chamber. Gilda couldn't help but wonder if he had overheard what had been said and was making a timely entrance to cut Philip off.

"Count Cedric told me you'd be meeting with Philip. I thought I'd come along to lend a hand, Lord Justin."

Gunthar nodded toward Gilda. They had met briefly after morning worship when he welcomed the two nuns from Saint Ives to Mainz. As he thumped into the room, Gilda couldn't help but remember that Freda had called him a toad. He had almost no neck, and his small head sat upon his large, short body.

Philip's expression made it clear he resented the intrusion, but the young man was silent. Justin sensed he would be reluctant to say more in front of the bishop. "Actually, we've finished talking with Philip, your grace. But perhaps we could have a few words with you."

Philip smiled at this, clearly eager to listen while someone else was questioned. Justin hated to disappoint him, but he knew he'd learn more from the bishop if Philip wasn't present. "We'll talk more later, Philip," Justin promised, making his dismissal clear.

The young man reluctantly took his leave as the bishop settled his bulk into a large chair. "What did Philip have to say?" he inquired.

"He's concerned about Lady Mariel," Justin answered. "You must know that he stood in for his brother at the marriage ceremony. Did you suggest the substitution to Count Cedric?"

"As I recall, there was a problem. Cedric was unable to travel to Bordeaux, and Lady Mariel's father was eager for the marriage to take place right after the Spring Assembly. I realize the practice is no longer in use, but I'm not aware it's against any papal edict."

Gilda watched Justin, wondering if he would press the issue. Instead he changed the subject. "After Lady Mariel arrived in Mainz, did she speak to you about her marriage?"

"No, she did not. That was one reason I did not object to the king sending you and Sister Gilda to look into the matter. Lady Mariel refused to speak to me. When I first heard that she had barred Cedric from her bedchamber, I tried to talk some sense into the willful woman. After that first day, she refused to see me."

His words, and the haughty way he spoke them, convinced Gilda that Lady Mariel showed very good sense in not confiding in the bishop. When Justin glanced over at her, she could tell that he agreed.

"I'm pleased to hear that you do not resent the work that Sister Gilda and I are here to do. Your attitude will make it easier for us to work together."

Justin watched the satisfied expression spread over the bishop's wide face before he continued. "There is something I'm curious about, your grace, and I hope you can help me. I understand from Count Cedric that he wishes the annulment so that he can pursue another match."

The satisfied expression disappeared. "He told you that?" the bishop burst out in a high squeal. Caught off guard, his face flushed. Slowly he seemed to regain his composure. "There is nothing settled, and I'm surprised the count would mention anything about it."

As Justin watched the bishop's eyes narrow, he could see that Gunthar realized he had been led into a trap. "Cedric did not say much, but we have heard rumors and he did not deny that he had other prospects. I haven't questioned anyone yet, but I'm sure we can find out more."

Gunthar must have decided it was best that Justin hear the story from him. "A local landowner is in poor health. He was a soldier in the service of Charlemagne and owns a large property south of Mainz. His only child is an older woman who never married. In order to secure her future, Lord Metcalf approached me to help him find a match worthy of Lady Emma. Until Cedric is free, nothing can be settled. That is why I prefer it be kept a secret."

Justin understood why the bishop would be eager to facilitate such an alliance. He and Cedric ruled Mainz together. Although the bishop was in charge of religious matters and the count secular affairs, in practice the two worked closely. Adding a large piece of farm property to the count's holdings would enhance the position and prestige of Mainz.

"Do you suppose Lady Mariel could have heard rumors about the possibility? Perhaps she was frightened that she would be put aside."

"How should I know? I've already told you the willful woman did not confide in me."

It was clear this line of questioning irritated the bishop. Justin didn't mind irritating him, but he wasn't sure it would gain him much information.

"I'm sure you did what you could to discover what was bothering Lady Mariel. Young women can be difficult in such situations. Do you know if there is anyone she did confide in?"

The bishop's large body had been quivering with anger, but at the change of subject and Justin's sympathetic tone, he stilled. "I don't know of anyone. I'm afraid I can't be of any more help to you on the subject of Lady Mariel."

"Thank you for your time, your grace. If you do think of someone Lady Mariel might have talked to, please let me know."

After the bishop had left the room, Gilda moved closer to Justin and repeated his words to the bishop. "Young women can be difficult in such situations."

"I was trying to smooth things over. It's called tact, and, as you may have noticed, it worked."

"I know. You managed the old toad brilliantly."

Justin's mouth fell open, and he glanced quickly around to make sure they were alone. "You're a nun like none I've ever known," he whispered.

"So you keep saying. Do you think we could go for a ride? There's a monastery nearby that Freda wishes to visit while we're here. We might learn something from the humble brothers."

"By all means. It'll be interesting to learn if they have heard anything about this affair."

CHAPTER FIVE

It was a short ride to the monastery located outside the walls of Mainz. Although Sister Freda had mentioned she was related to one of the monks, Gilda and Justin were unprepared to see a giant of a man approach her at the gates. He lifted Freda from her horse and swung her to the ground, then embraced the tall woman in huge arms that made her look tiny. Freda was blushing when she pushed him away.

As the cheery man laughed at her embarrassment, Freda said, "This is my nephew, Brother Arnulf. I sent him a message that I would stop to see him."

The monk had white hair but an unlined face that gave him a youthful appearance. "Welcome," he boomed. "I had already heard tales of the visitors to Mainz. On a mission from the king, I understand."

The monk looked from Justin to Gilda as he was introduced, and there was a sparkle in his eye. "It's a pleasure to meet the nun who is betrothed," he said.

Now it was Gilda's turn to become flustered. Several brothers in the courtyard glanced in her direction as they passed, and she wasn't sure she appreciated becoming a curiosity.

Justin cleared his throat to distract attention from Gilda. "Tales travel quickly." He knew people in isolated communities had a voracious appetite for news. He remembered there was a priest at the head table when Philip made his accusation.

Although Gilda was also familiar with the speed with which news spread, she had hoped to seek out rumors, not become the source of them. "We've come to speak with the Abbot," she said.

"Of course. I'm afraid he is busy at the moment. I will keep you company until he is free to see you."

They followed Arnulf to a community dining area, and Gilda was pleased to see it was empty. "My brothers and I are fasting," he said, "but I can arrange something for you if you are hungry."

Justin looked at Gilda. "I'm fine," she remarked, not wishing to eat in front of a fasting monk. "What we'd really appreciate is some information."

Brother Arnulf fairly glowed at the idea of discussing what he knew. Frowning at her nephew's eagerness to tell tales, Freda announced she would wait outside in the sun.

"I'm sure you know the reason we've been sent to Mainz," Justin began. "In speaking with Count Cedric, we learned that if his marriage to Mariel is annulled, he hopes to marry a local woman. Have you heard anything about a possible match?"

"It's common knowledge, although it was astonishing at the time the proposed match first came to light. The timing was all wrong, of course. The count already had a young bride on her way to Mainz when rumors began."

Gilda didn't bother to hide her surprise. "It was being discussed even before Mariel arrived?"

"Yes. You have to understand that Lord Metcalf, an old warrior, lives in his own world, never bothering about what is happening outside his manor. He has kept his daughter to himself all these years. All of a sudden he's looking for a husband for Lady Emma."

"Metcalf is a famous name," Justin said.

"Aye, I'm not surprised you've heard it. At one time he was one of Charlemagne's most famous soldiers. He was granted a large benefice for his loyal service."

Justin nodded. "I always wondered what happened to him. I remember hearing stories about his bravery in battle. He had retired to his manor before I arrived at court. Wasn't he seriously injured?"

"Yes, which is another reason he keeps to himself. He limps badly, and his face is terribly scarred. He doesn't like strangers to see him."

"Do you suppose Metcalf is aware that Count Cedric is already married?" Gilda asked.

"He's a crafty old man, interested in a match worthy of his daughter. He may know. If so, I suspect that Bishop Gunthar assured him the marriage would be annulled. Gunthar is as eager as Cedric is to have the rich farmland of Metcalf's property become a part of Mainz."

"What do you know of Lady Emma?" Gilda asked.

"Not much, as she stays close to home. Because of Metcalf's health, Lady Emma is the one who manages the estate. I do know the lady is well past the time when women usually marry. She must have at least thirty years. Women never have much say in these matters, of course. Although her father depends upon her to manage the manor, I imagine he still wants to know that a man will be in charge when he is gone."

"Perhaps Metcalf wants to be sure his daughter doesn't lose the property when he dies. It could return to the king," Justin pointed out.

"You may be right. But Lady Emma loses control in either case, as the count and the bishop will govern the land as part of Mainz if the marriage goes ahead. The king is more likely to forego claiming it for another warrior if the count takes it over."

The Abbot walked in as the holy brother was speaking. The monk flushed, no doubt embarrassed about being caught expressing himself so candidly. He introduced the visitors to the Abbot.

"Thank you, Brother Arnulf. Perhaps you have some chore you should be attending to," the Abbot said.

The monk left quickly, and the Abbot turned to the visitors. Justin and Gilda had jumped to their feet when the Abbot arrived, but he waved them to sit down.

"I suppose Brother Arnulf has given you most of the information you are seeking," the Abbot said, his expression disapproving.

"It's good of you to see us, Holy Father," Justin said, ignoring his reference to Brother Arnulf.

"I'm aware of your mission and was expecting a visit. However, now that you have talked to Brother Arnulf, I'm not sure I have any further information to offer you."

Hoping he could make the Abbot realize they weren't seeking idle rumors, Justin said, "Since you are aware of our mission, you know we have been instructed to determine whether there are grounds to annul the marriage of Count Cedric and Lady Mariel. It's our duty to speak with anyone who can give us information about the situation."

"I understand, Lord Justin. What do you wish from me?" he asked.

"The news that another match is already being discussed is pertinent information. We have learned from Brother Arnulf that the proposal is common knowledge."

"Yes, even in a secluded monastery the outside world intrudes continually. But though we can't avoid being prey to secular information, it has nothing to do with our mission."

Justin glanced at Gilda, hoping she would help him thaw out the stiff-necked Abbot, and Gilda took her cue.

"You're probably aware that Lady Mariel has taken refuge at the Convent of Saint Ives, Father Abbot. I spent some time with her and found her to be a very frightened woman. Did you have a chance to meet her during the short time she was at Mainz?"

"No. There would be no reason for me to meet her. If she needed spiritual guidance, she would have sought out a priest, or the bishop. I don't imagine it's unusual for a young woman who has fled her husband to be frightened."

The Abbot was studying her in a thoughtful way that made Gilda feel uneasy. When he spoke again, she realized what he was thinking.

"I understand that you yourself have become betrothed, Sister Gilda."

Her first thought was that for someone who disapproved of rumors, the Abbot certainly had made note of the one about her. Knowing she should deal with this herself, Gilda struggled to keep from looking to Justin for help.

"My father sent me to the Convent of Saint Ives to be educated. I grew up there and became a member of the community. However, I have not taken final vows, Holy Father." She prayed she wouldn't have to say more about it.

Aware that he was the one to blame for putting Gilda in an uncomfortable position, Justin spoke up. "I trust there is no restriction against a nun who has not taken her final vows from becoming betrothed, Holy Father."

"No, of course not," the Abbot conceded. "But Sister Gilda is still wearing her habit."

"Surely that is not unusual. I believe some priests are married and wear their habit," Justin pointed out, no longer trying to appease the Abbot.

"If they are, they are old men and they live with their wives as brothers and sisters, Lord Justin." The Abbot sat up straighter and narrowed his eyes. "Priests no longer marry, as I'm sure you know. And if nuns plan to marry, they leave the order."

"Sister Gilda is committed to finishing her mission for King Louis before she marries," Justin answered.

The Abbot glared at Gilda. "You represent the religious community in your mission, Sister Gilda. Do take care not to bring dishonor to that community."

Gilda spoke quickly to stop Justin from answering for her. "I hope to bring honor to my community by performing the duty assigned me by the king. What is between Lord Justin and myself will not affect my ability to accomplish the task." And she prayed with all her heart that she spoke the truth.

"Tales spread, Sister Gilda. You've seen examples of that today. Although you may be innocent of wrongdoing, the rumors can be damaging."

"Everyone is eager to hear tales, Holy Father," Gilda replied. "But it's important to distinguish between important information and frivolous rumors. Most people will be able to make that distinction. It would be very difficult to live our lives in a way to avoid all rumors."

There was a hint of softening in the Abbot's expression. "I take your point, Sister Gilda. My own choice has been to withdraw from the world. You may discover there is difficulty maintaining a foot in both the spiritual and secular worlds. I'll pray for the success of your mission."

On the ride back to Mainz, Gilda lagged behind the others. Brother Arnulf was accompanying Freda, and they had gone on ahead. Gilda couldn't forget the Abbot's words. She risked bringing dishonor to her community for a betrothal that was a contrivance. Deep in thought, she was startled when Justin spoke up and she realized he had waited for her to catch up to him.

"You're probably hungry," he said, as though to explain her low spirits. She saw that he was holding out a piece of cheese.

"Have you taken to bringing along bits of food to cheer me?" she asked, astonished at his offer.

He grinned, then asked, "Is it so disheartening, being betrothed?"

"For heaven's sake, Justin, it's all made-up," she reminded him as she nibbled on the cheese that he had given her. "How do you think the Abbot knew about it?"

"There was a priest at the head table last night. He no doubt raced to the monastery with the news."

Justin leaned over to take hold of her reins and pulled her horse to a halt. Gilda was riding sidesaddle with her legs on the far side of the horse. Before she could react, Justin pulled her from her saddle to sit upon his lap.

"What are you doing?" Gilda dropped the chunk of cheese and looked around to see if anyone could see them. Although they were in the woods, she knew the walls of Mainz were not far away.

"The others have gone ahead. I've thought of another way to cheer you. Sit still for a minute," he whispered in her ear.

"Are you mad? Let me go, Justin. You heard what the Abbot said about rumors."

"There is no one to see you. Stop wiggling about. All you're managing to do is arouse me."

Her whole body went still. His meaning was clear, and her cheeks turned pink.

"That's better," he said. "No one can see us here. I want you to come to my room tonight, Gilda."

"No. You are mad. Last night was a mistake."

"Was it?"

She was staring at him with startled eyes when he leaned forward and captured her lips in a hard kiss. When he felt her relax against him, he softened the kiss, teasing and exploring until she was kissing him back. Her mouth opened to accept his tongue, and her arms wrapped around his neck for a thorough kiss that had them both trembling. When he broke away, she moaned.

"It was no mistake—"

Before he could finish his words, Gilda nodded and kissed him, exploring his mouth with her tongue. She liked being on his lap, as her head was level with his. When she moved to kiss his eyes, he gasped for breath.

"Have you been with a man before, Gilda?" he whispered.

"No, of course not," she muttered as she leaned her head on his shoulder so she could kiss his neck.

"Your kisses don't seem those of a novice."

As soon as the words were out of his mouth, he realized he was reminding her that she was a nun. When she tried to pull away, he grasped her chin in his large hand.

"You're an exciting woman, Gilda. I loved the way you stood up to the Abbot, and I think he respected it too. If you decide to choose the nunnery, I won't stop you. But let me ask you this. Do you wish to take your vows without having experienced what it's like to be with a man?"

Instead of answering, she asked a question of her own. "Could you kiss me once more?"

Justin was quick to oblige, kissing her long and hard, and while her arms held him close, his hand moved to cup her breast. It was surprisingly full for a small woman, and his thumb moved over her taut nipple.

Gilda gasped, astonished at the charge his gesture sent through her body. She knew she wanted more and tried to press closer to him.

"Say you'll come to me," he whispered against her lips. "I promise I won't go further than you wish. I just want to hold you, Gilda. That's all I can think of."

It was what she wanted as well, but she hesitated to admit the need she felt but did not fully understand.

They heard the sound of a horse, but Justin still didn't release her. "Say yes," he demanded.

Gilda nodded, and he quickly slid her back onto her own horse. When Arnulf rode into sight, Gilda was settling herself in her saddle. The monk didn't say a word but turned back so they could follow him to Mainz.

Both Justin and Gilda breathed a sigh, but their relief was short-lived. In the courtyard of Mainz the porter who took their horses told them that Leonardo had returned and Lord Chetwynd was with him.

"You were so sure that Chetwynd would approve the match by letter," Gilda whispered as they rushed up the narrow staircase to their chambers. "Whatever did you say to him that brought him here?"

"I gave him a detailed account of how the betrothal came about. Under the circumstances I can't imagine why he would have a problem approving the match."

But Justin remembered the outrage he felt when Chetwynd married his sister Isabel, tricking their father into believing that Justin had approved the match. He told himself the circumstances were different. Chetwynd had been warming Queen Judith's bed a few months before he married Isabel. At the time there was plenty of reason for him to be upset with Chetwynd.

When they entered the outer chamber of their apartment, Chetwynd and Leonardo stood up. Chetwynd's face gave no hint of his feelings, but his greeting was cool.

"This is a pleasant surprise, Chetwynd," Gilda said.

"Is it? I'd like to speak with you alone, Gilda."

Leonardo, who had been talking with Chetwynd, disappeared quickly, but Justin moved closer and spoke in a controlled voice. "I'm the one who wrote the message that brought you here, Chetwynd. I think I should be with you when you talk to Gilda. I remember a similar situation a year ago. At that time, I spoke with you and Isabel together."

"Isabel and I were married, Justin. And Isabel was not a nun. I really don't think you can compare the situations. I want to be sure you are not using Gilda. You are a skilled manipulator and have a way of working situations to your advantage. Gilda has led a sheltered life."

Justin exploded. "You pompous ass. Do you really think I'd be able to manipulate Gilda, even if I wanted to? She may have grown up in a convent, but she knows people and has no trouble holding her own. Don't forget her work with abandoned women. She even shed her habit when you were stupid enough to get yourself thrown in the dungeon. Gilda can take care of herself. She doesn't need you rushing to her rescue."

Chetwynd didn't even try to hide his grin. "You used to have such an even temper, Justin, and often lectured me on keeping my own. I wonder what has happened to change that."

Realizing that Chetwynd was enjoying the situation, Justin's anger fled. "You provoked me on purpose. Is that why you rode all this way, to have a bit of revenge?"

"Not just to provoke you, but it was satisfying," Chetwynd replied. "The reason I came is that my wife believes you have been infatuated with Gilda since you met her. I never believed it, but now I'm beginning to wonder. The betrothal you described in your letter sounds like something invented as an excuse to enhance your fascination with Gilda."

Justin wondered if there was some truth in Chetwynd's words and forced himself to relax. "I explained how that happened. It wasn't planned, if that's what you mean."

"I believe you, Justin. Who would plan such a foolish sequence? But I'd still like to speak to Gilda alone."

Justin looked at Gilda. She had stepped away to let them have their say. There was no reason why he should object to Chetwynd's request, but he worried about it nonetheless.

Justin and Chetwynd had been friends since they were boys, and Chetwynd seemed to know what Justin was thinking. "I'm not against anything there might be between you and Gilda, Justin. Give me a few minutes alone with Gilda."

After Justin left, Chetwynd chuckled and embraced his sister. "He's not at all sure he wants me to talk to you."

They had always been close, but Gilda couldn't approve his approach to the situation. "You were a little hard on Justin, my lord."

"I know. He always takes everything so seriously, and I grew up being envious of his control. I couldn't help provoking him a bit."

"Is that the only reason you came, to have a little fun at Justin's expense?" Gilda asked.

Chetwynd's eyebrow rose. "You've been influenced by Justin. Getting right to the point is his method." He drew her to sit beside him on a bench.

"I came because I'm worried about you, Gilda. Before I met Isabel, I made some serious mistakes with the women I became involved with. But now I know what it's like to find a woman I can love with all my heart and soul.

"Betrothals are entered into for all kinds of reasons, and they seldom have anything to do with love. Many of them work well. But you already have a satisfying life in the convent, Gilda. I've seen you there, and I know about the work you do. You were a great comfort to me when I needed it. Don't leave that life unless you are sure you have found something that will be as satisfying."

As Gilda put her hand on her brother's face, she could feel the tears filling her eyes. "That's a beautiful speech, Chetwynd. Thank you for coming all this way to make it," she whispered.

Chetwynd was surprised at her tears. He'd never seen his calm, levelheaded sister cry. "Don't do that, Gilda," he begged, pulling her close.

"I'm just moved, Chetwynd. I know the kind of marriage you and Isabel share. Everyone around you can tell how you feel about each other, and it's a wonder to see. I won't marry unless I'm sure I'll have the same."

Chetwynd nodded. "Justin is a good man, Gilda. I've never known him to be disloyal, and everyone respects his talent for diplomacy."

Gilda smiled at her brother. "Now you're worried you scared me off him. I know his strengths." Suddenly she was thinking about Justin lifting her onto his lap and kissing her until she was senseless.

Chetwynd was studying her expression. "What is it, Gilda?"

"Nothing. I was just remembering something. I'm sure it's time for vespers. I hope it's a short one because I'm starving."

In the great hall, Gilda watched her brother and Justin at the high table. Chetwynd had golden hair that caught the candlelight. Justin was as dark as Chetwynd was fair, but he matched her brother in build. "They seem to stand out from the rest, don't they?" she commented to Freda.

"Aye, they're well made. Justin has relaxed somewhat. He was pacing around the courtyard while you were closeted with your brother. Was he warning you off?"

"Not exactly, Freda. But he knows how much I love my work. He doesn't think I should marry unless there is love involved."

"Hmmmm. Not everyone can be that lucky." She stared at Gilda's plate. "I don't know how you can eat so much. You don't look big enough to hold it all."

"I've always had a good appetite, and lately it's even stronger." Gilda lowered her voice. "What about lust, Freda? How important is that? I wanted to ask my brother, but it didn't seem appropriate."

"Thank the good Lord for that. You can satisfy lust without love, Gilda, but when they are combined, there is magic."

"I'm so glad Ermguerrd sent you along on this journey, Freda."

When Justin approached their table, the two nuns were smiling at each other. They both jumped when he said, "Gilda, I need to talk to you."

Outside, Justin took Gilda's arm. "What was that all about?"

"What do you mean?" she asked, feigning ignorance.

"You both looked guilty when I spoke to you. Never mind. Now that we've talked with Chetwynd, can we get back to the work that brought us here? I want to talk about what we learned from the Abbot."

He had led her to the ramparts, hoping to find a quiet place they could be alone. It was a clear night and Gilda stared at the stars overhead.

"Your brother is bedding with me tonight, so you can't come to my room," he said as he moved to stand closer. He wanted to hold her but was afraid someone would walk by.

"I thought you wanted to talk about our mission," she teased.

"I do, but you're distracting me," he admitted.

"Maybe we should go inside."

"No, not yet. I'll behave. I was thinking about what we learned from Brother Arnulf. According to him, the count and the bishop were presented with a tempting new alliance before Lady Mariel arrived at Mainz."

"That really surprised me, Justin. What a strange situation."

"I think it means that the count is telling the truth in at least one area. If he had plans to annul the marriage, he would have been careful not to bed Mariel."

"Of course. I didn't think of that. And the bishop would have advised him to stay away from her. But Mariel indicated she feared being pregnant. I don't think I could have misread her."

"If it wasn't Cedric who took her to bed . . ." Justin started.

"Philip. But he denies it also."

"I think we should have another talk with Philip."

Gilda nodded. "It's complicated, isn't it? If it was Philip who took her to bed, how would that affect an annulment?"

"The annulment could still be approved. But if it becomes known that Philip slept with his brother's bride, he will be in a great deal of trouble."

Gilda grabbed Justin's arm. "Let's not leap to conclusions about Philip. We don't wish to cause him any harm." She paused then asked, "What? Why are you smiling at me that way?"

"You're asking me not to leap to conclusions?"

"I see what you mean. I'm worried about this, Justin. A young man's life is in danger because he comforted a frightened girl on her way to an unknown husband. He held her, and they were probably overcome with longing as they lay together under the stars."

"Saints in heaven, Gilda. Stop that. You're going to drive me mad."

"Is there someplace we can go for some privacy?" she whispered.

He moved her back against the rampart wall with his body. "No. Your brother is in my bedchamber."

"It's just as well, just as well," she said, patting his shoulders. He was watching her mouth. "Don't say another word."

"All right. Why not?" she asked.

"Because your lips move in a way that makes me tremble."

"Don't *you* say another word," she countered.

Justin heard footsteps and pulled back. He ignored the interloper, hoping he would walk on. Instead, there was the sound of a throat being cleared.

"I wondered where you had gotten to," Chetwynd said in a cheery voice.

Justin turned to face his friend. "We were looking for a quiet place to discuss our work, Chetwynd."

"Is that a fact. It's a beautiful night, but wouldn't it be more effective to discuss work in your chambers?"

"It would, but I thought you'd be there," Justin pointed out.

"I stayed in the great hall to speak to the count. He asked a great many questions about the two of you. I suspect he wishes to uncover some information that he can use to persuade you to see things his way."

"Heavens, he clearly is desperate to obtain an annulment," Gilda said.

"What did you tell him about us?" Justin asked.

"That I had hoped for some time that the two of you would find each other. I pretended I was Isabel and said all the things about you that she would say. Then I pointed out that you were godparents for our child."

Gilda grinned at her brother. "Thanks for helping."

Chetwynd put his arm around Gilda, who was beginning

to shiver now that Justin had moved away from her. "Gunthar was paying great attention to the conversation. The bishop and the count are powerful men who are determined to have their way in this matter. The two of you should take care. I doubt they would be above harming your reputations if they thought it would be to their advantage."

Gilda leaned into her brother. "We already know we have to be careful, Chetwynd."

"Maybe you two should marry. My presence would be a good excuse."

"No." Gilda pulled away. "We won't marry to keep people from whispering about us."

"You could have more to worry about than whispering, Gilda," her brother said. "Your mission is in jeopardy. I suggest you find a way to pacify the count and the bishop."

"I agree with Chetwynd, Gilda. We have to reassure them in some way. Perhaps let them know we believe that the count did not consummate his marriage to Mariel. If they think we will work for an annulment, they will want to make sure our reputations remain intact."

"I hate to think we're giving in to the pressure," Gilda replied.

"Don't worry, Gilda, if we discover anything different, we'll do what needs to be done."

"It's a good plan," Chetwynd added. "Is there anything I can do before I return home?"

Justin was about to say no when he remembered what they had learned from the Abbot and Brother Arnulf. "Do you know Lord Metcalf?"

"I met him once. His reputation as a soldier was legend, but he was old by the time I joined the king's service. Why do you ask?"

"Perhaps you should pay him a visit before leaving Mainz. He might talk to you more freely than he would Gilda or me. You'd be a young knight paying his respects to an old warrior. See what you can find out for us."

"Justin, what a good idea." Gilda grabbed his arm then quickly let go as her brother watched her with a raised eyebrow.

"I'll find out what I can tomorrow morning," Chetwynd promised.

CHAPTER SIX

At breakfast Count Cedric informed Justin that he was available for a meeting that morning. Gilda and Justin took a few minutes to bid Chetwynd goodbye and then hurried off to the count's living quarters.

"Do you really think Chetwynd will discover anything useful by visiting Metcalf?" Gilda asked as they wound their way through the busy bailey.

"Probably not, but it gets him out from underfoot for a while. He has a keen eye, and so far, he has been using it to watch me."

Gilda chuckled. "To watch *us*. I've felt his eye on me as well. He should be returning home soon. Are you still planning to give the count some reassurance that we believe his story?"

"I want to ask a few questions first, but I think it's a good plan. It's not much of a compromise as we have come to believe his marriage to Mariel wasn't consummated."

Gilda shrugged. There was something about the count that still bothered her. Perhaps it had to do with his giving up on one marriage as soon as a more advantageous match presented itself.

Cedric's greeting was gruff. "I'm sorry I broke off our last meeting so abruptly. I did have another appointment."

Justin ignored his defensive manner. "Since our conversation, we have talked with both Bishop Gunthar and your brother Philip. I'd like clarification on a few of the things we discussed earlier, my lord. You said you had come to believe your marriage to Lady Mariel was a mistake."

"That's correct. The marriage should never have taken place."

"I wonder about the timing of your decision. From what we've heard, you had already decided it was a mistake before Mariel arrived. Yet you told us that Lady Mariel was the one who refused to consummate the marriage."

The count frowned. "She didn't want anything to do with me. I told you the truth."

"That may be," Justin replied. "The question I'm asking you is whether you made an attempt to consummate your marriage."

There was a long pause while Cedric considered his answer. "No, I did not," he finally admitted. "To tell the truth, I was happy that she did not wish the marriage any more than I did. But she did bar the door and made up her wild story about being married to Philip. Our marriage was never consummated; that's the important thing."

The count was still blaming Mariel, and his answer irritated Justin. "I can understand why you wouldn't want us to find out that you were seeking a different match before Mariel even arrived in Mainz, my lord." Justin's tone, as well as his words, revealed his feelings. "But did it not occur to you that sharing that information might have convinced us that your marriage was not consummated? After all, why would you bed Lady Mariel if you wished to have the marriage annulled?"

The count's eyes grew wide as he considered Justin's words. "I'm afraid I've made a tangle of things, Lord Justin. I thought you would believe I was trying to rid myself of Mariel so that I could marry Lady Emma."

The count's face flushed red at his own words, since that's exactly what he had been doing. Justin waited for the count to continue, curious about how he would cover the truth that his mouth had already poured out.

"I discussed the matter with Gunthar before Mariel arrived. By that time Metcalf had approached the bishop about a match with Lady Emma. We thought it best to seek an annulment and figured it would be an easy enough matter. The bishop advised me to stay away from Mariel, and I did."

Instead of letting his explanation stand, Cedric became defensive again. "But Lady Mariel acted strangely from the minute she arrived. I allowed her to go on a religious retreat, thinking that would help, but she refused to return. Instead she took refuge at the abbey."

If Cedric had not added his attack on Mariel's behavior, Justin would not have felt reluctant to give the count some indication they believed his story. He was not used to making concessions before all the information was in, but he remembered Chetwynd's concern for his sister's reputation. He knew he was to blame for any rumors that were circulating about Gilda.

"I thank you for being more open with us, my lord," Justin said, although the words did not come easily for him. They did believe Cedric had kept away from Mariel, so he should not mind saying it, but he did. "Sister Gilda and I . . ."

To Justin's surprise, Gilda finished his sentence for him. "Will consider all the facts when we speak to the archbishop."

From the way the count whipped his head around to glare at Gilda, Justin knew he resented her speaking out. Up to that moment, Gilda had been careful to let Justin conduct the interview.

Cedric narrowed his eyes. "You should also consider your own position, Sister Gilda. I wonder if the king knows he appointed a betrothed nun to be his emissary in this matter."

Furious, Justin was about to respond when Gilda spoke up for herself.

"It's not I who seeks to dissolve a marriage, Count Cedric. King Louis believes that marriage vows are sacred, as you well know. They are not to be put aside when a better offer appears. Since you referred to my position, let me say that when I marry, it will be for life."

Gilda stood tall in spite of her small stature. Justin wasn't sure whether he wanted to throttle her or hug her to him. For the moment the count was too stunned to respond, and Justin took advantage of his astonishment to try to remove the stinger from Gilda's words.

"Sister Gilda makes a valid point, my lord. I suggest you do your best to persuade her that your marriage was a mistake, not only for you, but for Mariel as well. She will make an excellent advocate if she feels it's in the best interest of both parties that an annulment be granted."

Cedric settled back into his chair and looked toward the ceiling. He was clearly making an effort to compose himself. Grasping on to the argument that Justin had given him, he said, "I'm sure Lady Mariel desires this annulment as much as I do, Sister Gilda. Perhaps more. She fled our marriage. You should bear that in mind."

"I will remember that, my lord." Gilda felt the fluttering in her stomach settle. She had felt compelled to speak up, but it wasn't easy for her to do so. Fortunately, Justin had come to her aid with his comment about Mariel. Each day her respect for his skill increased.

"We wish to speak to Philip once more," Justin said, eager to end the discussion while he had the count placated.

"I will send my brother to your chambers directly," Cedric answered. The count stood up and walked them to the door. "I hope you will remember I'm not the only one who wishes an end to this ill-fated marriage." He directed his comment toward Gilda.

Neither Gilda nor Justin spoke until they reached their chambers and Justin had closed the door behind them. He checked the apartment quickly to make sure they were alone. "What possessed you to stand up to the count, Gilda? You surprised me, but I was impressed."

Gilda laughed at his words. "I was afraid you'd be angry. His answers annoyed me, and I couldn't let you give him assurances for my sake."

"I was more stunned than angry. I didn't want to put his mind at ease any more than you did."

"You saved the situation, Justin. Pointing out that he would do well to get me on his side was excellent strategy."

"Did you mean it when you said, 'when I marry, it will be for life'?"

"Of course I meant it. But then I'll not marry unless I'm sure the decision I'm making is the right one for me, and for the one I wed."

He smiled at her and moved closer. "And on what do you plan to base your decision?" He spoke in a sensual whisper as he drew her into his arms. "Have you thought about that?"

Gilda allowed herself the pleasure of leaning against his chest and listening to his heartbeat. It was amazing to her how quickly she had developed a need for his touch. She didn't think it would be appropriate to admit that if she married it would be to someone who made her tremble with pleasure the way he did.

"Why didn't you marry Lady Lilith, Justin?" she whispered. She didn't even realize she was going to ask the question that had been in her mind until the words escaped her lips.

When Justin held her away from him so that he could stare into her face, Gilda almost groaned at the chill she felt at the separation. At least he kept his hands on her shoulders, and heat radiated from them.

"Why are you asking me that question now?"

"We're talking about marriage. Your name was linked to hers, and I wondered why you didn't marry her."

"Our attachment was convenient for both of us. We enjoyed each other's company, but neither of us was interested in marriage, Gilda. At least not to each other."

His words reminded Gilda of her own lack of experience, and she felt jealous of their connection. "It was convenient, you say. Do you mean because she was a widow and you could join her in her bed?"

His hands tightened on her shoulders, and it was all she could do not to grimace. "What I shared with Lilith has nothing to do with us." He loosened his grip then, as though realizing he was hurting her, and she pulled away from him.

"Don't do this, Gilda."

"We have to be careful. Philip should be arriving soon."

"That's not why you're putting up barriers between us. Why are you asking about Lady Lilith?"

She strode away from him, then turned and glared at him from the other side of the room. "I'm experiencing some disturbing sensations that I don't understand, Justin. Every time I'm near you I want to press closer. No, stay on that side of the room." He stopped his forward movement and she continued. "You've felt all these things before, but for me it's new. I guess I wish it was as new and amazing for you."

Again, he moved forward. Gilda stretched out her arm, but he didn't stop until his chest rested against her palm. "Believe me, Gilda, it's just as amazing for me. I've never felt like this before."

She could see by his expression that he meant what he said. "Give me some time, Justin. We have other things to think about right now. I fear that our feelings will interfere with what we need to do, and I don't wish to fail or cause you to fail. We have to be careful. Philip is on his way."

"I know," he said, backing up. "You're right. It's not the time. But we will return to this conversation," he promised.

Justin closed his eyes and tried to refocus his attention. "Do you think Philip was Mariel's lover?"

Justin's eyes opened, and they stared at each other for a minute. The topic of their investigation made it difficult to forget their own attraction. But they both knew they had to try.

"It seems a strong possibility," Gilda answered. "I'm sorry now I didn't spend more time speaking with Mariel."

"You said she was very upset. Besides, we had no way of knowing that there was anyone else involved. We'll have to return to the convent to speak to her before we go on to Reims and report to the archbishop. If she and Philip were lovers, it makes things complicated."

There was a loud knock on the door. When Justin pulled it open, expecting to find Philip, he was disappointed to find a messenger.

"Count Cedric wishes to speak with you, my lord."

"We just came from speaking with him," Justin protested, thinking the messenger was confused.

"I know, my lord. But something has happened, and he wishes you to return at once."

Puzzled, Justin and Gilda again hurried to the count's chamber. Bishop Gunthar and the count were in excited conversation when they arrived. Both men grew silent for a minute at their arrival, then the count spoke. "Philip has fled Mainz. The porter says he departed with his personal servant."

"What makes you think Philip fled? Couldn't he have just gone on an errand?" Justin asked.

Cedric shook his head. "When questioned about his destination, Philip refused to answer."

"Why did you have him questioned about his destination? Surely he is free to travel where he pleases," Justin said.

"I became suspicious when I discovered Philip followed Mariel to the convent. I decided to have him watched. I believe my brother betrayed me with Mariel."

Although Cedric appeared agitated, Justin noticed that the bishop had a satisfied smirk on his face. If what Cedric said was true, it would suit their purposes. For that reason, Justin was suspicious. "What makes you think that, my lord?" Justin asked the count, but he was already sure he knew what the two were thinking.

"It seems clear enough," the bishop intoned. "Philip took advantage of Lady Mariel, and rather than face questioning, he has run away. The lady was afraid of the consequences of their betrayal, which is why she took refuge at the convent."

Although Justin and Gilda had discussed a similar scenario, Justin wasn't willing to allow the possibility without more proof. "I think you might be reading too much into the fact that Philip has departed Mainz without telling you where he is headed, my lord."

Cedric ignored his suggestion. "His flight explains so much. I don't know why I didn't think of it sooner. Mariel insisted she was married to Philip, remember that." Cedric groaned as though in pain. "Without my knowledge, Philip went to the convent to see Lady Mariel. When he realized you recognized him, he claimed to be traveling on my behalf. We think he was seeking to be with Lady Mariel for his own reasons. No wonder she was so afraid to return to Mainz. They betrayed me."

Gilda bit her lip to keep from speaking. She suspected his anguish was affected for their benefit. Cedric wanted nothing to do with the woman he married, and now he pretended to be distraught because she had betrayed him. If what he claimed was true, he had only himself to blame for sending Philip to stand in for him at his marriage. Fortunately, she heard Justin speaking words that voiced her own feelings.

"This matter needs to be investigated, my lord. Although it may look bad for Philip, I don't think you should be so quick to accuse your brother. It was you who sent him in your stead for the marriage. Philip may have done nothing more than form a friendship with Lady Mariel."

The bishop was the one to answer. "The facts speak for themselves, Lord Justin. Philip fled because he is guilty of betraying his brother. I believe the count should report the situation to the archbishop and end this investigation."

Justin addressed the count. "I strongly disagree, my lord. Philip has only been gone a short time. You shouldn't leap to the conclusion that he has fled. All you have to go on is your own interpretation of the facts. Sister Gilda and I will return to the Convent at Saint Ives to speak with Lady Mariel. If we find evidence to support your conclusions, we will report the situation to the archbishop."

The count looked doubtful and glanced toward the bishop, who still appeared determined. "We think there is enough evidence to go to the archbishop now, Lord Justin," Cedric said, although he didn't sound as sure of himself as he had earlier.

"You could do that, Cedric. But consider this. The archbishop is expecting us to determine the merits of your request for an annulment. If we report in your favor, the case will be much stronger. If you go on your own, your report of a betrayal by your brother might be considered biased. As you know, the king is determined that marriages be for life and that the church fathers only grant annulments for specific reasons. You are going to need a strong case, and our support could very well be vital in ensuring the outcome you desire."

Gilda watched the effect that Justin's argument had on the two powerful men. They had been sure they had the evidence they needed to obtain their goal. But now the bishop's smirk was gone, and he appeared thoughtful.

"You'll return to the convent and question Lady Mariel?" Cedric asked.

"Yes. We have more information now and should be able to determine what is behind Lady Mariel's flight. I know that you are impatient to have things settled, but the archbishop is going to want to know all the facts. I sincerely believe it's in your best interest to allow us to continue our investigation."

Gunthar wasn't ready to give in completely. "You talked with Philip, and you've heard what we believe. You must credit that there is merit to our suspicions."

"I learned a long time ago that things are not always what they seem, your grace. You may have reason to be suspicious, but I don't believe you should act on suspicion alone. A young man's life is at stake here. As I said before, someone who has no personal interest in the outcome of the investigation can most forcefully present the facts. That's why we were appointed in the first place. I assure you we will find the truth and report it to the archbishop."

Justin's words were met with silence, and Gilda held her breath. When the bishop nodded to the count, she knew Justin had won them over to his view. She prayed they would stay convinced until she and Justin had a chance to talk to Mariel.

"I will leave the situation in your hands, Lord Justin," Cedric conceded. "But I can't tell you how upset I am by this betrayal. I have always treated Philip as a brother, in spite of the fact that we have different mothers."

"Try and keep an open mind, my lord," Justin urged. "If you love your brother, you will surely want to believe him innocent until proven otherwise. His future is at stake."

"Of course, you are right," Cedric replied, attempting to sound sincere.

Back in their chambers once again, Gilda watched Justin pace the floor. "What's the matter, Justin?"

"I don't like the way things are working out. Gunthar is prepared to brand Lady Mariel and Philip adulterers and win Cedric his annulment. The count seems prepared to go along with him. I have stalled them from acting for a while, but I'm not sure how long they will be patient. If Cedric really cared for Philip, I'd feel better. What do you think?"

"I don't know. Sometimes I think Cedric is sincere in his regard for his brother. He gives you all the right answers. Other times I feel he is playing a game. He's much more skilled than the bishop at hiding his feelings."

"What bothers me most, Gilda, is that what they say may be true. You said Mariel was worried she was pregnant."

"Yes, but I think you're right to want to wait until we can talk to Mariel. There have already been several surprises in this case, and I'm still suspicious of the count."

Later, when Chetwynd arrived in their chambers, he found Gilda and Justin in a thoughtful mood. "New developments in the investigation?" he asked in a cheerful tone.

"You might say that. Tell us about your visit with Lord Metcalf. Gilda and I need a distraction."

"The old warrior may be on his last legs, but he greeted me warmly. Mostly I think he wanted someone to talk to about the good old days when Charlemagne was alive. He said things were simpler when there was a strong leader in charge. He made me nostalgic for the old days I never experienced."

"We were led to believe he is on his death bed," Gilda said as she watched her brother settling himself on a bench and stretching out his long legs. "That's why he is now eager to find a husband for Lady Emma."

"Metcalf didn't appear well. He has a lot of scars and is a bit hard to look at until you get used to him. His energy faded as we talked, and I was afraid to stay too long."

Justin nodded. "That fits with what we have heard. Did you see Lady Emma?"

"I hinted several times that I'd like an introduction, but old Metcalf ignored me. She didn't seem to be anywhere around. But as I was leaving the manor, I came upon a group of peasants tanning some hides. It's a skill I admire, so I stayed to watch for a while. While I was there a beautiful woman on a magnificent horse raced by. One of the men muttered about another sighting of Lady Emma. I understood that I had seen the lady of the manor."

Gilda perked up at his words. "A beautiful woman? Brother Arnulf said she has thirty years and keeps to herself. Tell us more."

"I only had a glimpse, but her hair had come loose from its covering, and its russet color reminded me of turning leaves. Her face was lively with excitement. The lady was not alone." Chetwynd dropped the last tantalizing aside with a satisfied smirk.

"You seem to have surmised a lot from what you call a glimpse," Gilda said.

"Lady Emma didn't even glance in my direction. I would say she was completely preoccupied, and the man she was with was equally engaged."

"Are you trying to tell us that you think Lady Emma has a lover?" Justin asked.

"I don't believe it," Gilda said. "You're making it up, Chetwynd."

Her brother was laughing. "I thought you might be surprised. I spoke with the peasants about her. They were reluctant to speak at first, but one of the young women confirmed Lady Emma's identity. It seems the change in the lady of the manor has surprised them all. Apparently, she has become quite animated of late."

"If she has a lover, that doesn't necessarily change what we know of the situation," Justin pointed out. "Her father was the one negotiating the match with the bishop. Perhaps he wishes to separate her from an unsuitable love interest."

"There is one other thing, Justin. Last night I met the young man who was racing with Lady Emma. He sat beside the count at the high table."

"Philip!" Gilda and Justin spoke together.

"He hasn't fled Mainz," Gilda added.

"He didn't tell the porter where he was going because he was meeting Lady Emma," Justin added.

"Wait, wait. Let's slow down," Gilda pleaded. "Perhaps you misunderstood what you saw, Chetwynd. The discovery you made doesn't fit in with anything we know about the situation. Philip is impulsive and energetic, and also quite young. We thought he might have been involved with Mariel."

"I understand your problem, Gilda. But believe me, I know what I saw."

"Lady Emma is a woman of thirty years, Chetwynd. He's a young boy," Justin pointed out.

"He's not that young. I talked with Philip at breakfast this morning. He asked me a great number of questions about being a soldier in the service of the king and mentioned he had some training. He was very interested in my experiences. Perhaps he has been seeking advice from Metcalf and became acquainted with Lady Emma."

"That's possible," Justin agreed.

"That may be how they met, but I'd be surprised if there wasn't more to it. I can recognize when there is a special spark between two people." Chetwynd looked meaningfully from Gilda to Justin.

Gilda ignored her brother's suggestive look and spoke to Justin. "We have to rethink our assumptions. We can't leave for Saint Ives without learning more about the situation here."

"I'm wondering if Cedric and Gunthar have any idea of what's going on. Would Metcalf have approached them to propose a match with Lady Emma if she was involved with someone else?"

"You know as well as I do that women have little to say in the arrangement of marriages." Gilda frowned and shook her head. "Metcalf may not even know that Lady Emma and Philip are spending time together. Brother Arnulf, who seems well informed about everything, never suggested there was someone else paying court to Lady Emma."

Justin shook his head. "I still can't imagine Philip being involved with two women."

"Why not? He's full of youthful energy and pleasant to look at. I think he has an appealing quality that women would find endearing," Gilda replied.

Both Justin and Chetwynd were staring at Gilda with raised eyebrows. When she realized they were surprised, she laughed. "It's not as though nuns can't notice these things."

"And when was it you noticed, Gilda? The first night we were here, Philip accused you of improper behavior," Justin pointed out. "Then later he didn't want you in the room when I questioned him."

"That's true. But he wasn't hiding his feelings either time. And he changed his mind quickly, a sign of how flexible he can be."

"I guess he is flexible if he is making love to two women at once."

"Justin, you don't know that. Now who is jumping to conclusions?"

Chetwynd, who had been watching the building confrontation, said, "I'm going to the stables to make arrangements for my journey home." Neither Gilda nor Justin bothered to answer him.

When the door closed behind Chetwynd, Justin grinned. "I'm actually jealous. I've never been jealous in my life."

Pleased by his admission, Gilda grinned back. "You have no reason to be. I was just trying to say I find it quite possible that women find Philip attractive. His youth makes him more accessible, not threatening as an older man might be. That's all I meant."

"If your brother is not delusional and Philip is involved with Lady Emma, Gunthar and Cedric are going to be furious. What if they've gotten wind of Philip's visits to the lady? Perhaps that would explain their sudden interest in declaring that Philip has betrayed Cedric by seducing Mariel."

"Justin, Mariel is the key to all this. She is the only one who can tell us the name of the person she feared had made her pregnant. Perhaps we should return to the convent as we planned."

"I suppose you're right. Whatever is happening between Lady Emma and Philip doesn't really matter. Our concern is whether the marriage of Mariel and Cedric can be annulled."

When the door flew open, Gilda and Justin turned to frown at Chetwynd for the interruption. But the excited expression on his face changed their reaction to interest.

"Philip has returned. I was at the stables and approached him to see what I could learn. While we were speaking, he was grabbed by a couple of guards who hustled him away. I think Cedric means to imprison him."

CHAPTER SEVEN

Before Justin could respond to Chetwynd's news that Cedric's guards had seized Philip, Gilda was hurrying to the door. Knowing exactly where she was headed and poised to follow her, Justin spoke quickly to Chetwynd. "What makes you think Philip is in trouble?"

"The guards were rather rough with him. Philip resisted and earned himself a few blows. I stepped in, but some damage was already done. Gilda's description of Philip as impulsive seems accurate. Do you want me to stay around?"

"That's not necessary. I know you're eager to return home to Isabel. But we appreciate what you were able to find out. I better try and catch up to Gilda."

"I'm depending on you to keep Gilda safe, Justin. Just one warning, and it's not about the mess Philip is in. If Gilda means as much to you as I think she does, be careful you don't rush her and ruin your chance for a future together."

Chetwynd's words made Justin pause. He wished he had time to discuss the matter, but Gilda already had a head start on him, so he nodded solemnly to show that he understood Chetwynd's warning.

By the time he caught up to Gilda, Justin hardly had enough breath to speak. "Were you going to barge into Cedric's quarters on your own?"

"Of course not. I knew you'd catch up. I'm afraid Cedric will direct his frustration and anger at Philip, and we need to forestall that possibility."

"I know. But I have to warn you. Chetwynd told me that Philip reacted stubbornly when he was questioned. The guards retaliated."

Without a word Gilda moved even faster. There was a guard at the entrance to Cedric's quarters, but Gilda slipped by while Justin spoke to him. She looked quickly about the room and found only the count and the bishop huddled in hushed conversation. When she approached them, they stared at her, shocked by her boldness. Up until now she had been content to let Justin lead the way and do most of the talking.

"I'm sorry to disturb you, Count Cedric," Gilda said. "We understand that Philip has returned, and we wish to speak to him. It's important to our investigation."

While the two men were still recovering from their surprise at her entrance, Justin approached. He didn't look at Gilda, but he moved to stand in front of her. He was relieved when she moved to his side but stayed just behind him.

"I know you're eager for us to get to the bottom of this matter, Cedric, and the sooner we can talk to Philip, the better our chances," Justin said. "Lord Chetwynd informed us that Philip has returned, so of course we hurried over to speak with him." He thought it was best to allow Cedric and the bishop to think they didn't know Philip had been seized.

"The fool resisted the guards, Lord Justin." Cedric spoke in a clipped manner that revealed his impatience. "There was no need for violence. The guards have placed him in a cell so he can regain his composure. Perhaps you can see him tomorrow when he's had a chance to settle down."

"I understand. Young men can be impulsive and unreasonable. But Sister Gilda and I are eager to be on our way to speak with Lady Mariel and put an end to this business. We'd like a word with Philip now. He is an important link in our investigation. Once we have interviewed him, we can make our plans to return to the convent. I'm sure you agree that it's best to settle this matter as quickly as possible."

The count turned to the bishop, and Justin gave a silent sigh of relief when he saw that the bishop was not going to object. He suspected the two men knew nothing of Philip's involvement with Lady Emma. When the bishop spoke, his theory was confirmed.

"You should remember that Philip was the only one who was alone with Lady Mariel. He's an unreliable and rebellious young man, as you have seen. He may deny it, but we believe he betrayed his brother's trust. If you can't make him confess, we have our own ways of obtaining the truth."

Justin nodded at both men, wondering if Gilda would realize what the bishop meant. When she pinched his arm from behind, he knew she understood and wanted them to hurry to see Philip. "We are here to seek the truth, my lord. We need to be on our way to Philip. Please have a guard take us to him immediately."

Cedric nodded and instructed a guard to do as Justin requested. "Remember, he put up a fight when seized," he warned as he sent them on their way.

As they left Cedric's chambers, Justin rubbed his arm where Gilda had pinched him. "That hurt," he whispered.

"It was a tiny pinch," she whispered back.

They were led to the first level of the dungeon by the guard. Gilda shivered as she remembered Chetwynd being imprisoned in a similar cell and the beating he had received at that time. Like Philip, her brother had been impulsive. But Chetwynd had been defending Lady Isabel at the time. Gilda was puzzled about why Philip had lost control and antagonized the guards.

Justin remembered the same incident, and he wished to spare Gilda the sight of another beaten man. "You wait here, Gilda. I'll make sure Philip is ready to speak with us."

She didn't bother to answer Justin but stepped into the cell right behind him. Philip was slumped on a narrow bench, his face bloody, but he jumped up when he saw his visitors.

Before anyone could say a word, Gilda took charge. "Bring me some clean rags and fresh water," she ordered the guard as she eyed Philip's bloody face.

"Sister Gilda, what are you doing here?" the young man asked, clearly embarrassed to have her see him in such a condition.

"Tending the hurt, as I have done a hundred times, Philip. Now sit down."

"It's just a scratch, Sister. Don't be frightened."

"She's not frightened, Philip, so you may as well save your breath."

Although Justin had wanted Gilda to stay behind, he was beginning to realize that was not her style. He examined the cut on Philip's jaw. It was much more than a scratch, but it didn't seem serious. However, both eyes looked bruised, and he imagined Philip would have two black eyes by morning.

The guard returned with the rags and fresh water that Gilda requested. She waved Justin out of the way so she could get closer to Philip. Sitting on the bench beside him, she gently cleaned his face, avoiding the cut on his jaw until last. Philip pulled back a little when she finally cleaned around it, but he didn't make a sound.

"Face wounds bleed a lot. Now that looks better," she

assured him. In spite of her words, she saw that it was a deep cut and knew it should be stitched to avoid an ugly scar.

"I'll send Sister Freda to stitch the wound. The bleeding seems to have stopped, but it would be best if it were closed up."

"Please don't bother, Sister." Philip straightened up on the bench. "It'll be all right. I've had cuts before."

Rather than argue with him, Gilda decided to leave him to Freda. The older nun had a way about her that brooked no resistance. Instead she remained sitting beside Philip on the bench and signaled Justin with a look that he should begin.

Justin was leaning against the wall, his arms crossed in front of him. He had watched Gilda's handling of the reluctant patient and admired her skill. He knew it was his turn to employ his own skill and learn what role Philip played with Lady Mariel.

Pushing away from the wall, Justin decided on a blunt approach. "Your brother thinks you betrayed him with Lady Mariel. Did you seduce your brother's wife?"

Before he could continue, Philip jumped to his feet. "No. Of course not. I already told you what happened between us." He swayed a little from the sudden movement, and Gilda gently pulled him back to the bench. She kept her hand on his shoulder but removed it when Justin narrowed his eyes.

Philip lowered his head, covering his face with his hands. When he had recovered enough to look up, he asked in a calm voice, "Is that why Cedric has locked me up?"

His relieved manner puzzled Gilda. Perhaps Philip had been afraid his brother knew about his visit to Lady Emma. She wondered if Justin noticed the change.

"Your brother has become suspicious, Philip. You told him you went to the Convent at Saint Ives to persuade Mariel to return to him. Cedric now suspects that you went to see Mariel for your own reasons. When you wouldn't tell the guards where you were going today, he assumed you fled because we were close to the truth and you were guilty."

"I didn't want to tell the guards where I was going. What right do they have to keep track of me? I don't see how that makes me guilty of anything."

Justin hoped to shock Philip into responding honestly. "You should know that when Gilda spoke to Lady Mariel, she expressed fear of being pregnant. Could you be the father?"

"No, I swear it's not possible! If she said such a thing, she's mad. I was a friend to her, nothing more. You have to believe me." Philip turned from Justin to Gilda, appealing to her with wide eyes. "I swear to you that I speak the truth. I never touched Mariel in that way."

"Is there another reason why your brother might be angry with you?" Justin asked.

Before answering, Philip bit his lip and turned his face toward the cell door. "I don't know what you mean," he said.

Interpreting his nervous glance, Justin went to the barred window of the cell and spoke to the guard. "Seek out Sister Freda and bring her here. Tell her that Philip has a cut that needs stitching."

"I told you I don't need stitching," Philip complained when the guard was gone.

"You didn't want to talk while the guard was outside the door. Now he's gone. Talk to us," Justin replied.

Nodding nervously, Philip glanced at Gilda, then began to speak quickly. "I know Lord Chetwynd saw me with Lady Emma this afternoon. No doubt he informed you I was there. I'm in love with Emma and have been since I was ten years old. That's another reason you should believe that I never touched Mariel except as a friend."

Justin stared at the young man who now appeared almost defiant. He had to admire his nerve, although it bordered on lunacy. "You must know that Cedric hopes to marry Lady Emma when his marriage to Mariel is annulled. Apparently, Lord Metcalf himself suggested the match."

"Lady Emma does not wish to marry my brother. She assured me of that today. Her father waited until I was away, standing in for my brother at his wedding to Lady Mariel, before he arranged the match." Philip's voice became bitter as he spoke of Metcalf, and he kicked at the straw on the floor. "He knows I care for Lady Emma. It's his way of separating us. I thought he was my friend."

"Calm down, Philip," Gilda urged him. "Your cut is starting to bleed again. Perhaps it's best if you lie on the bench."

"I don't wish to lie down, Sister," he replied, but he held a cloth to his bleeding jaw. "And I don't need stitching."

"We'll see what Sister Freda says," Gilda replied. "Tell me how you came to know Lady Emma." She hoped to distract him and learn more about their relationship.

"I used to visit her father's manor to see the horses and ask him questions about his years as a warrior with Charlemagne. Metcalf loves to tell tales, and I loved to listen. My mother died when I was ten, and Emma was kind to me. I grew up visiting them. Emma didn't take my vows of love seriously until about a year ago. I think I wore her down." He grinned at Gilda.

"I understand the lady is many years older than you, Philip. I wonder if it's realistic for you to believe that she is serious in her feelings about you."

He straightened his back at her question. "I am no longer a lad, Sister Gilda. She has shown me that she loves me."

It was Gilda's turn to flush red when she realized what Philip meant. He was a bold young man, and his passion was likely to earn him a great deal of trouble. She met Justin's eyes. He raised his eyebrow at her obvious discomfort.

Although Justin was amused by Gilda's blush, he was also worried by Philip's boldness. "If your brother finds out that you're involved with Lady Emma, you will be in great danger, Philip. I don't know why he hasn't already learned of your attachment."

"When I was growing up Cedric encouraged me to spend time with Lord Metcalf. It was a way to keep me out from underfoot, I imagine. Because of our age difference, no one takes note of the time Emma and I spend together. As I said, I grew up in her company."

"That may have been true, but Lord Chetwynd took note and was able to guess your attachment. It won't be long before others notice as well. Especially if you continue to spend a lot of time alone with her."

"There is no turning back now, Lord Justin. Lady Emma finally accepts my love for what it is, and she returns it. I won't give her up."

When voices outside the cell caught his attention, Justin signaled Philip to be quiet. "It's Sister Freda," he said needlessly as the woman was let into the cell by the guard. "Philip has a deep cut that needs attention," he explained to the newcomer.

"I can see that." She used her hand to wave Gilda off the bench. "Lie down, young man."

"I don't need . . ."

"For heaven's sake, stop wasting my time and lie down." An experienced healer, Freda was already pulling out the supplies she needed from a sack fastened at her waist and setting up a small stool she had carried with her. "Gilda, put a little of this on the cut to dull the pain."

At the word *pain*, Philip closed his eyes. Although he clearly was afraid of Freda's needle, he seemed determined to be brave.

Gilda did as Freda instructed, wetting a clean cloth with the ingredients from a small bottle and applying it to his jaw. When Freda signaled her to remove the cloth, Gilda took Philip's hand, then watched in fascination. Sitting on her stool, Freda skillfully sewed the wound together, alternately catching small pieces of flesh from below and above the cut. She could have been mending a piece of clothing for all the emotion she displayed.

During the procedure Philip tightened his grip on Gilda's hand and mumbled a long prayer through partly closed lips. At least Gilda hoped it was a prayer. There seemed to be a number of different references to the Lord.

When Freda finished the last stitch, Gilda said, "It's done, Philip. Freda is a skilled seamstress. I doubt there will be much of a scar."

"Just lie still for a while," Freda instructed Philip, then turned to Gilda. "Are you coming to chapel?"

"You go ahead, Sister. Justin and I need to speak further with Philip."

Freda nodded, then looked at Philip. "You be more careful in the future, young man." Her tone was scolding, but then she patted him on the shoulder. "You were braver than most."

When Freda left, Justin and Gilda moved to a corner away from Philip, who had closed his eyes and seemed to be dozing. They kept their voices low. "I think we should try to convince Cedric to allow Philip to come with us to Saint Ives," Gilda said.

"I know you wish to keep him from harm. But I doubt Cedric is going to agree. For all we know, he already has heard about Philip and Lady Emma."

"You heard what Philip said. Cedric encouraged him to spend time at Metcalf's manor. I suspect Philip would have been beaten much worse if Cedric knew about the lovers."

Justin nodded agreement. Cedric gave no indication he knew about Lady Emma. "But he did lock up Philip. I doubt he'll agree to let us take him, Gilda."

"You can talk him into it, Justin. Your skill in managing Cedric is impressive. He is hoping Philip was involved with Mariel. All you have to do is convince him you need Philip to make your case for an annulment."

His eyebrows rose. "Oh, is that all I have to do?"

"You'll think of something. We can't leave him here. It won't be long before Cedric learns of his attachment to Emma."

"The young fool could use some time alone to think about the consequences of his actions. But I suppose you're right to think he's not safe here."

They were so intent on their conversation that they didn't notice that Philip had sat up until he spoke. "If you can get me out of here, Lady Emma will hide me."

"No!" they answered together.

"Philip, the only way I can move you from Mainz is to convince your brother that I need your help with Mariel. Gilda is right about that. But we're not going to rescue you from here to let you hurl yourself into more danger."

"I can take care of myself. I don't need you to protect me." Philip stood up as he spoke, but the quick motion caused him to sway unsteadily.

Justin shook his head in disgust. "Gilda, say something to this idiot."

"Sit down, Philip." She encouraged him by putting her hand on his shoulder and pushing him back on the bench. "You'll have no chance to win permission from Metcalf to marry Lady Emma if you are accused of betraying your brother. Cedric can keep you in here forever with accusations that you seduced Lady Mariel. We have to make him believe we need you to clear up that situation."

Philip frowned. "How are you going to do that?"

Justin was the one to answer. "By bringing you and Lady Mariel together. That's the argument I can use with Cedric. The annulment of his marriage is his primary goal. He doesn't have to know that we doubt his theory that you and Mariel were lovers."

Gilda nodded. "I'm sure Justin can convince him. I will stay here while he talks to Cedric."

Justin shook his head violently. "No, you will not! I'm not leaving you here, Gilda. Don't even think about it."

"It's the only way we can be sure that Philip will be safe. You know that as well as I do. The sooner you approach Cedric, the sooner you can get us both out of here."

Justin looked at the dirty straw strewn about on the floor and the smelly pot sitting in the corner. Gilda sat down on the bench beside Philip and folded her hands in her lap. Justin suspected that if he meant to remove her, he'd have to drag her from the cell. He was chagrined to see that Philip had an amused expression on his face.

"I don't like it, Gilda," Justin grumbled.

"Don't worry, I know you'll succeed. You have a better chance of convincing Cedric on your own. I seem to make him uneasy."

"I don't care how uneasy you make him. I'm concerned about leaving you here." He glared at Philip. "You take care of her." Justin was not a violent man, but he thought he could easily tear the young lad apart if anything happened to Gilda.

Philip nodded. "I'll guard her," he pronounced with boyish enthusiasm.

Justin narrowed his eyes and then, without moving toward it, stared at the door. Finally, he clasped Gilda by the hand and pulled her up from the bench. Gilda was afraid he was going to drag her from the cell, but instead he embraced her. "I'll be back as soon as I can," he whispered.

When Justin had departed, Philip said, "Is he always so intense?"

Moved by Justin's embrace, Gilda didn't reply for a minute. Then she said, "Justin is serious about everything, which is what makes him so very effective. How do you feel?"

Philip lifted his hand to his forehead. "I have a little headache. Do you really think Lord Justin can persuade my brother to let me leave with you? I'd hate to spend too much more time locked up."

For the first time Gilda sensed the fear he kept so well hidden. "Of course he can. Don't worry." She changed the subject. "Tell me about Lady Emma."

At once Philip's face relaxed into dreamy contentment. "Emma is the most amazing woman I've ever met. When I was ten, I followed her around as she managed her father's estate, and she was incredibly patient with me. She used to laugh when I told her I wanted to marry her, but she did it kindly. We were both lonely, and I appreciated her friendship. This spring, I noticed that she started to look at me in a different way." He grinned.

He was a handsome, well-made lad; Gilda could imagine Emma taking note of the change he must have undergone. "And she started to take you seriously?"

"Emma fought it at first, but I was persistent. I wore her down. Then her father decides to marry her off. It's so unfair. The old man kept her to himself all those years. I'm sure he only let me hang around because he thought I was no threat."

"And Cedric never knew how you felt about Emma?"

"No. We weren't close, and I didn't confide in him. I was sure he'd laugh. Cedric assumed it was the old warrior I went to see, and I encouraged his belief. Metcalf gave me some training, and I told Cedric I wanted to be a soldier."

Losing his enthusiasm, Philip leaned his head back against the wall. "Emma can't marry my brother," he whispered.

Gilda suspected that wasn't true. "Do you really wish to become a soldier, Philip?"

He nodded, but he had closed his eyes. Clearly, he wasn't interested in talking anymore. Gilda reached over to him. "Put your head on my lap, Philip."

She thought he would object, but he paused only a moment before doing as she suggested. He was soon asleep. Gilda leaned her own head against the wall and realized she was hungry. She was missing supper, and she fervently hoped Justin wouldn't be too long.

Justin returned to find both inhabitants of the cell asleep. Gilda's head covering was holding her head in place against the wall, and her face was tipped upward. He might have thought she was praying if he didn't know better. Philip looked entirely too comfortable. Justin clenched his teeth to keep from grabbing his shirt and pulling him forcibly from his position nestled on Gilda's lap. Instead he patted him gently on his shoulder.

Philip jerked upward, then put his hand to his head. Gilda had opened her eyes. "Are you all right?" she asked Philip.

"He's fine," Justin said. "We have to get Philip out of here."

Gilda blinked her eyes at him, then leaped up and hugged him. "You did it. I knew you would get us out of here."

In spite of his hurry to rescue them from the dungeon, Justin pulled her closer and slid his hands up under her veil to her hair. It had been difficult to talk Cedric into allowing Philip to travel with them, and he had feared Gilda would refuse to leave the cell if he had failed. That fact had given him extra incentive to persuade Cedric. When he saw that Philip was grinning at them, he released his hold on Gilda.

"What happened?" she asked.

"I'll tell you about it later. Right now, I want to get you out of here. We'll talk in our rooms."

Because Gilda read the urgency in Justin's expression, she didn't say anything further. As all three left the cell, Philip watched the guard, clearly afraid he would be stopped any minute. Only when they were safely behind a closed door did Philip relax and look to Justin for an explanation.

Justin addressed Gilda. "Cedric has agreed to let us take Philip with us. But I'm worried. Any minute he could find out about Emma and Philip. He's going to be angry, and there is no telling what his next step will be. Rather than wait until morning, I think we should leave for Saint Ives tonight."

"But Philip's been hurt. He could use a night's rest before we leave," Gilda pointed out.

"I'm fine, Sister. I think Lord Justin is right. We need to leave now."

Having the impulsive Philip agree with him did not reassure Justin. He could see that the cut on Philip's jaw was still red and raw looking. "You said before that Lady Emma would hide you. Just how could she manage that?"

"There is a secluded cottage on the manor. We have used it many times. The tenant farmers who live nearby are devoted to Emma and won't give us away." Philip was grinning widely at the thought of seeing Emma.

"What are you thinking, Justin?" Gilda asked.

"Philip and I could spend the night at this cottage, then be on our way in the morning. That way Philip will be out of Cedric's reach. You and the rest of our party can start out tomorrow morning, and we'll arrange a place to meet on the way to Saint Ives."

"It sounds like a good plan. But I want to go with you tonight, Justin."

"That won't work, Gilda. We'd have to take Freda with us if you're going. It's best that you stay with the others."

Gilda knew it would be inappropriate for a young nun to travel alone with two men. If for some reason they didn't meet up with the others as planned, she would draw unwanted attention to herself.

"I want to keep an eye on Philip's injury," she said. "I'll borrow some of Philip's clothes and travel as a lad."

Justin knew it wasn't the first time Gilda had discarded her habit and donned a disguise. The first time he saw her she was dressed as a noblewoman to help her brother. He remembered how angry he had been to discover she was a nun. The elegant noblewoman had caught his eye, and he realized now that he had been deeply disappointed to find she was unavailable.

Before Justin could reply, Philip asked in a disbelieving tone, "Are you going to let her do that?"

Gilda narrowed her eyes at the young man, and Justin laughed. He was learning it was futile to argue with her if she felt strongly about something. His guess was that this was one of those cases. "Sister Gilda is my partner. We have to stay together." As he answered Philip, Justin wondered what Gilda would look like dressed as a lad.

"I'll go with Philip to find some clothes for you, Gilda. You inform Leonardo and Freda of our plan. They should be in the great hall. Also gather some food, in case there is nothing to eat at the cottage."

"Good idea," Gilda replied, beaming at Justin. She had been prepared for an argument about accompanying them and was more than a little surprised when she didn't receive one.

Later in the dining hall, even Sister Freda seemed resigned to the plan. "I think you're right to rush Philip away from here," Freda said after she heard Gilda's explanation. "Lord Cedric is glaring in our direction. Perhaps we have overstayed our welcome."

Gilda had kept her eyes from looking toward the high table, but now she stole a glance and grimaced at the expression on Cedric's face. "Will you be all right traveling with Leonardo until we meet up tomorrow?"

"Of course. But I draw the line at dressing as a man. At my age I attract no attention. Don't concern yourself. We'll meet up with you soon enough. Just be careful, Gilda."

"I have Justin with me."

Freda searched Gilda's face and must have seen something that disturbed her. "As I said, be careful."

CHAPTER EIGHT

As Philip had promised, the cottage he led them to was secluded. Tall trees blocked out the light from the moon and stars, and Justin wasn't sure he would be able to find his way back even in the daylight. But Philip must have memorized the winding route, as he guided them skillfully to a small clearing. No doubt it was a place he used often to meet Lady Emma.

Inside, the thatched-roof cottage was divided into two rooms, and the main one had a rustic fireplace. Because the spring evening was cool, Justin set a fire going while Philip took care of the horses. Justin checked to see that the shutters at the windows were closed, then watched Gilda open the sack of provisions and spread the food out in front of the fire. He knew that from a distance no one but he would recognize that Gilda was a woman. Her hair was securely captured under a woolen cap, and one of Philip's doublets hung loosely on her body. The only possible giveaways to close scrutiny were her face, which was much too sweet even for a young lad, and her legs, whose form in the clingy tights drew his notice. Although boots covered her slim ankles, the shape of her thighs and calves were definitely feminine.

When Philip entered the cottage, Justin tore his eyes away from Gilda. "It's cool outside," he said, to cover the fact that he had been studying Gilda. Philip nodded and flopped down on the floor by the fire. He sat with his legs bent and crossed in front of him. Gilda observed the way Philip was seated and imitated his position.

They ate the bread, roasted fowl, and fruit they carried with them in silence until their hunger had been sated, each busy with private thoughts. Philip was the first to speak. "How did you persuade my brother to release me from the dungeon, Lord Justin?"

"The count is eager to have his annulment, so I appealed to his desire to have an end to our investigation. He is sure we will learn that Lady Mariel was unfaithful and you were her partner. He seemed pleased when I went along with his thoughts on the matter."

A stricken look clouded the young man's face. "I hope you were pretending to believe that story. I befriended the lady, but I didn't bed her."

"To tell you the truth, Philip, I don't know what to believe. But I intend to discover the truth."

Justin's voice betrayed his impatience, and Gilda saw that Philip appeared even more downcast. Although she didn't want to contradict Justin's words, she spoke gently to comfort Philip. "Perhaps you should get some rest, Philip. We'll have to leave early tomorrow for Saint Ives."

"I hope you believe me, Sister Gilda. Compared to Lady Emma, Mariel is a child. I would never touch her."

Gilda felt Justin's eyes on her. "We have to keep an open mind while looking into this matter, Philip. That doesn't mean we believe you are guilty of anything."

Philip seemed only slightly reassured. "There's a small

room at the back. I'll sleep there. You two can settle in front of the fire." Then before leaving he appealed one last time to both Justin and Gilda. "You will discover that I showed Mariel nothing but friendship."

Gilda watched Philip close the door behind him. "Why were you so impatient with him, Justin?" she whispered when they were alone.

"If Mariel feared she might be pregnant, someone lay with her. I think Philip is the most likely person. He has charming ways, as I'm sure you've noticed."

His terse tone of voice made Gilda ask, "What do you mean by that?"

"You know what I mean, Gilda. You stayed in the cell with him, and I found him asleep on your lap when I returned. A charming sight."

"You're being ridiculous," she chided.

Justin knew she was right. He was tired and jealous. In addition, he had to fight the urge to pull off her cap and gather her into his arms. Chetwynd had warned him to be patient, but it wasn't easy. His frustration was causing him to behave irrationally. He prided himself on being a man of reason, but lately his emotions seemed to be running wild.

"I'm sorry, Gilda. But consider this. Philip is a young man with impulsive urges. Mariel is a beautiful young woman. When men and women are thrown together in intimate circumstances, it's natural to be tempted."

"Tempted," she repeated. She stared into his eyes and realized he was speaking of himself as well as Philip.

When Gilda turned away from him, Justin knew he had revealed more than he meant to. "It's been a long day," he said. "Settle your blanket in front of the fire. I'll go to the other side of the room. Do you wish to go outside first?"

Gilda nodded and hurried out. When it was his turn, Justin stayed outside as long as he could, giving himself time to get his feelings under control. When he returned to the cottage, Gilda appeared to be asleep. He could see that she had removed her cap, and her hair resembled a pile of gold as the light from the fire flickered upon it. When he settled on his blanket with his back turned to her, the shine of her hair and the gentle curve of her body appeared behind his closed eyelids.

Justin's groan caused Gilda to burrow deeper into her blankets. She knew that if she went to him, there would be no denying the need she felt to be wrapped in his arms. In order to fight temptation, she reminded herself that Philip was in the next room.

Gilda wasn't sure how much later she heard a noise and felt a draft. Turning her head, she saw the cottage door slowly closing. It seemed odd to her that Justin would go outside, and she got up to have a look. On her way to the window, she saw that Justin was still asleep on the floor and knew at once that it was Philip who had left the cottage.

Instead of waking Justin immediately, she gave in to the temptation to study his face. He lay on his side, and his dark, curly hair hung over his eyes. Crouching beside him she gently pushed the hair back from his face, then held it there so she could see better. Concentrating on his full lips, it was a few seconds before she realized his eyes had opened. Without a word he rolled to his back, reached out, and pulled her down on top of him.

The fire had died down, but there was enough light for Gilda to see his sleepy, half-closed eyes. He hesitated only a second before placing his hands on either side of her face and slowly moving her closer until his lips met hers. His gentle kiss was different from any he had given her before. He opened his mouth and slowly teased her lips with his tongue until she opened up and accepted it into her own mouth.

The kiss went on and on as he drank from her lips and encouraged her to respond. Gilda lost herself to the dreamlike sensation. He was making love to her mouth, and she was soon imitating his thrusts. She heard a purring sound and wasn't sure which one of them it was coming from. The desire to have their bodies as fused as their mouths made her move restlessly on top of him. She wanted to feel the heat of him.

Suddenly Justin lifted her face away from his, and when she tried to regain his mouth, he held her face above him. "This isn't a dream, is it?" he whispered.

"Just kiss me," she pleaded, then became aware of what he was asking.

Gilda propelled herself off him with such force that she bumped her sore hip on the hard floor. "Ohhh," she whimpered. "I'm no good at this."

"Believe me, you're very good at this. But Philip is in the next room."

Justin cursed himself for being so practical. Philip was making love to at least one woman, perhaps two. It had been a dream kiss, and he wanted to taste it again. They would be quiet. But when he again reached for Gilda, she scrambled to her feet.

"That's what I wanted to tell you. Philip left. I heard the door close and thought it was you."

Without a word Justin sprang up and pushed open the door to the back room. After a quick search he slammed the door and let loose with a string of curses.

Gilda grimaced at his words. "Philip probably wanted to say goodbye to Lady Emma," she suggested.

"Don't make excuses for him, Gilda. I got him out of the dungeon, and he's shown his appreciation by running away. He's my responsibility. I made promises to obtain his release."

Justin's fury was understandable, Gilda thought. Philip had left them in a terrible predicament, and if he didn't return, their assignment would be in jeopardy. Although she hoped Philip would appear in the morning, she didn't dare to suggest it would happen. Rather than say anything, she moved to the fire and added a few logs.

Regaining control of his emotions, Justin sat beside Gilda, being careful not to touch her. He knew his anger was as much a result of sexual frustration as Philip's disappearance. "If Philip is guilty of seducing Mariel, he won't be back. We might as well accept that fact," he said as he stared into the fire.

Gilda nodded, but she didn't look at Justin. She was reliving the kiss they had shared. In order to distract herself, she picked up the woolen cap and started to cover her hair.

"Don't do that, Gilda." Justin's plea was hoarse with emotion, and she put away the cap.

"I can't believe Philip would sneak off like that," she said.

When Justin didn't answer, she asked, "What are we going to do?"

"Hope he returns. We can't do anything else until morning. I can't find my way out of here in the dark, and even if I could, I wouldn't know where to go. If he doesn't come back, I'm not sure what we should do. I keep thinking that if I hadn't let him know I doubted his word about Lady Mariel, he might not have run away."

"You have no reason to blame yourself, Justin. I know you don't think he'll return, but try to see things from his point of view. Cedric is going to be making accusations against him and his connection to Mariel. No doubt Philip wants to find Lady Emma and tell her about what is happening. After loving her since he was ten, he has finally convinced her to return his love, and he won't want to risk losing what he has gained."

Justin took her hand. "You have a great deal of faith in people, Gilda. Do you really believe that Lady Emma, who from what we have heard is at least ten years older than Philip, is the love of his life?"

"It's very possible. There is no lack of examples of couples who seem hopelessly mismatched but share a deep love for each other." Gilda looked at her small hand lying in his large one and thought about their own case. Did Justin love her? she wondered. "Let's find something more to eat," she whispered.

Holding her hand tightly, Justin ignored her request. "You are a fanciful person, Gilda. I haven't known many couples who share the type of devotion you speak of."

"What about my brother Chetwynd and your sister Isabel? You know them."

"Yes, I know them. But there is nothing mismatched about your brother and my sister. The puzzling thing about them is they took so long to find each other."

Gilda nodded her agreement and relaxed. The mismatched couple she wished to discuss was the nun and the diplomat, but she was afraid of where that discussion might lead. "Perhaps we should talk of something else to pass the time."

"You really think that might help?"

"No, and neither will eating. Maybe we should try and sleep. It's a long time until morning," she pointed out.

"If I promise to do nothing more than hold you, will you lie in my arms?"

Gilda hesitated briefly, then turned her back and moved closer to him. Justin fitted his body to hers, pulling her close so that she curled into him. Her head tucked neatly under his chin, and when he draped his arm over her stomach, his elbow rested on her hip. It was heaven to hold her, and he knew it would be torture to keep his promise, but he wouldn't change a thing. It felt right.

When Justin awoke, sunlight was seeping into the cottage from the edge of the window covering. He couldn't believe he had fallen asleep. The last thing he remembered was hearing Gilda's steady breathing and feeling her body relax as she nodded off.

Without moving, Justin took stock of how he was holding her. His hand was now cupping her breast. As he became aware of his own arousal, he knew he should pull back before Gilda woke up. Instead he closed his eyes and concentrated on all the places their bodies touched and the heat that touching generated. He told himself that if he moved, he would wake her, and she needed her sleep.

At the same time, he worried about what she would think when she did awake and felt his stiff member resting against her bottom. Perhaps she wouldn't notice, he reasoned. She was a nun, unfamiliar with the workings of a man's body.

But Gilda was not dull-witted. Helping abused and cast-off wives, she was bound to have picked up a great deal of knowledge about men. Justin gently lifted his hand from her breast and moved his body slowly away from hers.

When cool air replaced the warmth at her back, Gilda turned toward the retreating heat source. Blinking open her eyes, she saw Justin pulling away from her. She reached out her hand and placed it at the side of his face. "Where are you going?" she asked.

"It's morning. We should get up." He turned his mouth into her hand and kissed her palm.

"Hmmmm. I had such a lovely dream," she said.

"Did you?" Her half-closed eyes and languid smile were impossible to resist. He pulled her against him again. "What did you dream, Gilda?"

"I dreamed of the way you kissed me when I woke you in the middle of the night. You'd never kissed me like that before. In my dream it was like your whole body was kissing me."

"Do you realize what you're saying?" he whispered against her temple.

"Show me, Justin. Show me what it's like to be together with you like that." She lifted her face, offering her lips.

It would have been so easy to do what she asked. Justin certainly wanted to. But he knew Gilda wasn't fully awake, and he remembered how easy it was to lose control in that state. It wasn't that he doubted the fact that she wanted him, it was just that he feared she would be sorry if he allowed her to give in to her desire. She had never been with a man, and she might regret it later. Her brother had been right to warn him that he must be careful.

"We can't do this, Gilda." His words fell upon her like a bucket of cold water.

Forcing herself to pull free of his arms, Gilda sat with her back to him and tried not to feel rejected. "You're right," she whispered as she straightened her clothes. "I forgot myself."

"Look at me, Gilda. We need to talk about this. It's important that we reach some decision about our future before we let our emotions drag us where we aren't ready to go. Can't you look at me?"

"No, not at this moment. I'm going outside."

Gilda scrambled up and was gone before he could say another word. He had done the right thing, he told himself. Two days ago, he had thought he could make love to her and that would be the end of it. She seemed eager to learn what love was about, and he was certainly eager to show her. But now he wanted more. It wasn't just her body he wanted last night as they lay together in front of the fire. He wanted to talk to her, comfort her, and share a future with her. But he wasn't sure she wanted the same thing. She had made no secret of the fact that her life as a nun suited her.

Gilda was gone so long that Justin was about to go look for her when the door opened. He breathed a sigh of relief when he saw the wide smile on her face, but in the next minute he realized the reason for her happiness, and it had nothing to do with him. Philip was behind her.

"Where did you go?" Justin demanded harshly at the same time as he saw that Philip wasn't alone.

The woman beside Philip seemed taken aback by the bark of Justin's greeting. She stood as tall as Philip, and strands of russet hair hung below her head covering. In spite of the fact that she was a beautiful woman, the way she hung back, holding Philip's hand, gave the impression that she was the shyer of the two.

"I had to speak with Lady Emma," Philip explained. "I left without telling you because I wasn't sure you'd let me go. Lord Justin, this is Lady Emma, daughter of Lord Metcalf."

"My lady," Justin said, nodding his head. Sensing her fear, and knowing he was to blame, he tried to put her at ease. "I hope you don't mind that we used one of your cottages for the evening."

She shook her head but still didn't say anything. Philip spoke for her. "Emma was pleased we stayed here. When we met Sister Gilda outside, we told her that we have brought some fresh bread and cheese for breakfast."

"That would explain the pleased expression on Sister Gilda's face," Justin replied, determined to make up for his earlier harsh greeting.

Emma relaxed enough to say, "Thank you for rescuing Philip from the dungeon, Lord Justin." She looked at Philip's battered face with a sad expression.

"Sister Freda and Sister Gilda tended his wounds," Justin pointed out.

Gilda slipped past him and bent to pick up her cap as Lady Emma, her eyes wide, watched. Philip must have explained the situation to her, but the lady clearly didn't know what to make of a nun dressed as a lad.

Emma seemed fascinated by the sight of Gilda's hair disappearing under the cap. "Are you really a nun?" she asked Gilda.

"I am. I'm only dressed this way because we needed to leave Mainz quickly. I imagine Philip told you the circumstances."

"Yes. Philip explained. But I was expecting . . ." Emma paused as she searched for the right words. "I guess I expected you to be different."

It was clear to Justin that what she meant was she didn't expect to find a beautiful woman. Before he could suggest that Emma return home before she was missed, Philip spoke up, urging the same thing.

"Emma, you should probably get back before Lord Metcalf discovers your absence," he said, appearing nervous as he realized how interested Emma was in Sister Gilda.

Lady Emma smiled at him, but she seemed in no hurry and all signs of shyness had disappeared. She spoke again to Gilda. "You have a lot of freedom for a nun. I didn't realize nuns could travel about as you are doing."

"In spite of what you see, I don't travel about dressed as a lad," Gilda said. "But it's not at all unusual for nuns to travel in our work."

"You have more freedom than I have, Sister Gilda. I've never been away from my father's manor," Emma said. Then another thought seemed to occur to her. "You don't have to worry about your father deciding to marry you off to someone you have no interest in marrying. You are fortunate, Sister Gilda."

"That's true," Gilda replied with a smile.

"What's it like being a nun?" Emma asked.

As she thought about how to answer, Gilda became aware of the two men watching her. She knew Justin didn't understand her life as a nun any more than Emma did. She wanted them both to know how she became a nun and why she loved it.

"My father didn't send me to the convent to be a nun, but rather as a young girl to be educated. As I grew older, I began to teach other younger girls who came from all parts of the empire. That was an education in itself. Listening to their tales, I learned almost as much as I taught. When my father decided it was time I married, I told him I wished to stay at the convent. He wasn't pleased with my decision, but the abbess convinced him that it was the life for me."

As Gilda talked, she forgot the men watching and concentrated on Emma. "Perhaps the greatest advantage of being a nun is being free from the dictates of a father or husband. I understand that your father wishes you to marry Count Cedric."

"Yes. But I have no intention of marrying the count. If I can't dissuade my father, perhaps I can become a nun."

Startled by her words, Philip interrupted their conversation. "You don't have to become a nun. I will take you away, Emma."

The lady looked at his cut and bruised face, her eyes full of sadness. "I would like nothing more, Philip. But I worry about putting you in more danger."

"Emma, please, we've talked about this. Your father can't force you to marry my brother while he's still married. Give me time to work out a plan for us to be together. I know I can do it."

Gilda was also startled by Emma's words. "Being a nun is a vocation that gives a woman a chance to help people and to find spiritual peace. It's a very satisfying life, but it's not for everyone. I don't recommend it as a solution for resolving your conflict with your father. It's a choice you should make for other reasons."

Emma nodded. "I understand what you are telling me, Sister Gilda. I want to be with Philip. But if that isn't possible, I can flee to a convent as Lady Mariel did."

"I hope things work out for you and Philip," Gilda replied. Although she was glad Emma understood that there was something she could do to escape marrying Cedric, Gilda didn't want to encourage flight while Philip was staring at her in dismay.

Philip took Emma's arm. "I wish to say goodbye to Lady Emma in private. I'll be back in a minute," he said as he moved through the door quickly, not giving Justin a chance to object.

As soon as they were alone, Justin turned to Gilda. "You shouldn't have encouraged Lady Emma to join a convent. That's not the answer for every woman who has a problem."

"It certainly isn't, and I did not encourage her to join a convent to solve her problem. If you were listening carefully, you would know I said the opposite." To avoid his piercing stare, she turned to help herself to a piece of the fresh bread Emma had left on a bench.

"You made the life seem ideal. All that freedom from the dictates of husbands and fathers. That's all she is going to remember."

"Emma is a clever woman, and I think she understood what I was saying, even if you didn't."

With a violent movement, Justin ripped a piece of bread from the loaf in front of them. "Oh, I understand all right. You love the freedom you enjoy as a nun with no father or husband to worry about."

Gilda stopped chewing and threw her bread down. "That's it, isn't it? You aren't worried about my misleading Emma. You're angry because I'm satisfied with my life as a nun."

"You receive satisfaction from other things, too, Gilda. You like being kissed, being touched. How do you plan to fit that in with your love for your vocation? Answer me that."

"Lower your voice," she hissed. "Yes, you have taught me to appreciate those things. What are you trying to say?"

"I want to know what your intentions are. Are you going to make love to me to satisfy your curiosity, then return to the convent? Is that your plan?"

"I don't have a plan, Justin."

"All right. I can accept that. But what if I had given you what you wanted this morning? What would you have done?"

"But you didn't give me what I wanted, did you? Because you knew it would have been wrong. And you were right, Justin. Thank you for having the control and good sense to stop."

"Holy mother. You are turning this around on me. Are you angry because I stopped?"

Gilda paused to consider his question. "Maybe a little. But please believe me, it was the right thing. I'm the one who made a mistake. I forgot who I am."

"It doesn't feel right now." He took a step toward her, but before he could reach out to touch her, the door opened, and Philip strode in.

The young man glared at Gilda. "Did you have to put ideas in Emma's head about becoming a nun?"

Before Gilda could reply, Justin spoke harshly to Philip. "You forget yourself. You shouldn't have brought Emma here, and you shouldn't have left in the middle of the night. I hope you got some rest because we're leaving."

Philip looked like he wanted to say more, but Justin's fierce expression discouraged him. When Justin began to gather together the few belongings they had brought to the cottage, Philip moved forward to help.

Gilda followed their lead, packing up the food she no longer had an interest in eating. Justin was being unreasonable, but he had made a good point. That morning she had acted recklessly. If Justin had made love to her, as she had all but begged him to do, she could have become pregnant. If that happened, she'd lose all control over her decision about the future.

Her involvement with Justin was threatening her freedom to choose. She stole a look at his face and could see that he wasn't happy with her. But at least Philip hadn't stayed angry.

"Let me help you with that," he said as he lifted her pack.

"For heaven's sake, let's get going. The others will be way ahead of us," Justin complained, causing Philip to look at Gilda and shake his head.

CHAPTER NINE

Philip, Justin, and Gilda rode in gloomy silence as they
made their way along the road that would lead them to
the Convent of Saint Ives. Philip, who was upset at having to say
goodbye to Lady Emma, took a while to realize that he wasn't
the only one in a melancholy mood. When he did notice that
Gilda trailed behind and Justin rode well ahead, he urged his
horse forward until he reached Justin.

"Is something amiss?" the young man asked Justin in a
quiet voice.

"No," Justin answered, keeping his eyes on the road ahead.

The curt reply kept Philip silent for a few minutes, but he
finally spoke again. "Sometimes it helps to speak of the things
that are bothering you."

When Justin turned his eyes upon Philip, one eyebrow was
raised. Unaffected by the wary look, the young man persisted,
"Perhaps I can be of help."

It was on the tip of Justin's tongue to ask Philip how he
could possibly be of any help. It was ridiculous. Philip was
accused of seducing his brother's wife. If that wasn't bad enough,
he was in love with a woman whom he was unlikely to be able

to marry. Although Justin was skeptical of Philip's qualifications for helping anyone, the young man's offer seemed sincere. For the first time Justin suspected Philip might be more than a reckless, charming youth.

"You were telling the truth, weren't you, Philip? You weren't intimate with Mariel."

"No, I wasn't." The young man beamed. "You believe me. The only woman I ever lay with was Emma. It was the first time for both of us. It was rather awkward and amazing at the same time."

That was a little more detail than Justin wanted to hear, but at the same time it confirmed his growing trust in Philip's word. "I'm glad to hear that, Philip, but let's keep that information between us. We still have to find out who was intimate with Lady Mariel. I'm not sure your presence will help with that task, but at least your brother will be unable to lay hands on you as long as you are with us."

"I know it's for the best that I get away for a while. But I hated leaving Lady Emma. She fears that we are destined to be separated, but I know we'll be together one day. No matter how hard I try, I can't convince her of that."

Justin didn't respond. Although he thought Philip's optimism was sadly misplaced, he didn't wish to be the one to say so. He looked back at Gilda. Although she had been watching them, she lowered her eyes when he turned. He could almost feel her pushing a wedge between them. Dressed as a lad, she didn't look like a nun, but he suspected she was reminding herself that she was one. When she was talking with Lady Emma about her vocation, he could almost see her remembering why she had rejected the marriages her father had proposed.

The sun was high in the sky when they came upon a roadside shrine that was a popular resting place for travelers. The thatched hut that housed sacred relics was set back in a little grove, but there was a covered area beside the road where it was possible to escape the rain or sun while stopping for a meal.

It was Justin's intention to ask the monk who tended the shrine whether he had seen Leonardo and Sister Freda. Unfortunately, there was a small party already occupying the open shelter. Justin didn't wish to take the chance that someone would realize that the young lad trailing behind him was a woman, but before he could signal his party to keep moving, a familiar voice called to him.

"Lord Justin, is that really you? Wherever have you been?"

"Lady Placida," Justin said, then nodded to the others in her party who had turned to see who approached.

"We were just remarking the other day that you hadn't been seen at court for an age," she continued. "There was much speculation about what errand the king had sent you on this time. I'm glad that we stopped for refreshments. Now I can report back to a certain person who expressed an interest in your whereabouts."

Lady Placida was well known for circulating tales, and it occurred to Justin that he might not want to hear who was seeking information about him. Gilda and Philip had caught up to him and would be sure to hear everything she had to say.

"I've been away on assignment," Justin replied, determined to say as little as possible about the nature of that assignment. "We have just stopped for a minute to speak with the local caretaker."

Before Justin could move away to seek the monk, Placida spoke again. "Since you have been out of touch, I have news I'm sure will be of interest to you, Lord Justin. Lady Lilith is a widow again. Her husband had a hunting accident, and the poor man has passed over."

The relish with which she told of his death was completely inappropriate. Justin was aware that Gilda, who already knew about his affair with Lady Lilith, had halted her horse just behind him. "I'm sorry to hear that," he replied.

"I'm sure the lady needs cheering up. Will you be back to court soon?"

"No," Justin replied as he got down from his horse. There was no point now in trying to rush away. He turned to help Gilda from her horse, then realized it would be inappropriate to help a young lad. Fortunately, she was already dismounting.

"We'll stop for refreshments," Justin said to Philip.

"We have plenty of provisions with us," Lady Placida offered. "And there is a spring nearby. Perhaps your servant could fill a jug for us."

It took a minute for Justin to realize that Placida was speaking of Gilda, and he couldn't think of a reason to refuse her request. Placida's traveling companions were two lords and another lady, and the lords were clearly above being ordered to fetch water.

As Justin was wondering if he should offer his services, Gilda, keeping her head bent toward the ground, snatched up the large water jug that Placida indicated and headed for the spring.

Philip, who had watched the exchange with wide eyes, said, "I need to stretch my legs. I'll go along and have a look at the spring."

Because Placida was watching Gilda move out of sight, Justin decided it best to distract her. "The death of her husband came so soon after their marriage. How is Lady Lilith holding up?"

Placida smiled at him. "I knew you'd be interested. Lilith is doing very well in spite of putting on a show of extreme grief. I suspect that she married the count to benefit her children."

One of the lords laughed and the other woman giggled at Placida's words. Justin was wishing he had an excuse to follow

Gilda and Philip. He listened to them gossip further about the situation with one ear and wondered how anyone could think that Gilda was a lad. It irritated him that Philip had been the one to follow her.

When Gilda and Philip returned, Philip was carrying the large jug and Gilda was following with an exaggerated limp, no doubt a plan they had devised to explain why Gilda wasn't carrying the water. In spite of his earlier irritation, Justin had to grin at their ploy.

The lords and ladies were generous in sharing their food supply. They discussed a visit at a nearby manor house, recommending the local wine to Justin and Philip, and took no further notice of Gilda. When she moved out of sight, Justin relaxed. She had no doubt gone to find the caretaker to learn if there had been any sign of Leonardo and Sister Freda.

Justin introduced Philip but neglected to identify him as Count Cedric's brother in case gossip about the count had reached court. Although Lady Placida smiled encouragingly at the young man, her main interest seemed to be in teasing Justin about the possibility of his reunion with Lady Lilith.

Aware that Philip listened carefully to her gossip, Justin hoped she would tire of the subject. He could see by the speculative look in Philip's eyes that the young man was used to court gossip and understood what was going on.

Lady Placida's party was just preparing to leave the shelter when Sister Freda and Leonardo approached. "Here come more travelers in need of respite," Lady Placida commented. "Is that a nun traveling alone with a man?"

One of the lords in her party was clearly becoming impatient with her chatter. "She's an old woman, Placida. No source for gossip there. We need to be on our way. Let's leave the shelter to the new arrivals."

As they watched the noble party move out of sight, Philip remarked, "That was a close one. I can't believe they didn't see through Sister Gilda's disguise. Discovering her true identity would have made that gossipy woman quiver with excitement."

Justin knew Philip was right in his assessment of Lady Placida. The arrival of Leonardo and Sister Freda couldn't have been better timed.

After dismounting, Sister Freda looked around for Gilda, but before she could ask, the younger nun came running from the thatched hut. Barely breaking her forward motion, Gilda embraced Freda and almost knocked them both over.

Surprised, Freda laughed, held on for a minute to get her balance, and then pushed Gilda away so that she could look at her. "You make a convincing lad. Not only do you look like one, you move like one. You almost knocked me over."

"I want to change into my habit," Gilda answered, heading for the bundle on her horse.

Justin frowned at the two women. "We should get moving. The weather is good, and we can cross the mountains if we get there in time. It's important that we put as much distance as possible between us and Mainz."

Gilda knew he was worried about Cedric sending someone after Philip. It was only a matter of time before the count discovered Philip had been with Lady Emma. But Gilda was determined to change.

"I only need a minute," she said, pulling her habit from the saddle pack.

"Can't you do that tonight?" Justin asked, displaying more impatience than he meant to do.

"No, I want to do it now. Freda and Leonardo need refreshment, then we will be off."

Gilda disappeared, and the others became busy. Leonardo and Freda took the food that Philip offered, in spite of the fact that they had some of their own. Aware of his bad mood, no one looked at Justin.

Gilda was true to her promise and returned in a few minutes. The monk, who had joined them, watched her return dressed as a nun with a puzzled look on his weathered face, and Justin glared at her disapprovingly. Without a word, she mounted her horse and the party quickly took their leave of the shrine.

They reached the mountains with about two hours of daylight left. Because the weather was dry and mild, they made the decision to cross. The day they had struggled along the pass in fog and heavy rain was vivid in everyone's mind. But this time they made good progress. By the time they were descending the other side, the sun was gone, and it was dark as they set up camp.

Justin knew everyone was aware of the tension between him and Gilda. It was affecting the whole party. Fearing Gilda might be determined to give up her assignment and remain at the convent, he wanted to persuade her otherwise. As he was debating what to say to convince her to marry him, she went off with Freda.

Although Gilda was aware of Justin's eyes following her, she needed to put some space between them. Sister Freda knew something was wrong, but she waited for Gilda to speak.

"I'm in deep trouble," Gilda finally blurted out at the same time she stumbled over a tree root. Her foot had caught in her habit, and she shook her leg until it was free.

Freda grabbed her arm and led her to some boulders where they could sit.

"Dressing as a lad did make it easier to move. I fear I have gotten used to the freedom," Gilda said to explain her clumsiness.

"It's too dark to walk about," Freda said. Once they were settled, they both stared up at the stars. Freda waited a minute for Gilda to confide in her. When Gilda remained silent, Freda expressed her impatience. "Out with it, Gilda. We both need our rest."

"I have grown to care deeply for Lord Justin," Gilda admitted. "He's wise, and wonderful at understanding people and how they think. In addition to admiring his abilities with people, I long for his touch, and even a glance will make me go soft inside."

"Yes, I suspected you felt that way, Gilda. Does he feel the same way about you?"

"I believe he does. He wants our betrothal to be real, and I know he wants me in his bed." Gilda hung her head.

Freda watched her for a while in silence, then said, "You knew from the beginning there was something between the two of you, and yet you came on this journey. I thought you wanted to see how things would develop. Now you have found out, and yet you are troubled."

"Yes. I'm troubled because since I was quite young I've never lived anywhere but the convent. Teaching children and helping abandoned women is what I do. I feel useful and I like that. If I married Justin, my life would change. I've visited court, and the life of the lords and ladies there never appealed to me."

Gilda thought about her recent glimpse of court life. "Before you arrived, we met a group of nobles at the shrine, and the encounter reminded me of how shallow they can be. One of the ladies was gleefully telling Justin that Lady Lilith's husband just died. She was matchmaking while the earth on the dead man's grave is still fresh."

"Gilda, you can't judge a group of people by a few you met on the road. You know better than that."

"There's more. Justin knew Lady Lilith when she was a widow. He knew her very well and for a long time before she married again." Gilda was sure Freda would get her meaning.

"But he didn't marry her, did he? Perhaps that means she did not mean as much to him as you do."

"Or perhaps he wasn't rich enough for her to marry. She may be richer now that she has survived a second husband." Gilda was surprised to hear the bitterness in her own voice.

"Gilda, we don't really know what went on between Justin and Lady Lilith, and it was a while ago. He wants to marry you. And you believe he cares for you, is that right?"

Gilda nodded.

"Well, you have a choice to make. I think you are fortunate, as you are torn between two things you love. Others don't have such luxury. I know it will be hard, but you have to choose. Then you live with your choice and throw all your energy into making it the right one."

Freda paused, rethinking her words. "Forgive me, Gilda, I make it sound easy, and it isn't. Perhaps I'm a little jealous. You need to talk to Justin."

Gilda smiled at her friend. "I appreciate your honesty and understanding. Lord Justin and I have to concentrate on resolving the question of Count Cedric's annulment. I can't be distracted now."

"You are already distracted, Gilda. Don't wait too long to speak with Justin."

The next day as they rode through the gates of the Convent of Saint Ives, Gilda breathed a sigh of relief at being home. Her smile was wide when a few of the sisters and young children ran to greet her and Freda.

As Justin watched her reception, his expression was sober. Then he noticed a few of the girls looking at him and giggling behind their hands. They didn't leave Gilda's side, but their interest was clear.

Gilda saw the children's reaction to Justin. He was a handsome figure, and even Philip did not receive as much attention from the school children. When Gilda grinned at him, Justin lost some of his reserve and came to walk beside her.

As Gilda and Justin headed for the community hall, the same girls followed, staying a short distance behind. The one exception was a round-faced cherub who followed on Justin's heels, inspecting him closely. She even reached out a chubby finger to touch the fur piece that lined the knife sheath hanging by his side. He smiled down at her, and she ran back to join the others. Justin saw her laughing while her friends patted her back.

"What was that all about?" Justin asked.

"No doubt the girls dared Hilary to touch the rabbit fur. Maybe for good luck, or just to see how it felt," Gilda replied.

"Are they always this curious?" he asked Gilda.

"Oh, yes. That's why it's such fun teaching them."

"I can understand why you feel that way." He paused a minute, then leaned toward her to whisper, "You could teach your own children, you know."

Pretending not to hear him, Gilda suddenly felt very warm. In spite of Freda's advice, Gilda had avoided talking about their future. Now she was home, and it felt good. But the longing she had for the man beside her had not gone away.

It wasn't until after vespers and supper that they had a chance to speak with Abbess Ermguerrd. As the abbess welcomed them back, Gilda felt the force of her observant eyes watching them as they related all that had happened at Mainz. Justin spoke of interviewing Count Cedric and Bishop Gunthar, and Gilda filled in the details and made it clear how clever

Justin had been in learning that the count hoped to wed another. When they related the story of Philip filling in for Cedric at his wedding ceremony, Justin credited Gilda with realizing that Mariel, rather than being afraid of Philip, had arranged to meet him in the garden shed.

"Clearly you have worked well together, as King Louis had hoped." It did not escape the abbess's notice that both Gilda and Justin spoke well of the other's contribution. "If Mariel thought she married Philip, surely he is the one most likely to have bedded her."

"I don't think so," Gilda replied. "He admitted befriending her, but he is devoted to Lady Emma. Count Cedric could be lying."

Justin was shaking his head. "It is just as unlikely that Cedric was intimate with the lady. He had plans to marry Lady Emma even before Lady Mariel arrived in Mainz. Bishop Gunthar, who also favors the alliance with Lady Emma, would have warned Cedric not to touch Mariel if he wished an annulment. I don't know the answer, but I'd like to be there when Lady Mariel is questioned."

Staring at Justin, Gilda held her tongue. She doubted the abbess would allow Justin to observe the questioning of an already unstable Mariel about a matter of such delicacy. The abbess's next words proved her correct.

"I think nothing useful will be gained by your presence, Lord Justin, and it might even do some damage. It's pretty straightforward, after all, but it's also a private matter that Mariel will be more comfortable talking about to Gilda and me. I will have Lady Mariel brought back to the convent tomorrow. She has been staying with a family we trust to protect her."

Justin nodded, and Gilda assumed the interview was over, but Justin didn't make a move to leave. Instead he addressed the abbess. "There was a situation that came up while we were at Mainz that I think you should know about."

Telling herself that Justin wouldn't dare speak of their pretend betrothal, Gilda watched him with wide eyes as he continued.

"You may remember that after we discovered Lady Mariel in the garden shed, two men approached. At the time I thought they had followed me. We hid Lady Mariel, and to distract the men, I embraced Sister Gilda as they opened the door." He paused a minute to let that news sink in.

"As we have already explained, when we arrived in Mainz one of the men turned out to be Philip. At the high table that first night, I confronted Philip. Angry that I had told his brother that he had come to Saint Ives, Philip told Count Cedric about the embrace he witnessed in the shed, no doubt to discredit us. To explain the situation, I said that Sister Gilda and I were betrothed."

Ermguerrd looked from one to the other, a questioning frown on her face. "And did Count Cedric accept your explanation?"

"He did. If he chose to reject our mission, he would have had to request that the king send new envoys. I suspect he wanted us to deal with his case without delay and therefore accepted the situation."

There was a long silence, and just as Gilda was about to say something to fill the awkward pause, the abbess spoke up.

"I imagine the tale served its purpose. Why are you telling me this, Lord Justin?"

"Two reasons. I thought you might hear of the unusual betrothal and wanted you to hear it from me first. I also wished to know if you believe there is any regulation against such a betrothal."

"It was a ruse, Justin," Gilda said, before the abbess could answer.

He nodded his agreement. "At first, yes. I made up the story to protect your reputation, as well as my own. But later we consulted your brother about the situation and received his approval of the betrothal. We also discovered we had feelings for each other."

Amazed at Justin's words and feeling the abbess's eyes upon her, Gilda bit her lip. "That's all true, Justin, but I never agreed to marry you."

"No, you didn't. In fact, I told you that you were free to break the betrothal anytime you wished. So far you haven't talked to me about doing this. Now I want to know from the abbess whether it is against any rules for you to be betrothed to me."

They both looked at Abbess Ermguerrd. "It's unusual for this to happen, but nuns have left the convent to marry before. While I appreciate your telling me the circumstances, it's a matter between the two of you." She looked from one to the other. "I suspect you have some talking to do. I will leave you here so that you will have some privacy."

As soon as the abbess left the room, Gilda turned on Justin. "Why did you do that?"

"Keep your voice down," he answered, pointing to the door that the abbess had left open. "As I said to the abbess, we have come to care for each other. You can't deny that."

Gilda narrowed her eyes. "I'm not marrying you, Justin. Our betrothal has served its purpose, and it is ended."

Working hard to keep his deep hurt from showing, he spoke casually. "Well, at least you're talking to me, which is more than you have been willing to do since we left Mainz."

"Here's what I have to say to you. If you want to get married, go to the palace and find Lady Lilith. Apparently, she is pining away for you."

Gilda's blue eyes were flashing, and her hands were clenched into fists. Justin had seen her angry before, but never to the point that her body trembled. Wondering if she could be jealous, he grinned.

It was the wrong thing to do, as Gilda spun away from him. Justin managed to grab her arm before she could sail through the open door.

Well aware that his grin meant he knew she was jealous, Gilda was humiliated. In spite of her earlier words, the thought of Justin with another woman tore her apart. She refused to meet his eyes.

"I'm going to release your arm, Gilda, before someone passes by the door and sees us. Please don't leave."

As soon as he dropped her arm, she moved away from the door and back into the workroom. No longer wishing to flee, she faced him. "I know you wanted to make sure being betrothed was a real possibility, I believe that. But did you have to tell the abbess that we came to care for each other? Ermguerrd has a good imagination and can figure out what you meant."

"I thought she'd be a good person to talk to. You told her about the kiss we shared."

"Yes—and remember how angry you were to hear I had done that."

"You have a point. I wanted you to talk to me, Gilda. You're back at the convent, and until a minute ago I had no idea what you were thinking. Now you say you won't marry me. Are you just going to forget me and return to your life here?"

"I will never forget you," she whispered.

His face fell. "You've already decided, haven't you? Without even talking to me about what our life together could be, you've made up your mind." He reached out his hand to touch her cheek and had some hope when a tear slid down to wet his fingers.

"This is as hard for me as it is for you, Justin. I will listen to what you have to say tomorrow, when we'll have an answer from Mariel. The mystery will be solved, and our investigation will be complete. After that, I promise I won't avoid you any longer."

Justin knew enough not to press for more. It was true they were approaching the end of what they had been asked to do. If Philip had been intimate with Mariel, Cedric would be free to seek an annulment. On the other hand, if Cedric bedded her, no annulment would be granted. In the meantime, he'd have to think of a way to keep Gilda with him.

CHAPTER TEN

The first thing Gilda noticed about Lady Mariel was that she was much calmer than the last time she saw her. Sister Freda escorted her into the room, and Abbess Ermguerrd indicated that Freda should stay. At the abbess's urging Mariel sat on a bench and even managed a small smile for Gilda, who sat down facing her.

"It's good to see you looking so well, Lady Mariel," Gilda said.

"Thank you, Sister," she replied in a soft voice that was minus the tremor that Gilda remembered.

It had been decided that Gilda would do most of the questioning, and the abbess would step in if she thought of something to add.

"As you know, I have just returned from Mainz, where I met with Count Cedric and Lord Philip. There I learned that Philip stood in for his brother during your marriage ceremony."

"I'm married to Philip," Mariel said, lifting her chin in the air.

Instead of contradicting her, Gilda continued. "The custom of having a surrogate stand in during a wedding ceremony has for the most part been discontinued because misunderstandings can occur. This is what seems to have happened in your case, Mariel. Count Cedric was unable to travel to Bordeaux, so he sent Philip as a surrogate. Do you understand what that means?"

Mariel frowned, then repeated, "I'm married to Philip. He has to be my husband."

"Before the ceremony, did your father speak to you about the man you were going to marry?"

"All he said was that my future husband was wealthy, and I should be pleased he had done so well in finding me a husband. I didn't really want to marry, but Philip was kind to me on the journey to Mainz."

Gilda's anger at Mariel's unfeeling father was growing with each word Mariel said. It was a story she had heard too many times. The authority of a father was above question, and in this case, he wielded that power with little consideration for his daughter. It seems he didn't even take the time to introduce her to Philip and explain that he was a surrogate for Count Cedric.

"What happened when you arrived at Mainz, Mariel?"

Her young face clouded. "It was a nightmare. Everyone kept saying I was married to Count Cedric. Philip disappeared. The count has a cold face and angry eyes. I hated him on sight and barred him from my bedchamber. At first, I was afraid he would insist and there would be nothing I could do. But he left me alone, thank the good lord."

It was the most Gilda had heard her say at one time, but the information was not what she expected. "Count Cedric never entered your bedchamber all the time you were at Mainz?"

"Never."

"And what about Philip? Did you see him at Mainz?"

"No. I expected him to come and straighten out this terrible misunderstanding, but he didn't. All I could think of was fleeing Mainz, but I was locked away in my room."

"Yes, I can understand your feelings," Gilda said. "What happened next?"

"Lady Millicent, the count's sister, came to my bedchamber several times. She was kind to me. She's never been married and seemed to understand my reluctance to accept marriage to the count. When I learned she planned a religious retreat to Saint Ives, I asked to join her. To my surprise my request was granted."

Lady Millicent, a frequent visitor to the convent, was well known to the sisters. It was no surprise to Gilda that she would help Mariel.

"After you had been here a while, Philip finally sought you out, didn't he?" Gilda asked.

Mariel smiled then. "Yes, my husband came, and I promised to meet him at the garden shed. For some reason he wanted to keep our meeting a secret." Her smile then disappeared and she said, "He never came."

"Why did you take the sleeping potion?" Gilda asked.

"I was nervous, and my stomach hurt. I remembered the potion and thought it might ease the pain. I just wanted to escape into sleep for a while. I lit the candles in case Philip did come to me. I didn't realize how strong the potion would be."

Gilda, unhappy about where the questioning was headed, looked at the abbess. At her nod Gilda forced herself to continue. "When we talked to you the next day, you were very confused. You talked about a baby. Did you think you were with child?"

"Yes. I lay with my husband on the journey. But I discovered there was no child." Mariel whispered the rest. "The pains were the beginning of my monthly flow."

There was no doubt in Gilda's mind that Mariel was telling the truth, but that meant that Philip had lied to her. Gilda wondered how he had managed to convince her that he was an innocent. While she was berating herself for being taken in, the abbess spoke up.

"Mariel, I wonder if you would mind telling me more of your journey with Philip. Did he lay with you each night?"

The young woman looked down, but Gilda could see the pink flush coloring her cheeks. "No, Mother Superior. Just one night when there was a storm and I was upset."

"He came to comfort you." When Mariel nodded, the abbess continued. "When Philip was lying with you, did you remove your clothes?"

Mariel's face lifted at that. "No, certainly not."

"This is important, Mariel. Did Philip remove your clothes?"

"No, why would he do that?"

Gilda's mouth fell open. Was it possible that all Philip did was sleep beside Mariel?

The abbess continued her questioning. "Mariel, did your mother tell you how a child is conceived?"

"My mother died when I was young, but my father's sister talked to me. She said a child would come after I lay with my husband." Mariel seemed puzzled by the direction of the questioning.

"It's not quite that simple, Mariel. Were there not animals where you lived? Did you not see them coming together?"

"Holy Mother, those are animals. Humans would never do such a thing," Mariel said, smiling confidently.

Gilda sighed with relief, but she wanted to make sure there was no mistake this time. "Mariel, neither you nor Philip removed any of your clothes?"

"Of course not. We were also wrapped in blankets."

Gilda's admiration for Abbess Ermguerrd grew even greater, if that were possible. Although Gilda had known the education of a woman about to marry was often sadly neglected, it had never occurred to her that Mariel would take her aunt's words so literally. But of course, it made all the sense in the world. Gentlewomen were often protected from the realities of life.

While Gilda sat there grinning, the abbess hid her own smile and spoke to Mariel. "Sister Freda will give you the information that you should have received before you were married. After you understand the situation, we'll talk again about your future."

The young woman was not as simple as she appeared, and Gilda could see that she was beginning to understand that something was missing in her knowledge of marriage. "Have I made a mistake?" she asked.

"No, my dear, the mistake is not yours," the abbess assured her. "Your family neglected your education. It's not the first time this has happened, and it won't be the last. Sister Freda will help you understand."

Before leaving the room, Freda and Mariel bowed their heads to the abbess. Once alone, Gilda was unable to contain her pleasure, and she impulsively embraced the abbess. Just as quickly she pulled back, a sheepish grin on her face.

"What now?" Gilda asked to cover her embarrassment.

"What indeed. Lady Mariel is a virgin, and since she has no fondness for Count Cedric, I suspect he will qualify for an annulment. Perhaps Lady Mariel will stay with us for a while until she makes up her mind whether she wants to return to the home of her father."

"I should hope not," Gilda blurted out.

"That will be her decision, Sister Gilda."

"Yes, of course, but if she goes home, she will not be making any more decisions for herself. Her father will marry her off again."

The abbess nodded to acknowledge the truth of her statement. "I'm glad that Philip is innocent, as I know it means a great deal to you, Gilda. I'll summon Lord Justin, and you can tell him the outcome."

When Justin arrived, he knew immediately by the sparkle in Gilda's eyes that the news was good. His own eyes grew wide as Gilda explained the situation and he came to understand that neither Philip nor Cedric had lied about bedding Lady Mariel.

"I can't imagine how you obtained that information, and I'm glad I wasn't present to listen to it," he said with a grin.

"It was the abbess who knew the right questions to ask," Gilda said. "Mariel must have grown up in a protected household."

The abbess had been quiet while Gilda spoke, but now she said, "Yes, but protected in the wrong way." Then she turned to Justin. "Am I correct in assuming that Count Cedric will be successful in obtaining his annulment?"

"Yes, I think that's very likely. From what you tell me, Lady Mariel will not object to ending her marriage. That would be the only reason for denying an annulment."

"In that case, I imagine you will be leaving soon to report your findings."

Justin glanced at Gilda. Seeing the color drain from her face, he was afraid she wasn't planning on joining him. He spoke to the abbess. "I think Sister Gilda should come with me to explain the delicate information you obtained from Lady Mariel. I doubt I could make the parties involved believe that the lady thought she could conceive by lying beside a man."

Justin knew he was grasping at straws, but he was hoping that Gilda would agree to see the investigation through to its finish. In fact, she appeared torn, but it was the abbess who spoke. "The decision is up to Sister Gilda. I'm gratified with the outcome of this affair, Lord Justin. Hopefully, both Count Cedric and Lady Mariel will obtain what they wish. Stay and discuss the matter as long as you wish." This time the abbess closed the door when she left the room.

Justin spoke before Gilda had a chance to say anything. "I want you to come with me, Gilda." He raised his hand to keep her from replying. "I know you're going to say I can explain the situation, but in fact it would be much easier with you present. We started this assignment together, and we should report our findings together."

"What you say would be true if there was any controversy. But the matter is clear. The count did not bed his bride, and Mariel does not wish to be married to him. In fact, she thought she was married to someone else. You don't need me, Justin. Shouldn't we give some thought to the fate of Lord Philip and Lady Emma? His half brother will move quickly to marry Emma once you report our findings to the king and the annulment is announced."

"But I do need you, Gilda." He decided to risk being truthful. "I want you to marry me."

"I need more time, Justin. I won't be rushed into a decision." Her voice was sad but determined.

Unwilling to give up, Justin paced the floor in front of Gilda, searching for an argument to convince her to come with him. "Your instincts are good, Gilda, and I need your talent in reading people. You were right about Philip. I was sure of his guilt, but he was completely innocent all along."

"I must admit I was worried when Mariel insisted that she was married to Philip and Cedric had not come to her bedchamber. It was the abbess who continued the questioning and arrived at the truth."

"The abbess is a wise woman."

Gilda nodded. "When Cedric realizes what happened, he will know that Philip did not seduce Mariel. But will Philip be safe?"

Justin suddenly stopped his pacing and stared down at Gilda. "Not at all. Once Cedric is free of Mariel, he will seek to wed Lady Emma. Philip will be safe only as long as he accepts that marriage. He is sure to try to sabotage the union and land in the dungeon again."

Gilda frowned, and Justin pressed forward with what he hoped would be the situation that would make her want to join him. "I think Philip is going to be in even greater danger than before. If Cedric learns Philip and Emma were intimate, he might even put his young stepbrother to death. It's important that we protect him."

"Good lord, you're right. We have to make sure that Lord Metcalf allows Lady Emma to marry Philip."

Amazed at the leap she had taken, Justin shook his head. "That's going a bit far, Gilda. I think the best Philip can hope for is to escape with his life. We have to persuade him to flee Mainz."

"Nonsense. There has to be a way to make Lord Metcalf see that Count Cedric is not a proper match for Lady Emma. The count is an old man who has survived two wives and is now putting aside a third."

Justin knew her expectations were too high. "And how is that to be accomplished?"

"I'm not sure," she admitted. "But there has to be a way. I'll come to Mainz with you."

Justin had hoped to persuade Gilda to come along and help protect Philip, but it was clear her purpose was much more ambitious. Although her goal did not seem realistic to him, Justin was quite happy with her decision to accompany him.

He hoped he could reason with her later about how to protect Philip from harm. "Will the abbess agree with your plan?"

"She did say it was my decision," Gilda answered.

But later when Gilda sought out the abbess, her superior asked some difficult questions. "Is it really necessary that you go with Lord Justin, or does your decision have to do with how you feel about the man?"

"I want to see the matter to completion, Mother Superior. My fear is that once Count Cedric is free of Mariel, he will seek to marry Lady Emma. Philip will attempt to stop him, and the conflict will lead to tragedy. If I go to Mainz, I may be able to convince Lord Metcalf to allow his daughter to marry Philip."

"Sister Gilda, I'm sure you know that your plan has nothing to do with the task the king has given you."

Gilda was silent for a few minutes. "What you say is true. But there are connections. Mariel's father forced her, against her will, to marry Count Cedric. Now Lord Metcalf plans to see Emma married to the count, again against her will. Since I was asked to investigate the first case, it seems only right that I keep the same injustice from happening again."

The abbess shook her head, but there was an indulgent smile on her lips. "You are exaggerating the connection, Gilda. You know that fathers can marry their daughters to whomever they wish. The king will not see that as an injustice."

"It's so unfair. I'm sure some fathers must be more considerate of their daughters. Perhaps Lord Metcalf is one of those."

"I understand your desire to do all that you can to avert tragedy. But you haven't answered my question about Lord Justin. I assumed that you would have made up your mind about him by now. I suspect he wants you to marry him, Gilda."

"I know. I have to make up my mind. Sister Freda urged me to do that, but to tell you the truth, I do not wish to give up my vocation. Being a nun is important to me. On the other hand, the thought of not seeing Lord Justin again is painful to imagine."

The abbess sighed. "You wish to keep both options open for a little longer."

Gilda jumped up from her bench. "I swear to you it's not just my inability to make up my mind, Mother Superior. Philip is headed for disaster. I have to do something to help."

"I fear the task is more than even you can manage, Sister Gilda. I'm reluctant to see you go off on a wild errand."

"I'll be able to do something. I know it. Lord Metcalf was one of the king's most talented knights. Sister Freda knew of him when she was at court. My brother Chetwynd had also heard of him and visited with him when he came to Mainz while we were there.

"For years Lady Emma managed her father's manor and he never encouraged her to marry, but now that he is not well perhaps he worries that his estate will revert to the king when he dies. Metcalf knows Philip and even encouraged him in his desire to be a warrior. I must try to convince Metcalf that allowing Emma to marry Philip is best for everyone concerned."

There was a long pause, and Gilda wondered what other objections her superior would present. "You will need Sister Freda to go with you," the abbess said. "I will speak to her."

It took Gilda a minute to realize that Ermguerrd had been convinced by her words; then, all she could do was bow her head to hide her tears. "Thank you," she whispered.

"Be careful, Sister Gilda. Count Cedric is a powerful man, and you will be thwarting his plans if you succeed in your mission. I will pray for you."

After leaving the abbess, Gilda walked to the garden where she had been turning soil the day that Lord Justin had arrived at the convent. That day seemed so long ago. Other nuns had finished the hoeing, and the planting was well under way.

Yesterday's return to the convent had been a happy occasion, but already she was planning to leave. This had been her home, the place that nourished her as she was growing up. Was it time she made her life somewhere else? Lord Justin had said she could teach her own children. Would being his wife, bearing his children, fulfill her as being a nun had done?

Deep in thought, Gilda didn't hear Justin approach until he was standing at her elbow. She looked up at his dear face, saw the worry lines marking his forehead, and couldn't help but smile.

Impatient at having to search her out, Justin said, "Tell me what the abbess said, Gilda."

"Sister Freda and I are going with you to Mainz."

Justin closed his eyes for a minute, but his frown did not disappear. "I thought Abbess Ermguerrd would talk you out of accompanying me."

"No, she didn't do that, although she had a number of questions about my reasons for returning with you. I know I have to make up my mind about whether I wish to remain a nun or become your wife. I desire both."

"That's impossible, and you know it," he said.

"Give me a little more time. Can you do that?"

Justin sighed. "Yes, I can do that. But I've been thinking while I was waiting for you, Gilda. I talked you into coming with me by pointing out that Philip will be in danger. But you are not going to be satisfied with keeping him safe. Now I'm afraid you will put yourself in harm's way. I hate to admit it, but it may be best that you stay here. I will come back when things are settled and perhaps you will have made up your mind."

Unable to speak for a minute, Gilda stared at Justin. When she regained her voice, she said, "You can't mean what you say."

"You expect too much, Gilda. We might be able to help Philip, but I can't believe we can persuade Lord Metcalf to allow Lady Emma to marry him. I know that's what you intend. I don't wish to take the chance that you'll make enemies of Count Cedric and Bishop Gunthar. It's too dangerous."

Gilda sank down to sit on a stone wall, and when Justin sat beside her, she refused to look at him. Watching one of the sisters planting seeds, she said, "I could tell you I won't try to persuade Lord Metcalf to change his mind, but it would be a lie. This is important to me, Justin, and important to our future. I want you to give me a chance to help Philip and Emma. I want you to trust that I can make a difference."

When he remained silent, Gilda turned toward him. "You said my instincts are good. I think we can do this."

"I don't know, Gilda. I can't bear the thought of something happening to you. You might be the one to end up in the dungeon."

"I've been in dangerous situations before. There have been several times I've come between an abusive husband and his wife. I know how to take care of myself."

She waited for him to think through what she had said. As she was about to continue, he said, "We'd have to work together, Gilda. You'll have to agree not to try anything on your own. And if I believe we have to retreat, you have to trust me."

"I agree. We'll work together, and I'll trust you, Justin."

He was no longer frowning. "All right," he said. "But you must remember your promise."

Covering her action with her habit, Gilda took his hand. "I'd cover you with kisses, but there are too many people around."

Justin finally smiled. "Keep that thought for later," he said.

CHAPTER ELEVEN

The weather was favorable, and the return journey to Mainz was accomplished without incident. Most of the time the travelers were absorbed in anticipation of their arrival at Mainz and speculating on how events would unfold once Gilda and Justin had reported to Count Cedric. Justin had cautioned Gilda about giving Philip false hope, so she had not spoken to Philip about her plans to approach Lord Metcalf.

Although Philip was at first happy that he had been cleared of any misdeed involving Lady Mariel, he soon realized that his brother was sure to receive the annulment he wished. Since he knew that meant the count would seek to marry Emma, his spirits plummeted. Philip rode at the end of the small caravan, as though delaying as long as possible his arrival at Mainz.

As they neared their destination, Justin, still uneasy about allowing Gilda to come along, spent time with Leonardo, alerting him of the possibility of danger. "If for any reason I become separated from Sister Gilda, I want you to keep an eye on her. She promised to stay with me, but she is determined to help Philip, and I fear she might be planning to approach Lord Metcalf on his behalf."

Leonardo looked back at where Gilda was in conversation with Sister Freda. "Perhaps you should have left her at the convent, Justin."

"Believe me, I tried," he answered, but he knew his try had been half-hearted.

Leonardo's mouth twisted into a grin that caused Justin to frown. "What?" he asked the young soldier.

"My wager is on Sister Gilda finding a way to help Philip. You and she make a formidable pair, and don't discount the strength of Sister Freda. She kept me entertained during the time we spent traveling together. You should hear her opinion of Bishop Gunthar and his desire to expand his domain."

"Yes, I can imagine what she'd have to say. I just wish the bishop and Cedric weren't so greedy. They can be dangerous if thwarted."

"I'll keep my eyes open, Justin. Rest assured about that. Is the good sister going to marry you?"

"I hope so," Justin replied, then examined the handsome soldier at his side. Leonardo had been his companion on many journeys. Women found him appealing, and he never seemed to lack for invitations to warm their beds. "Have you ever thought of marrying, Leonardo?"

"Good heavens, no," he said with a laugh. Then after a minute, he added, "But then I never met anyone like Sister Gilda."

Justin nodded. "I'm sure there is not another woman like Gilda."

While Justin was worrying about her safety, Gilda was questioning Freda, hoping to obtain some ideas for how to approach Lord Metcalf. "Did you ever meet Emma's father during the years you were at court?"

"No, but he was a friend of the man I loved, so I heard a great deal about him. Apparently, he was skilled with a sword and known for putting the fear of God into the enemy. He won respect on the battlefield defending the empire against the Saracens."

"Do you remember any personal information?"

"He was a handsome man before he was injured. The rumor was that women at court often sought his favor, but they had no luck. I understand he was faithful to his wife."

"Now that might be a useful bit of information."

"Yes, I suppose a man who is faithful to his wife might wish the best for his daughter. But if that's the case, why would Metcalf have sought to match her with Count Cedric?"

Gilda remembered what her brother had to say on the matter. "After Chetwynd visited him, he reported that Metcalf, although eager to talk of his days as a warrior, tired easily. Chetwynd judged him to be unwell. Perhaps the bishop, or the count himself, approached him to suggest the match, although they claim it was the other way around."

"I take it you are planning to seek out Metcalf. If you wish, I could accompany you. He might respond to someone nearer his own age. He might remember the soldier I loved."

A worried expression on his face, Justin was peering back at them, and Gilda smiled at him. "I'll keep that in mind, Freda. Justin is wary of my hope to help Philip. He insists I do nothing without him, and I gave him my promise. But I think he'll be interested in what you say and your offer."

They rode in silence for a while, and it was clear from the relaxed expression on Justin's face that he was happier when Gilda and Freda weren't talking. Gilda wondered if he feared they were planning a scheme of which he wouldn't approve.

It was difficult for Gilda to be silent for long. "I didn't ask how your discussion with Mariel went, Freda. All I know is that you were successful."

"The poor girl was surprised then embarrassed by the information she lacked. I think the reason she held so fiercely to her belief that she was married to Philip was that they had lain together. As far as she was concerned, that is what married people did. As we talked, her embarrassment was replaced by anger at her family for not preparing her for marriage."

"I think that's appropriate," Gilda remarked.

As they were about to enter Mainz, Philip, without a word to anyone, headed off to Metcalf's manor. Justin considered sending Leonardo after him, but he decided to let Philip have some time with Emma to explain the situation.

Gilda moved to ride beside Justin, and Leonardo dropped back to join Freda. "You know that Philip has left us," she said.

"Yes. Hopefully he'll be careful."

"We can't wait too long to visit Metcalf, Justin. Philip is going to be trying to persuade Emma to run away with him."

Justin's frown was back. "And how would you know that? Did he speak to you about it?"

"No, but as you've said yourself many times, Philip is impulsive and reckless."

Justin nodded. "Lady Emma is the more mature of the two. I don't imagine she'll be eager to make him a hunted man by running away with him. But before we can consider how to approach Metcalf, we have to meet with Count Cedric and Bishop Gunthar. Even though we are bringing them good news, I'm not looking forward to it."

Upon their arrival, Lord Justin and Sister Gilda were shown to the same quarters they had occupied on their last visit to Mainz. This time the count was eager to meet them, and they just had time to settle their belongings before they were summoned into his presence.

Bishop Gunthar and Cedric stood as soon as they entered the room. Greetings were dispensed with quickly, and then the count said, "What news do you have for us?"

Justin was just as eager to deal with their business. "In talking to Lady Mariel, she made it clear that your marriage was not consummated. In addition, she does not wish to remain in the marriage any more than you do. In fact, she would like to stay at the convent, where she can further her education. There should be no problem with annulling the marriage."

There were broad smiles on the faces of both Gunthar and the count. "And what about Philip? Was he intimate with Lady Mariel?" Cedric asked.

"No, he was not," Justin said.

Gilda held her breath, wondering if the two powerful men would accept Justin's word.

"But Lady Mariel claimed she was married to him," the bishop said. "That's what she told everyone."

"Mariel's father did not bother to explain the surrogate situation to Lady Mariel." Justin addressed the bishop. "That's why having stand-ins for marriage is discouraged." He could have said that Gunthar had made a mistake in recommending it, but he could see by the shifty expression in the bishop's eyes that he understood what Justin was implying.

"So, it was all just a misunderstanding by that silly country girl," Cedric concluded, his satisfied smile still in place.

Justin held his tongue and prayed that Gilda would do the same. It would be best to keep Cedric happy with them until they could attempt to help Philip. He was relieved when she remained silent.

"What happens next?" Cedric asked.

"We will report our findings to Archbishop Humbert, as it is up to him to grant an annulment," Justin replied. "But the evidence is straightforward and not in dispute by either party. I will also report to King Louis when I return to Aachen."

The count was clearly pleased. "Excellent," he said.

Bishop Gunthar came forward then, looking from Sister Gilda to Lord Justin. "Now that you have accomplished your task of investigating the situation, will you be marrying soon?"

Since Justin had no idea whether Gilda would marry him, he nodded and hoped that was answer enough for the bishop.

"You have both done a great service to Mainz, and I wish to reward you. I will marry you here."

It was a great honor to be married by a bishop, and Gunthar's expression made it clear he expected them to be overjoyed by his magnanimous offer. But Justin was sure Gilda, even if she agreed to marry him, would never consent to have the bishop oversee their vows. Unfortunately, he wasn't sure how to refuse the offer without offending a man who could become a powerful enemy. Before he could think of some way to delay giving an answer, he was surprised to hear Gilda replying.

"That is a very generous offer, Bishop Gunthar. We would be happy to accept, but we were married at the Convent of Saint Ives." She saw the puzzled look on the bishop's face as he glanced down at her habit, and she rushed on. "We wish to keep the marriage a secret, which is why Lord Justin didn't say anything. It seemed wise to do that until a report has been made to Archbishop Humbert."

When the bishop turned to Justin for confirmation, Justin swallowed the lump that her surprising statement had lodged in his throat and said, "It is as Sister Gilda says. We don't want anyone to think there has been any distraction from our mission. I'm sure we can depend upon you to keep our secret until our report has been made."

Gunthar was still frowning, but Count Cedric spoke up. "It

appears you are acting in my best interest, Lord Justin. I thank you for that. Will you be leaving for Reims tomorrow morning?"

"I'd like to stay one more day to give everyone a rest. Be assured we will be on our way as soon as possible," Justin replied.

The count seemed disappointed at the delay, but he agreed. "I won't keep you any longer, Lord Justin. It's almost time for vespers."

Justin didn't speak to Gilda until they were in their quarters, then his words burst forth. "What were you thinking? You just told the bishop we are married, and you haven't even made up your mind whether you'll marry me. You can't depend on Gunthar keeping a secret if we anger him in any way. Everyone will think we are married. It's a story that will spread quickly."

"We'll get married," she answered.

Justin frowned at her. "You are willing to be married to delay our stay here just to be able to help Philip?"

"No. That's not it at all. I want to marry you, Justin, I do."

"Since when?" he asked, not at all convinced.

"Since you stood up to Count Cedric and protected Lady Mariel by not telling of her ignorance. Since you put the blame for the mix-up on Bishop Gunthar and Mariel's father, where it belonged. As I watched you dealing with them, I knew I need not fear marrying you."

"Ever since we met you have been surprising me, Gilda." Although he was pleased by how quickly she made up her mind, he wanted her decision to be based on something more than respect for how he dealt with others. "What else? Are there other reasons for your eagerness to wed?"

"How about my powerful desire to do this?" Gilda moved close and pulled his head down to kiss him full on the lips.

It took only a second for Justin to respond, then he lifted her off the floor so that she could wrap her arms around his neck. He fitted his body close to hers and returned her kiss, all the while edging her toward his bedchamber.

Reading his mind, Gilda whispered, "Wait."

Justin groaned as his vision of taking her to bed disappeared. But her explanation had him wide-eyed again. "We have to rush to the monastery and find someone to marry us."

Justin lowered her so that her feet were on the floor. "Are you sure about this, Gilda? When we were at the convent, I thought you wanted to stay there. I know you were torn."

"Yes, I did think about staying, I won't deny that. And it was hard for me to ride away. But even then, I think I knew I'd made my choice."

Still in doubt as to her quick reversal, Justin took her face in his hands. "I want to marry you more than anything in the world, but we don't have to rush to marry, Gilda."

"Please believe me, Justin, I'm sure about this, and I don't want my lie to the bishop to be a lie for any longer than necessary. The only reason I was able to tell it in the first place is that I knew I wanted to marry you. The bishop is utterly contemptible, and the idea of his marrying us called for drastic action."

Justin embraced her again and twirled her around. They had whirled full circle when they saw Freda at the door. She appeared to be about to leave when Gilda called to her, "Wait, Freda. We need your help."

"It looks like you are doing fine without any help from me," the nun replied. "I was just going to remind you it's time for vespers."

"We're going to be married," Gilda blurted out.

"Good. Now it's time for vespers."

"No, you don't understand. We need to go to the monastery to find someone to marry us. Bishop Gunthar offered to do it, and I said we were already married. I didn't feel that I was lying because in my heart I feel married to Justin. Now we have to make sure that's the truth. I'm hoping your nephew, Brother Arnulf, will help us."

Freda's lips had curled into a grin as she listened to an excited Gilda explain herself. "It's something I'm sure he would enjoy doing. Perhaps we should leave while the others are at vespers."

Justin gave the elderly nun a quick hug, then said, "I'll go see if I can find Leonardo to go with us."

"That won't be necessary." Gilda, Justin, and Freda spun around to see Leonardo in the doorway of the bedchamber. He was grinning. "I was trying to rest, but there was too much noise coming from this room."

The idea of the energetic Leonardo needing a rest baffled Justin. Nodding toward the bedchamber, he asked, "Are you alone?"

Justin's question had Gilda and Freda staring at Leonardo, who shrugged his shoulders and blushed. Gilda had a hard time keeping a straight face as she remembered Justin trying to move her into the bedchamber. It would have been crowded in there. "Did you hear everything?" she asked.

When Leonardo nodded, she said, "Let's get going. I want to be married as soon as possible."

The evening was mild, and it didn't take long to ride to the monastery. Vespers had just concluded, and the brothers were exiting the chapel. It was easy to pick out Brother Arnulf, as he towered over the others.

"Welcome!" the monk shouted as he came toward them.

When Freda slipped behind Gilda to avoid the embrace that he had treated her to at their last visit, Brother Arnulf grinned at her. "A pleasure to see you again, dear aunt."

Justin maneuvered Arnulf away from the other brothers. "We need some help," he said.

"Always happy to help. What can I do?"

Justin glanced at Gilda and she spoke. "We need a priest to marry us."

Arnulf clapped his hands with delight. "I can help with that. How soon were you thinking? We'll set a day and I'll find someone."

"You don't understand. Tonight. We need to be married tonight," Gilda said, suddenly realizing how insane that sounded.

Arnulf scowled. "What have you done?"

Impatient, Freda jumped in to say, "They haven't done anything, Arnulf. Can you find someone or not?"

Intent on their conversation, the small group didn't notice that the Abbot had approached them until he spoke. "Sister Gilda and Lord Justin. It is good to see you again. What brings you back to visit us?"

There was a long pause before Lord Justin spoke. "We have come to find someone to marry us, Holy Father. It has to be right away. Tonight."

The stern expression was back on the Abbot's face. "What is the hurry?"

"It's my fault," Gilda offered, eager to set him straight. "Bishop Gunthar offered to marry us, and I pretended we were already married so as not to offend him. Since we both wished to be married, I didn't think it was much of a sin, but now I'd like my words to become true."

"And the bishop believed you?"

"Yes, I think so. I said I would wear my habit until our mission for the king was complete."

"You do not wish to have the bishop marry you?" the Abbot asked.

"No," Gilda answered simply.

"Would you like me to hear your vows?"

A sudden smile lit Gilda's face, and Justin sighed his relief at the Abbot's words. "Yes," Gilda and Justin said in unison.

"Come to the porch of the chapel. I will marry you, and then we can go to supper."

Justin grasped Gilda's hand as they followed the Abbot for the few steps necessary to reach the porch. There, with Sister Freda, Brother Arnulf, and Leonardo standing beside them, Gilda and Justin said the words that bound them together and received the Abbot's blessing.

When the Abbot was finished, he said, "Go into the chapel and say prayers to ask God's blessing on your union, then come to the dining hall."

Kneeling beside Justin in the chapel, Gilda was overwhelmed by the tenderness she felt for him, and suddenly tears streamed down her face. She seldom cried and tried to hide the evidence of her emotion by wiping away the tears on her sleeve.

As Justin became aware that Gilda was weeping, he was struck by a sudden fear. "Are you having regrets?" he forced himself to ask.

"No! No! Justin, please don't think that. I have known for some time that I wanted to be your wife. The only reason I hesitated so long was because I also wanted to remain a nun."

"What about your fear of losing your freedom, Gilda? Your words to Lady Emma about a nun being free of the dictates of a father or husband have haunted me since you spoke them."

"I admit I wondered if it would work out for us. But I know you are meant to be my partner and husband, Justin. We complement each other in so many ways, and I've come to trust you. Besides, I love you more than I thought it was possible to love anyone."

Still kneeling in the candlelit chapel, Justin kissed his wife, and she clung to him for a long time. Then he heard a rumbling from her stomach. "You're hungry," he said with a grin.

"Starving. Never been so hungry."

In the dining hall there seemed to be a great deal of excited conversation, and all heads turned toward the entering couple, who joined Sister Freda and Leonardo at one of the long tables.

"I thought this marriage was supposed to be a secret," Justin whispered to Brother Arnulf.

"Don't worry. Monks know how to keep a secret. But little happens at the monastery that is not observed by someone. The Abbot made a short speech calling for a vow of silence on the matter, without even saying what the matter was."

"He is being very helpful. I'm surprised he offered to marry us," Justin said.

Brother Arnulf grinned. "There is no brotherly love between the Abbot and Bishop Gunthar, although the Abbot would never admit it."

Gilda was attacking the food in her trencher. Sister Freda poked her arm and said, "I see being married hasn't diminished your appetite." When Gilda only grinned in reply, Freda added, "I'm glad you made up your mind, Gilda. I know you made the right choice."

At that Gilda did pause in her eating. "Justin never ceases to amaze me. At first all I knew was that I desired him," she whispered. "I didn't trust myself to make a decision based on desire. But he means much more to me now that I know the kind of man he is."

"I hope you are better prepared for marriage than Lady Mariel was," Freda said with a smile.

Gilda returned the smile. "I've worked with women long enough to have learned a great deal."

Justin noticed the exchange of smiles and wondered what it was about. He had been watching Gilda tear into her food, and the sight made him eager to have her to himself and satisfy some of his own appetite. "We should head back to Mainz as soon as possible," he said to them all.

"Why don't you and Gilda go ahead," Leonardo suggested. "Sister Freda and I will follow after a long visit with Brother Arnulf." He emphasized the word *long*.

Gilda had sprung to her feet. "I think that's a fine idea."

Leonardo whispered to Justin, "You are a fortunate man."

CHAPTER TWELVE

R iding their horses at a sedate pace, Justin and Gilda waited until they were out of view of the monastery to give the animals their head and race toward Mainz. Once at the castle they rushed up the stairs and were almost to their room when Philip appeared out of the dark shadows of the hallway.

"I need to speak to you," the young man pleaded.

"Tomorrow," Justin replied, pulling Gilda toward their rooms.

"I'm in trouble," Philip said. "I've been hiding out, waiting for your return. It's urgent, Justin."

When Gilda looked from one man to the other, her concern clear, Justin relented. "Come in," he offered.

Once the door was closed, Gilda said, "Be quick about it, Philip. We have no time for a long tale."

Justin would have grinned at her words if he wasn't so irritated at the interruption.

"I've waited for an hour, hiding in the hall. Where have you been?" Philip asked.

Justin's frown deepened as he glared at Philip. "That's none of your concern. If you don't tell us immediately what trouble you are in this time, I'm tossing you out the door."

Philip finally seemed to realize that his presence was only barely tolerated. "I tried to see Emma, but I was met by her father, who ordered me off his property. When I arrived at Mainz, a friendly porter warned me that Cedric is furious with me and asked the guards to watch for my return."

"Any idea why that might be?" Justin asked.

"I think Emma may have spoken to her father about me, and he must have sent word to Cedric. If Cedric knows about Emma and me, I fear I'll end up in the dungeon again."

Justin suspected the young man might be in more danger than even he knew. If Cedric was still determined to marry Lady Emma and he learned about Philip's relationship with her, Philip's life was in danger, not just his freedom. In the eyes of the church it would be considered incest for one brother to bed a woman another brother had been intimate with. Only if Philip was dead could Cedric still hope to marry Emma. The only alternative was to pretend nothing happened between the young couple, but Justin doubted Philip would go along with that. One way or another, Cedric would have to see that Philip disappeared.

"Can you find someone to hide you until morning?" Justin asked, but even as he spoke, his hopes of spending the evening alone with Gilda were fading.

"Cedric knows who my friends are. I hate to put them in danger."

"How thoughtful," Justin said, making no effort to hide his cynicism. "Give me a minute with Gilda. Go into my bed-chamber and stay there until I call you."

As soon as Philip had closed the door, Gilda took Justin's hand and pulled him to sit close beside her. "Do you think he's in immediate danger?" she asked.

"I'm afraid so. The fact that he has had a relationship with Emma may already be known."

"Can we do anything to help him?"

"I hope so, but we'll have to be careful. We don't know how long Cedric will continue to trust us. He'll remember I spoke up for Philip last time."

"Surely we are safe until we make our report to the archbishop."

"I'm depending on that," replied Justin. "But Cedric can make things unpleasant for us."

"What can we do?"

"I hate to admit it, but I think we'd better take Philip away from here tonight."

Gilda nodded. Still not feeling close enough to him, she moved to sit on Justin's lap. As he held her tightly, she whispered into his ear, "You are a good man, and I love you more and more each minute."

Justin groaned as she clung to him. "I had wonderful plans for you this night," he said.

"Don't forget any of them. Hopefully you can show me all of them soon," she replied.

Setting Gilda aside, it took Justin a minute to refocus on the task at hand. He knew that the only way he could be alone with Gilda was to deal with the problem and leave Mainz behind. Because they didn't have time to wait for Leonardo and Freda to return, Justin wrote a brief message to explain their absence. He left it in Freda's bed, hoping no one else would find it.

While he was doing that, Gilda gathered a few necessities. As soon as they were ready, Justin alerted Philip. "We have to leave Mainz at once. Do you think the cottage you took us to before is still a safe hiding place?"

"Yes. Emma wouldn't have told anyone about it."

"In the morning Gilda and I will visit Metcalf and see if we can persuade him to favor your suit over that of your brother's."

For a moment, relief flooded Philip's face, then he asked, "What if he refuses?"

"Philip, don't press me. Right now, I want you to follow my orders. You and Gilda will go on ahead. I'll follow to make sure you get away, then make an appearance in the dining hall so that Cedric will not suspect anything. I'll join you as soon as I can."

Gilda grabbed his arm and turned him to face her. "No, Justin, you must come with us. I don't wish to leave without you."

"I'll join you as soon as possible, but we must be cautious. I want to hold back in case someone tries to stop you and Philip. With Leonardo gone there is no one to act as a rear guard."

Gilda wasn't happy, but she finally said, "We'll wait outside the walls until you come."

"If there is a long delay, go with Philip to the cottage," Justin urged. "I have to know you'll be safe, Gilda. Cedric may detain me, but I won't be in danger. Please, do as I say."

Gilda nodded her agreement, then clung to him one last time.

Justin watched Gilda and Philip descend by a back staircase that was lit by only a few torches. He followed at a distance until he saw them mount horses supplied by a friendly porter. He sighed with relief and made his way back to the great hall.

The large room echoed with loud, boisterous talk, no doubt in celebration of the news he and Gilda had given Cedric earlier. Although the meal seemed long over, men loitered at the tables, drinking and gossiping. When Count Cedric saw Justin, he waved him to the head table. "Where have you been, Lord Justin? I wished to drink your health."

"Sister Freda wished to visit her nephew at the monastery, and we accompanied her. We just returned," he answered.

"I'm glad you're here, as I have a question for you. Why didn't Philip return with you?"

"Perhaps he was still angry about being thrown in the dungeon, Cedric. I imagine he will appear before long."

Cedric's eyes narrowed, and he slammed his fist on the table, spilling the wine in front of him. "You persuaded me to let you take him with you to the convent, but he hasn't returned. I hold you responsible for his appearance."

"I needed Philip with me to discover the truth about Lady Mariel. He was proven free of any guilt. I don't understand your concern," Justin said.

Justin's words seemed to enflame Cedric. "Do you not?" he shouted.

In spite of his bulk, the bishop moved quickly from the other end of the table to stand beside Justin. He addressed Cedric, "My lord, it's been a long evening. Perhaps you should leave this discussion with Lord Justin until morning."

"I do not think so," Cedric answered, but he looked around at the faces turned in his direction. "We will move to a more private room, Lord Justin."

"I agree with Bishop Gunthar that we should wait until morning," Justin answered.

"Now!" Cedric bellowed, and two of his guards moved to stand on either side of Justin. There didn't seem to be any choice but to follow the count.

Outside the walls Gilda and Philip watched for Justin to follow them. It didn't take Gilda long to regret she had gone along with Justin's plan. Philip was also impatient, and after some time had passed, he said, "Perhaps we should go ahead as Justin suggested."

"No. We are waiting for my husband."

"Your husband?"

Gilda was amazed at how easily the word *husband* flowed from her lips. "Yes, we were married this evening at the monastery," she answered, no longer caring who knew about their secret wedding.

To give him credit, Philip looked embarrassed. "I'm so sorry, Sister Gilda. I had no idea."

"And if you did, would you have done anything different?" she asked.

After a minute, Philip said, "You must think me very selfish." Gilda relented. "No, it's not your fault. But we are waiting for Justin."

Philip nodded his agreement.

But as time passed Gilda began to question her own decision. She was about to give in and follow Justin's plan when they saw riders approaching Mainz. "It's Leonardo and Sister Freda," she told Philip.

"Stay hidden," Gilda ordered, then on foot she raced from the cover of trees and approached her surprised friends. "What are you doing out here?" Leonardo asked as his eyes searched around for Justin.

"Follow me," she answered, and led them to where Philip still hid. It took only a few minutes to explain the situation.

"This is how you are spending your wedding night?" Freda asked.

"Don't remind me," Gilda said. "What can we do? Why hasn't Justin followed us?"

Leonardo was the one to answer her. "I'll find out. You go on to the cottage, and we'll follow."

"It's secluded. No one but Philip can find it. We'll have to wait for you," Gilda said.

Leonardo glanced around at their hiding place. "I don't like to leave you here. This is too close to the walls of the city."

Philip spoke up then. "I'll lead Gilda and Sister Freda to the cottage, then come back to wait for you and Justin."

"The idea was to spirit you away from Mainz, Philip. Now you're talking of coming back here," Gilda pointed out.

"The plan is not perfect, but it's the best we can do," Philip replied, determined to prove he didn't always think about himself.

Leonardo agreed with Philip. "It's the only way, Gilda. I have to find Justin." As he spoke, he remembered promising Justin that he would watch out for Gilda, and he hesitated. "I promised Justin I'd take care of you if you were separated from him."

"I'll take care of her," Philip promised.

Leonardo frowned, then turned to Freda. "Make sure nothing happens to her," he said.

The matter was decided, and Gilda, Freda, and Philip headed for the secluded cottage. As they approached their destination, it occurred to Gilda that it might no longer be a safe hiding place. But all was dark, as it had been the night they had spent there. Inside, Philip hurriedly lit a fire for Freda and Gilda.

"I'll bring Justin back to you, Gilda," he vowed as he left the cottage.

Gilda stared at the closed door. "He had better keep that promise," she muttered.

"Let's try and get some rest," Freda said. "It's been a long day, and we'll need our strength for tomorrow's meeting with Lord Metcalf."

Gilda nodded, sure it would be impossible for her but hoping Freda would be able to sleep.

"What if something happens to Justin?" she couldn't help asking after they were settled on the floor in front of the fire. "I'll never forgive myself, Freda. I'm the one who first persuaded him to help Philip."

"Lord Justin is one of King Louis's most favored ministers, Gilda. Cedric may be dangerous, but I doubt even he would do anything to harm Lord Justin."

"I hope you're right. Justin thinks we are safe until he makes his report to the archbishop."

"I'm sure he's correct, Gilda. Try and get some rest now."

Hours later Gilda was still awake when she heard the cottage door open. She sprung to her feet. "Justin, is that you?" she whispered, so as not to wake Freda.

"No, Gilda," Leonardo answered. "It's me and Philip."

Before he could say more, Gilda grabbed his sleeve and demanded, "Where is Justin? Did you come away without him?"

"Yes. Don't worry. Justin is fine, but . . ."

"Then why isn't he here?"

"Give me a chance to explain, Gilda. Justin stayed at Mainz. It turns out Cedric was told by Lord Metcalf that Philip had been visiting Emma, pressing her to marry him. Cedric wants Lord Justin to visit Metcalf and explain that his marriage to Lady Mariel will be annulled, freeing him to marry Lady Emma."

"We suspected that might happen, Leonardo. But why didn't Justin return with you?"

Leonardo and Philip exchanged glances, then Leonardo continued. "The count learned that you and Philip had left Mainz together. He insists Justin stay with him until they can visit Metcalf together tomorrow. Cedric suspects you have been helping Philip. He wants to keep Justin with him."

His words awakened all Gilda's worst fears. Cedric was keeping Justin as a guarantee that he couldn't join Gilda in her effort to help Philip. Justin may have even suspected this might happen when he sent her ahead. "Why didn't you stay with Justin, Leonardo?" she asked. "He might need you."

"Justin insisted I come to be with you, Gilda. He said to tell you he will be with you tomorrow and not to do anything on your own."

"Is that all he said? What does Justin plan to do?"

Leonardo took her arm and made her sit on a bench. "He didn't have time to tell me his plans."

"Because Cedric was there?"

"Yes, he was nearby. I suspect Justin has some ideas, but we weren't free to talk."

Gilda nodded, her mind racing. "Justin will visit Metcalf with Cedric, and perhaps even Bishop Gunthar will go along. Cedric may even bring some guards."

Leonardo sat beside her. "What are you thinking, Gilda? Justin told me to make sure you don't do anything without him."

"You'll just have to take his place, Leonardo. We are already on Metcalf's property, and we can get to him before the count arrives."

Freda was sitting by the fire, and Philip was crouching beside her. Their eyes were on Gilda, waiting for her to continue.

"We'll have to convince Lord Metcalf that Philip is a more appropriate match for Lady Emma."

Leonardo shook his head. "How are we going to do that? I think you better leave it to Lord Justin."

Gilda hadn't formed a plan, but she kept talking, hoping something would occur to her. "Freda knows a bit about Metcalf. He loved his wife. That may be something we can use."

"That's not much to work with, Gilda," Leonardo said. "I think I should follow Justin's orders and keep you safe."

Gilda narrowed her eyes. "Who is going to keep Justin safe? The best possible outcome is to convince Metcalf before the count arrives with his men. That means that we must be ready to approach him by first light."

Philip finally spoke up. "I know you're trying to help me, Gilda. But I don't wish to put you in danger. It will be safer for you if I try to kidnap Emma while the count is speaking with her father."

"Gilda has the more sensible plan." All eyes turned to Sister Freda, who had been watching them in silence. "From what I remember, Metcalf was an honorable and daring warrior. I predict he will admire Sister Gilda's courage in facing him. She has a good chance of convincing Metcalf that Count Cedric is not the husband he would wish for Emma."

"Metcalf is an old man, Freda. I doubt he resembles the warrior you remember," Leonardo pointed out.

"Few people change their basic values just because they grow old, Leonardo. I'll go along with Sister Gilda. There is no danger from Metcalf. He isn't going to be disrespectful to a pair of nuns."

Gilda smiled, hoping she was right. "Thank you, Freda."

Leonardo also smiled at the older nun. "I bow to your wise counsel, Sister Freda. I just hope Justin doesn't kill me."

They had agreed to try to get some sleep, but it seemed to Gilda that she had just nodded off when Freda was shaking her arm. "It's starting to become light," she said.

Gilda jumped up. "I'm awake," she said.

"I hope they give us some breakfast," Leonardo muttered as he straightened his clothes.

"If Emma is there, she will feed us," Philip said.

Gilda turned to him. "Not you, Philip. You lead us there, then disappear. It's important that we do not antagonize Metcalf before we can talk to him."

Philip paused only a moment, then nodded. "I'll do what you say. Metcalf used to be my friend, but that no longer seems to be true. But I won't be far away if you need me. I still have friends in his household."

As they approached the manor house, Gilda noticed there was an elaborate garden near the door and an apple orchard that stretched into the distance toward the west. She remembered Philip telling her that Emma worked hard to oversee her father's property.

When they entered the courtyard, two servants rushed to greet them. They were taking their horses when a woman appeared at the door. Gilda recognized Emma. There was a hint of the auburn hair beneath her head covering and a puzzled expression on her face.

"Sister Gilda, what are you doing here?" Emma asked, looking from her to Sister Freda and Leonardo.

"We wish to speak with your father. It's rather urgent as Count Cedric is due to arrive soon." Gilda saw her startled expression and rushed on. "He wishes to press his suit for your hand in marriage. It's our plan to suggest that Philip is a better match."

"My father is not well. He has already made up his mind, and I fear you will be unable to change it."

"What do you wish, Lady Emma? Do you want to marry Count Cedric?"

"No. I've never wished that. I remember our talk, Sister Gilda, and I thought of seeking sanctuary at a convent, but I do not want to hurt my father. He is not well and needs me," Emma said.

"Just give us a chance to speak to him before Cedric arrives. Sister Freda knew your father many years ago and may be able to help," Gilda said, exaggerating the connection to convince Emma.

Emma looked over at the older nun, then nodded. "I'll see if my father will see you. Come in and have some refreshment while I speak with him."

Freda whispered to Gilda as they moved into the great hall. "I didn't know him. I knew of him, as you are well aware." Gilda nodded. "We'll work with what we have," she answered.

The visitors sat at a long table and were served soup, fresh bread, and ale. When they heard some shouts coming from behind the door Emma had entered, they exchanged worried glances.

"His shouts are fairly robust," Freda commented. "Lord Metcalf can't be feeling too poorly this morning."

"You make it sound like that's a good thing," Leonardo said, fortifying himself with a long drink of ale.

Emma returned and sat beside Gilda. "He insisted I tell him why you want to see him. I had to tell him you are friends of Philip. Are you sure you want to go ahead with this, Gilda?"

"Yes. Has he agreed to see us?"

"He did, but only after I told him one of the nuns knew him from his days at court. I suspect otherwise he would have refused."

Sister Freda stood up. "This is our chance. If Count Cedric arrives before we are finished talking with your father, try and delay him," Freda said to Emma.

"I'll do my best, Sister. Don't you need me with you?"

"It might be best if we talk to him alone," Gilda answered. "Leonardo will wait with you."

"I told Justin I'd keep my eye on you, Gilda. I must go with you," Leonardo said.

Gilda and Freda exchanged glances. Leonardo was a handsome young man, much as Metcalf had been in his youth. Gilda didn't want him to distract Metcalf with thoughts of what used to be.

"I think Metcalf will be more comfortable with just the two of us," Gilda said.

Sister Freda smiled at the worried young man. "I agree with Gilda. But don't fret, I think I'll be able to protect her from an ailing Lord Metcalf."

Leonardo looked toward heaven. "Lord Justin will surely kill me," he said.

CHAPTER THIRTEEN

As Gilda and Freda entered Lord Metcalf's private chamber, Gilda remembered her brother telling her that the old warrior was hard to look at because of his scars. When she saw that Metcalf's face was red and puckered on the left side, she wished she had warned Freda. But she need not have been concerned as Freda's composed expression never changed.

Metcalf used a thick staff at his side to push himself to a standing position. Although he towered over Gilda, Freda was only a head shorter than he was. After a glance at Gilda, Metcalf held Freda's eyes. "Do I know you?" he asked.

His blunt question didn't faze Freda. "We were at court at the same time. I knew one of your men, a soldier named Gregor."

Metcalf narrowed his eyes and stared at her face as though searching for a clue. "A worthy warrior. He died young. Are you his wife?"

"No. He was already wed when we met."

Metcalf nodded, as though understanding that Gregor meant something to her. "That was many years ago," he said. Then he turned to Gilda. "I certainly didn't know you at court. You're much too young."

"No, but you met my brother, Lord Chetwynd. He stopped to see you not many days ago."

"Yes, I remember Lord Chetwynd. We had a good talk." He paused, then continued, "So neither one of you is an old acquaintance. It was rather bold to represent yourself as such."

Since he sounded more curious than angry, Gilda said, "I'm afraid the situation called for bold measures, my lord."

Unfortunately, her reply turned him suspicious. "Just what situation are you referring to?"

Since it was too late to soften her approach, Gilda said, "We wish to speak to you about Lady Emma and your plan to have her wed Count Cedric. Are you aware that the count recently married Lady Mariel of Bordeaux?"

Metcalf's dark eyes glared under his bushy eyebrows. "The man made a mistake. These things happen. The count wishes to marry my Emma, and she will have a place of honor as his wife. What possible business is this of yours?"

"I happen to know that Emma wishes to marry another."

He held up his hand to halt her words. "Philip! He is too young to be a suitable husband. Since you have never married, perhaps you don't know that it is a father's duty to arrange his daughter's match and a daughter's duty to accept his will."

"I am well aware of that, Lord Metcalf. But I also believe that it's a father's duty to make the best decision possible for his daughter. Is Philip's age the only reason you do not wish him to marry Emma?"

Gesturing with his staff, he shouted. "You're questioning my judgment! I've had enough of this. Out of here, the both of you."

Gilda took a step back at his attack, but Freda stood firm and addressed Metcalf. "Your words show a different man than the one I remember," she said.

Freda seemed to throw him off-balance. "We didn't know each other. What are you talking of now?"

"At court your fame made you the subject of much gossip. You were rumored to be faithful to your wife, in spite of many temptations. You respected your marriage vows. I always admired that about you, Lord Metcalf."

"What do I care for your opinion of me?" he replied. But his face softened, and he sat down. "Did you know my Emilia?"

"We met a few times. She was very beautiful and looked much as your daughter does today."

"Yes, Emma is much like her. I kept my daughter to myself too long." He looked into Freda's eyes as though seeking her understanding. "Because my end is near, I wish her married and settled. When she marries Cedric, she will become a countess."

Gilda's eyes widened when Freda sat beside Metcalf on the bench. Because her own words had upset him, Gilda moved to the side to keep out of his line of vision as she watched her friend.

"Clearly you care a great deal for your daughter. Is it your wish that Emma bear children, my lord?" Freda asked.

"Of course. I remember how happy Emilia was when Emma was born." He seemed lost in thought for a minute. "She told me she felt fulfilled and that I had made her the happiest woman in the world."

"Did you know that Cedric was married twice before he married Lady Mariel?"

Gilda saw Metcalf stiffen. "You go too far," he said.

In spite of his reaction, Freda continued. "I'm sure you know that Count Cedric never did produce an heir. You think Philip is too young for Emma, but perhaps you should be considering that Cedric is too old."

Metcalf looked from Freda to Gilda. "What kind of nuns are you? You should be saying prayers and helping the poor, not interfering with a father's decision for his daughter."

In spite of his words, he wasn't as angry as when he ordered them out of his chamber. Gilda wondered if Freda's words had affected him. Before either one of them could reply to his question, Emma appeared at the door.

"Sorry for the interruption, Father, but Count Cedric wishes to speak to you at once," Emma said. She closed the door behind her and whispered, "He has some men with him and seems impatient."

When Lord Metcalf struggled to his feet, Freda put her hand on his elbow to help him. He acknowledged her assistance with a curt nod. "I will speak to him in the dining hall, Emma. Serve the men some ale." He turned to Freda and Gilda. "Do you wish to join us, or do you wish to keep your visit to me a secret?" he asked, making it clear he suspected the latter.

"We will wait a few minutes to enter the hall, if that is all right with you," Freda answered.

"Do as you wish. It seems you are used to doing just that," he muttered as he followed Emma out of the chamber.

As soon as they were alone, Gilda embraced Freda. "You were wonderful," she whispered.

"I'm not sure how much good it did to point out the count's shortcomings."

"At least it gave Metcalf something to think about. You seem to be the one with the best instincts in this situation. What do we do now?"

"There is not much more we can do," Freda said. "Why don't we go to the dining hall and sit quietly in the background as we are expected to do? If nothing else, that will throw everyone off."

Gilda grinned at the prospect. "In minutes I will see Justin. I hope he will not be too shocked at my presence here."

"I suspect that Lord Justin may be getting used to being shocked by you, Gilda."

In the main hall Count Cedric was explaining Justin's presence to Lord Metcalf. The count had four of his guards with him, as well as Bishop Gunthar and Justin. These guards gave the impression they were watching for trouble as they stood behind the other men seated at the table. The guards were the only ones to notice Gilda and Freda slip into the room, but they said nothing as the count was speaking.

"I have brought Lord Justin with me as he was appointed by King Louis to investigate my request for an annulment. I wish him to explain to you his findings and the report he will make to the Archbishop of Reims."

Metcalf was the first one at the table to notice Gilda and Freda, no doubt because he was expecting to see them. Justin saw that Metcalf's attention had shifted, and his own eyes widened when he looked where Metcalf was looking.

Justin's startled expression made it clear that he didn't know Gilda and Freda were at the manor. While Cedric, still oblivious to her presence, was waiting for Justin to explain the situation to Lord Metcalf, Justin kept his eyes on Gilda. He stood up as he began talking. "What Count Cedric said about my investigation is true, but the king appointed two of us, Lord Metcalf. I am his secular representative, and Sister Gilda, a nun from the Convent of Saint Ives, represents the clergy. Please join us at the head table, Sister Gilda."

Cedric's head whipped around at Justin's invitation to Gilda. His face turned red and he shouted, "What is she doing here?"

Bishop Gunthar laid a hand on the count's arm, no doubt hoping to calm him, but Cedric pushed his hand away and appealed directly to Lord Metcalf. "Sister Gilda has befriended my stepbrother Philip. I suspect she has come to disrupt my plans to wed Lady Emma."

Since Lord Metcalf already knew this, he didn't comment on Cedric's accusation. Instead he said, "If Sister Gilda was appointed by King Louis, she should join us at the head table. Let's get on with it, Count Cedric. I wish to hear what their investigation has uncovered."

Walking the short distance to reach Justin's side, Gilda tried to stay focused on the business at hand. But all she could think about was moving closer to her husband, and she hoped the longing she felt for his touch wasn't visible to everyone present.

Justin didn't miss the special light in her eyes, and his voice was a little hoarse as he said, "Excuse me, Lord Metcalf, but I need a minute to confer with my associate in private before I begin to relate the details of our investigation."

Cedric was fuming, but he had apparently overcome his surprise at seeing Sister Gilda and gained enough self-control not to make an objection. Metcalf studied the pair as they moved toward one another, then said, "Emma will show you to a private chamber."

As soon as the door closed behind them, Gilda threw herself into Justin's arms and whispered, "I was going mad with worry when you didn't join us last night."

He silenced her with a kiss, and as his mouth moved hungrily on hers, his hands moved to her hips to draw her closer. Gilda still wasn't close enough, and she pushed aside his doublet so she could better feel his chest against her breast.

When they had to break their kiss in order to breathe, Justin took her face in his hands and stared into her eyes. "Why didn't you wait at the cottage? You promised to do nothing without me. My heart nearly stopped when I saw you."

"I had no choice, Justin. Leonardo came with us."

"Where is he now? I didn't see him."

"He stayed with Emma when Freda and I went to speak with Lord Metcalf," she answered, then kissed his mouth, nipping his lower lip and making him groan. She continued, moving her lips against his as she talked. "Leonardo told us you and Cedric would be coming here in the morning. We wanted to make a case for Philip before you arrived."

Justin pulled his face away from hers. "And what of your promise to do nothing without me?" he asked, although he had already reconciled himself to the fact that she had ignored that promise.

"The circumstances called for action," she muttered as she used her fingertips to caress his face.

Justin pushed her headcover off and ran his hands through her hair. "It always does with you. Did you succeed?"

"I don't know. Freda talked of Metcalf's wife, whom he clearly loved very much. They seemed to make a connection. Then she asked him if he wished Emma to have children, and when he said yes, she pointed out that Cedric has been married twice and has produced no heirs. She was brilliant."

Kissing first one eye, then the other, Justin said, "I suppose she pointed out that Philip was younger and more energetic. Did her ploy work?"

Gilda kissed his neck and inhaled his scent. "Not exactly. He said we should be saying prayers and helping the poor, not interfering with a father's decision for his daughter. He reminded me of you when he said that."

"I guess I did say something like that once. It was long ago."

A knock on the door caused the lovers to pull apart. After a discreet minute Freda entered the room. "Cedric is about to explode. I think you better rejoin us."

"We may need Leonardo. Where is he?" Justin asked. "I didn't see him when we arrived, which is why I was so surprised to see Gilda."

"Emma told me she asked Leonardo to join Philip at the cottage. She was afraid that Philip wouldn't be able to stay away. It must have taken some convincing as Leonardo was determined to watch over Gilda," Freda replied. "What's the plan?"

When neither Gilda nor Justin answered, Freda said, "You were supposed to be in here forming a plan." Then she grinned at them, shaking her head. "Fix your headcover, Sister Gilda."

While Gilda blushed and tugged at her headcover, Justin cleared his throat and spoke as though they had discussed a plan. "I'll explain the results of our investigation. Hopefully, Lord Metcalf will be smart enough to evaluate Cedric's past actions and change his mind about promoting a marriage between Cedric and Emma. I take it you have already planted a few seeds of doubt about Cedric's vitality, Sister Freda."

"I did what I could, but like most men Metcalf doesn't like his authority challenged. I think you are on the right track. We do what we can and hope he'll see the light."

Justin led the way back to the main hall where Count Cedric, his eyes narrowed, was watching for him. It was clear from his wary expression that his humor had not improved. Lord Metcalf, on the other hand, was leaning back in his chair, his mouth slightly curled at the edges as though he was patiently waiting to see what would happen next.

When Justin indicated that Gilda and Freda should join them at the table, they took seats at the end farthest from Cedric and Gunthar.

Justin stood and spoke directly to their host. "As Count Cedric has told you, King Louis requested that Sister Gilda and I investigate whether there were grounds to annul the marriage between Count Cedric and Lady Mariel. Since the lady was very confused by the fact that Philip was a surrogate for the count during the marriage ceremony, it took a while to learn what had happened. She believed that it was Philip she had married, and as a result acted very strangely when everyone insisted her husband was Count Cedric. She finally took refuge at the Convent of Saint Ives but gave little information about what had happened during the short time she was at Mainz."

Cedric couldn't resist injecting his view. "Lady Mariel is a simple country girl with little sense."

Seeing that Gilda was opening her mouth to reply, Justin spoke quickly. "The misunderstanding could have been avoided if her father had fully explained the marriage arrangement to Lady Mariel. No one bothered to do that, and as a result she was confused and endured a great deal of suffering. Fortunately for her, she is happy at the Convent of Saint Ives and is as eager for her marriage to be annulled as Count Cedric."

"Are you saying the misunderstanding was all the father's fault?" asked Lord Metcalf, one eyebrow raised.

Justin wondered if he had made an error in judging the father so harshly in front of Metcalf. To soften his words, he said, "Others could have explained the situation to Lady Mariel before the wedding. But she did not even meet Philip until the ceremony, and once it was completed the couple started back to Mainz." Having said that, Justin felt strongly enough to press his point. "But the father has the final responsibility, as he is the one who arranged the match. With the authority to decide goes the responsibility to do well by his daughter."

Metcalf's face darkened, making it clear he was aware that Justin was talking in general terms as well as about this particular case.

Impatient with what he considered a distraction from the main point, Cedric spoke up. "Explain your conclusion and the report you will make to the archbishop, Lord Justin."

"The conclusion Sister Gilda and I reached is that there is no reason to deny Count Cedric the annulment he seeks. The marriage was never consummated, and both parties wish it ended."

Now Cedric was smiling and nodding at Lord Metcalf. But Metcalf was still frowning. "And what of the father of Lady Mariel? What does he think about the ending of the marriage he arranged for his daughter?"

Justin nodded to Gilda, indicating that she should answer Metcalf's question.

"At the Convent of Saint Ives Lady Mariel is beyond her father's authority. She has asked for sanctuary. But my guess is that Lady Mariel's father, when he learns what has happened, will consider what is best for his daughter. Most fathers will do that," she said, knowing she was exaggerating but hoping to soften the argument she and Justin were making about fathers and their responsibilities.

Unaware of the underlying points being made by Justin and Gilda, Count Cedric tried once again to bring the discussion back to his concerns. "The annulment will go ahead quickly once Lord Justin has made his report. After that, nothing will stand in the way of my marriage to Lady Emma."

Metcalf had sunk down in his chair and seemed to be suddenly overcome with fatigue. In a hoarse whisper he said, "I wish to think on this matter, Count Cedric. We will talk again."

Beginning to be aware that the meeting was not going as well as he had hoped, Cedric's panic was evident in the expression on his face as he asked, "What more is there to talk about?"

But Lord Metcalf had lost all concentration on the matter and ignored Cedric's question. Freda was not the only one to notice the sudden change in Metcalf, but she was the first to act. She stood up and addressed their host in a respectful manner. "Lord Metcalf, would you like to have a little privacy to think over what you have heard?"

Without saying a word, Metcalf struggled to his feet, trying his best to disguise his weakness. He took the arm Freda offered.

A puzzled Count Cedric watched Metcalf's back as he was helped from the room. "What does he mean, talk some more?" he asked, addressing no one in particular.

Bishop Gunthar, who had been unusually quiet up to now, spoke up. "You can't rush matters, Cedric. You have made your point by bringing Lord Justin here. Lord Metcalf knows he has made a commitment to you, and I'm sure he will honor it."

Lady Emma, who had followed her father from the room, now returned. "My father is not well and tires easily. He needs to rest now."

It was clear from the disappointed expression on Count Cedric's face that he was not pleased by the fact that there wasn't a conclusion to their meeting. "I am sorry your father is unwell, Lady Emma. But it is important that an agreement is reached between us. I need to speak to him for a few minutes."

"My father has already taken a potion that will allow him to sleep without pain. Your business with him must wait until tomorrow," Emma replied.

"It's your business as well, Lady Emma. I want our betrothal to be settled," Cedric reminded her.

Lady Emma had always been shy in the count's presence, but today she looked him in the eye and said, "I believe it would be fitting that a betrothal wait until the archbishop has granted your annulment, Count Cedric."

Cedric's face turned red and his eyes narrowed, but before he could reply, Bishop Gunthar spoke up. "Although what you say makes sense, Lady Emma, an understanding should be reached as soon as possible. Your father is gravely ill, and your position should be protected by settling the matter before he passes on."

When Justin saw that Lady Emma was biting her lip at the mention of her father's worsening health, he knew he had been patient long enough. "Count Cedric, Bishop Gunthar, I think you have accomplished all you can here today. It is time for you to return to Mainz. Sister Freda is needed here to help Lady Emma. Sister Gilda and I will stay in case either of them needs our help."

"Leave the women if you wish, but you should return with us, Lord Justin," the count replied.

"I have completed my investigation at Mainz, Cedric. As soon as I see that Lord Metcalf is well, Sister Gilda and I plan to leave for Reims. I stayed with you last night, at your insistence, to come with you to disclose my findings to Metcalf. I have done that, and now it is time for me to complete my mission for King Louis."

Although Justin had made it clear he was responsible to a higher authority than Count Cedric, there were a few tense minutes while the count considered whether it was worth trying to force Lord Justin to come with him. The matter was decided when Bishop Gunthar said, "You have done well in uncovering the facts of the matter and proving that Count Cedric is within his rights to seek an annulment, Lord Justin."

"Sister Gilda and I worked together to discover the facts of the case, Bishop Gunthar."

"Of course," he answered, nodding to acknowledge Gilda.

"Thank you both," Count Cedric finally said, although his dark expression did not match his polite words. Once the decision to leave was made, the farewells were quickly accomplished.

Sharing a feeling of relief, Gilda and Justin stood at the open door of the manor and watched the count's party depart. Then Gilda turned to Emma. "Is Lord Metcalf seriously ill?" she asked.

"It's hard to say. He has had these spells before." Emma hesitated a minute, then continued. "I appreciate what you have tried to do for me, Sister Gilda. But this has been an upsetting experience for my father, and I fear it has made him even more frail." Emma's eyes filled with tears as she spoke of her father's health. "He is a sick man, and I will not go against his wishes. If he is determined that I marry Count Cedric, I will do that."

"I understand and respect your decision to honor the wishes of your father, Lady Emma," Gilda replied. "I hope that our actions today did not worsen his health, but I still think we did the right thing by speaking to Lord Metcalf on your behalf."

"I agree with Gilda," Justin said. "It is your father's decision, and he will make it with more knowledge than he had before. I will go back to the cottage and alert Philip as to what is happening and make sure he stays out of sight until things are settled."

Sister Freda appeared as Justin was speaking. "Lord Metcalf is sleeping peacefully now. I'll stay here with Emma. You go along with Justin, Gilda."

Although she wanted nothing more, Gilda hesitated. "Are you sure you don't need me?" she asked.

"Go with your husband," Freda insisted.

CHAPTER FOURTEEN

As soon as Gilda and Justin approached the cottage, Philip burst through the door to greet them. Leonardo was close behind, and his face lit up when he saw Justin.

"Thank the good lord you're here," Leonardo said to Justin, then rushed to explain why he hadn't kept his promise. "I tried to stay with Gilda, but she and Freda insisted on seeing Metcalf alone. Then Emma insisted I seek out Philip."

Remembering how many times he had been distracted from an objective by Gilda, Justin grinned at his worried friend. "I completely understand how that can happen."

Relieved by Justin's reply, Leonardo said, "I wasn't idle. I had to keep Philip from storming the manor, a task that has tried my patience. What has happened?"

Philip echoed Leonardo's question. "What happened? Did you see Emma?"

"Let's move inside and I'll tell you," Justin answered. He and Gilda had discussed how to handle Philip on the way, and Justin was determined to wait until they were settled in the cottage before dealing with what he knew would be upsetting information.

The wait increased Philip's anxiety as he began to suspect

the news wasn't going to be good. When he had finally settled nervously in his seat, Justin met his eyes and began to speak.

"Cedric came to the manor to discuss his betrothal to Lady Emma, and he brought me along to assure Metcalf that his annulment would be granted. Gilda and Freda had already talked with Emma's father by the time we arrived, but Metcalf was not pleased to have them questioning his authority.

"After Cedric introduced me, Metcalf listened to my explanation of our mission to investigate whether there were grounds for an annulment and the conclusion we had reached. Although he may have some misgivings about Cedric, Metcalf did not comment on our findings. He is not a well man, as I'm sure you know, and the meeting came to an abrupt halt when he became ill. All Metcalf would say was that he would talk more about it later. Although Cedric was unhappy that he didn't receive some commitment from Metcalf and tried to press for further discussion, he finally departed for Mainz.

"When Gilda and I left the manor to come here, Freda and Emma were attending Metcalf. But I have to tell you that Emma is not prepared to do anything to upset her father and has said she will accept his wishes. If you hope to have any chance with her, you must stay away until she summons you."

Clearly this was not the news Philip had hoped to hear, and he put his face in his hands. "I know Emma loves her father. But she loves me too."

Afraid to give Philip false hope, Justin didn't mention that Gilda and Freda had pressed his case or that at least Freda had made some connection with the old warrior. "I'm sorry, Philip. I just can't predict how things will turn out. We will return to the manor tomorrow morning. Until then you must stay here with us."

When Philip raised his face from his hands, his eyes had lost their sparkle. "You have both done a great deal to help me.

I promise I'll stay away from Lord Metcalf and Emma until I hear I'm welcome. But I won't stay here with you."

In spite of Philip's promise, Justin was suspicious. "Where will you go?" he asked.

"Leonardo and I will keep out of trouble and out of your way until tomorrow morning. Then we will return here."

Leonardo immediately objected. "I'm not leaving Justin and Gilda on their own," he replied.

As soon as the words had left Leonardo's mouth, he realized what he was saying and guessed that Philip's intention was to give the newlywed couple some privacy. A slight smile on his lips, Leonardo corrected himself, "I think Philip has the right idea. I'll go with him."

Neither Gilda nor Justin tried to dissuade them.

The two men were quick to take their leave, and Gilda and Justin were finally alone. The room was suddenly quiet, and Justin, who had followed the men to the door, turned to find that Gilda stood across the room from him. Justin saw that she avoided meeting his eyes.

"Philip has matured in the short time we've known him," Gilda said, glancing out the window to where the men had disappeared.

"Yes, I guess he has," Justin agreed, moving a few steps closer to her.

Still not looking directly at him, Gilda backed away. "Do you think there is a chance for him and Emma?"

"It doesn't look good at the moment," he said as he advanced a few more steps.

"No, it doesn't. But there is still a chance, don't you think? They are very much in love." This time she backed up slowly, as though to disguise her retreat.

"Gilda, I don't want to talk about Philip any longer. What I want to do is make love to my wife."

Gilda's eyes widened. "But it's still light outside, Justin," she replied, clearly believing this was a problem. Her move away from him was suddenly brought to an abrupt halt when her back thumped against the wall.

His next few steps brought him close enough to pin her against the wall with his body. "If the light bothers you, close your eyes," he whispered, then grinned when he saw her squeeze her eyes shut. His hands pushed away her head covering, and his fingers slid into her silky hair.

The feel of Justin's hands in her hair eased Gilda's hesitancy. She kept her eyes closed, content to passively let him kiss her, while she enjoyed the feel of his lips on her mouth and his hips pressing against her body. She relaxed even more as the pleasure of his nearness spread through her limbs.

As Gilda became aroused, sleepily enjoying his attention wasn't enough. Eager to see him, her eyes flew open. She pushed him just far enough away to be able to loosen his doublet and bare his chest so that she could run her hand through the dark hair she found there.

At her touch, Justin became impatient. "Help me here," he whispered.

"What?" she replied, still absorbed in watching the way his dark chest hair curled around her pale fingers.

"How do I get this off?" Justin asked. Unfamiliar with a nun's habit, he was pulling at the neck of her garment.

Gilda pushed him away again, and for a minute Justin thought she had remembered it was still light outside and wanted him to stop. As he was about to again suggest she close her eyes, he saw her performing some magic that caused her habit to fall away and pool around her feet. He had no trouble removing the light shift that remained, and she stood before him without a thread of clothing. The sight of her small, perfectly shaped body stopped him abruptly. He stared at her a long time, watching as her face turned a becoming shade of pink. When he regained his ability to move, he gathered her up in his arms and carried her to the bed in the next room.

Flat on her back on the narrow bed, Gilda watched as Justin quickly rid himself of his clothing. The sight of his aroused body startled her, and she wondered how they would ever fit together. But before she could be afraid, he covered her body with his own, being careful not to let her bear his full weight. He held her gently and loosely until she got used to the feel of him, then he caressed her, arousing them both.

Much later Gilda had her eyes closed again, and Justin saw that tears had wet her cheeks. "Did I hurt you very much?" Justin asked, wiping the moisture away with his fingers.

"Only at first. I can't believe how well we fit together, Justin. It was lovely."

"Yes, it was," he whispered, kissing her damp eyes. "Now you are truly my wife."

Gilda smiled. "We have to thank Philip for leaving us alone," she suggested.

"I suppose you're right," he answered, but he didn't want to think about Philip just yet. "It's well past the supper hour. Would you like me to find you something to eat?"

"Not just now. I like lying with you like this." She felt his arousal against her leg and nudged him a bit with her knee. "Does that mean we can do it again?" she asked.

Justin laughed. "It appears your appetite has grown to include more than food."

All through the evening and the night, Gilda and Justin continued to enjoy being close, free to do what they pleased. They made love, they fed each other what food they could find, and they slept in each other's arms. At first light, Justin watched

Gilda sleep and marveled at how wonderful it had been making her his wife. He grinned as he remembered how quickly she had overcome her shyness.

When Justin finally pulled away to get up, Gilda opened her eyes. "Where are you going?" she asked. "It's cold without you. Come back to bed."

Justin was ready to do just that, but he heard a noise from the outer room. "Someone is here," he said.

Expecting to find Leonardo or Philip, Justin pulled on his pants and opened the door. Instead he found a servant he recognized from the manor. The man seemed embarrassed at the sight of Justin's bare chest, and he rushed through his message.

"Pardon me, Lord Justin. Lady Emma wishes you and Sister Gilda to return to the manor at once. She says to bring Lord Philip with you."

"Philip isn't here, but we will come," Justin replied.

"I saw Philip and another man on the way. They are camped not far from here. I'll send them to you while you finish dressing," the servant said, flushing red at his own words. Then he rushed from the cottage before Justin had a chance to question him.

Gilda had heard everything and was already pulling on her habit when Justin returned to the bedroom. "Perhaps Lord Metcalf is dying," she said. "Do you think we were too harsh with him yesterday?"

"No, I don't. Metcalf may be ill, but he's been a tough warrior all his life. Hearing what we had to say, even if he didn't like it, isn't going to hasten his death. Emma said he's had these spells before, and even Chetwynd mentioned his tiring suddenly."

By the time they had finished dressing, Leonardo and Philip had arrived at the cottage. Gilda was prepared for some teasing remarks from the two men, but they were both sobered by the news that everyone had been summoned to the manor.

"What do you suppose it means that Emma wants me there?" Philip asked.

"I have no idea," Justin answered truthfully.

Unsure what to expect, the small party hurried to the manor house. At the door the same servant who had summoned them invited them to the dining hall. Much to the surprise of the visitors, Lord Metcalf sat at the head table with Sister Freda on one side and Lady Emma on the other.

"Don't stand there with your mouths hanging open," Metcalf said, his grin making it clear that he was enjoying their astonishment. "Come in, come in."

Justin was the first to recover. "I'm pleased to see you have regained your health, Lord Metcalf," he said.

"Thank you, Lord Justin. As you can see, rumors of my death have been greatly exaggerated," he replied with a chuckle.

Philip had hung back behind the others, uncertain of his welcome. He was still unsure when Metcalf caught sight of him and said, "Come up here, Philip. It is you I wish to speak with." From Metcalf's expression it was impossible to tell what his feelings for Philip might be.

Emma stood up, making it clear she was offering her seat to Philip. Her eyes swam with tears at the sight of him, but she managed a shy smile. The young man stared at her and wondered if this might be his last view of her. Unable to tear his eyes away from her face, he stumbled toward the seat she indicated.

"Sit!" Metcalf shouted in a commanding manner that forced Philip to turn from Emma and obey his order.

Staring at the lord of the manor who used to be his friend, Philip said, "I am sorry you have been ill, Lord Metcalf."

"Are you, indeed?" Metcalf answered. "I thought you might be pleased to have me out of the way."

Shocked, Philip replied, "Not at all, my lord."

Metcalf waved his hand to dismiss the subject. Servants had entered the hall and Metcalf was silent, waiting for everyone to be served a thick soup and fresh bread. Ignoring the others at the table, Gilda and Justin were tearing into the food set in front of them, but Philip hardly touched his spoon to the bowl. The young man was remembering that he and Metcalf had once been close, but it had been a while since he had been welcomed at the lord's table.

Metcalf must have decided it was time to put Philip out of his misery and finally said, "You have made it clear in the past that you wished to marry my daughter. I didn't take your suit seriously as I saw several problems with the match. I still see problems. However, I shouldn't have dismissed your suit without talking to you about it. Are you still serious about seeking to wed Emma?"

"Yes, sir." Philip pushed the words through a throat constricted with emotion.

"I wonder what kind of life you can offer her. Your brother is determined to marry Emma, and I understand he has already thrown you in prison once. I'm told that even now he has men looking for you, no doubt because he knows of your feelings for Emma."

Looking over to where Emma sat watching him, Philip seemed to have come to some conclusion. He straightened in his chair, his jaw hardened, and when he spoke it was in a clear, determined voice.

"I know it would not be safe for me to stay in Mainz, my lord. But if you approved our marriage, Emma and I could go to court. I have trained to be a soldier, and some of that training was at your hands, so you know I am able."

Philip took a quick breath, then rushed on before he could be interrupted. "I have only stayed in Mainz this long hoping for your approval to wed Emma. King Louis is always in need of soldiers to protect his empire from the Saracens in the south and the tribes in the east and north. As you well know, he never has enough armies. I love Emma, and I will do everything in my power to provide her a good and happy life."

The room went quiet as heads turned toward Metcalf. "Count Cedric is a threat to your union," the lord reminded Philip.

"My brother has much power in Mainz and is one of the king's officers. But I have done him no wrong, and he has no legitimate reason to pursue me. Lord Justin and Sister Gilda know I did not betray him with Lady Mariel. As you know, I have loved Emma long before Cedric knew of her existence. I swear to you that I will make her a much better husband than Cedric ever could."

Philip's voice had gained power as he spoke, and everyone seemed to be holding their breath as the young man held Metcalf's eyes. A long silence seemed to last forever before Metcalf replied.

"I still have friends at court," the lord of the manor said rather casually. "They could help you get started and make sure you are safe from your brother."

Prepared for rejection, Philip didn't at first grasp Metcalf's meaning. Then as he realized that Metcalf was offering to help him, he lost the power of speech.

There was a soft murmur of voices in the hall as the others realized what Metcalf was suggesting. The lord of the manor ignored it and continued. "You and Emma must be married right away to avoid clashing with your brother when he comes back seeking a commitment from me. After that, the two of you can leave immediately for Aachen to approach King Louis."

In an anguished voice Emma broke the quiet that followed his words, making it clear her father had not confided his plans to her. "I can't leave you now, Father. You are ill and need me," she said, clearly torn between the man she loved and her father.

"You have done your duty to me many times over, Emma," her father replied with a loving smile. "But just so that you don't worry, Sister Freda has agreed to stay with me for a while."

This announcement caused all eyes to seek Sister Freda, who sat inconspicuously beside Lord Metcalf until he mentioned her name. The only hint that she was aware of the curious stares was a slight pink tint that crept over her cheeks.

This final surprising announcement from Lord Metcalf set the room into action. When Emma rushed to Philip's side, he closed his eyes to shut out the rest of the world and embraced her. Gilda sprang from her seat and pushed herself into a place beside Freda.

Once settled beside her friend, Gilda leaned close and whispered, "Is this what you wish, Freda? I thought you'd be eager to return to the convent."

"Yes, Gilda, I wish to stay. There is much Metcalf and I have in common, and I enjoy his company."

"He's an ill-tempered man."

Freda laughed at Gilda's puzzled expression. "We share a lot of memories of how things used to be in the days of Charlemagne. Staying here and managing his manor as Emma has been doing will be a fulfilling task."

"But he is very ill," Gilda said. When Freda raised one eyebrow, Gilda's mouth fell open. She looked over at Metcalf, who was watching Philip and Emma's display of affection with a tolerant expression, then back at Freda. "Was his illness a ruse?" Gilda demanded to know.

"Keep your voice down, Gilda. Let's just say that like his death, his illness was exaggerated."

"You could have told me. I was worried that we were too harsh with him."

"You need not worry about that. Lord Metcalf was upset by how close he came to a terrible mistake by approving a match between Emma and Count Cedric, but he's not on his deathbed. He's still the honorable and courageous man I remembered."

Gilda, surprised by the softening she heard in her friend's voice, leaned toward Freda again. "I know you always admired Lord Metcalf. Do you have feelings for the man?" she whispered.

"We are too old for such things," Freda replied, but she didn't meet Gilda's eyes. "What of you and Justin? Did you manage to spend some time alone?" she asked to change the subject.

Instead of answering Gilda glanced over at her husband and smiled at the memory of the night they spent together. Justin must have felt her eyes on him, as he looked up from his conversation with Leonardo and returned her smile.

"Yes, I can see that you did," Freda said. "I'm glad things worked out for you and Justin. I know you'll be off on the last leg of your journey soon, and I'll miss traveling with you."

"Will you be safe here?" Gilda asked. "I think we must stay around until we see how Count Cedric will react to the news that Emma and Philip will be wed."

"There is no need. Metcalf spoke with the manor priest this morning. He has already sent Philip and Emma off to see him. After they are married, they will go into hiding until arrangements can be made for their journey to court and an interview with King Louis."

Turning around to look for the young couple, Gilda saw that they were nowhere in sight. "Lord Metcalf seems to have arranged everything, no doubt with help from you. I suspect you'll suit each other."

A servant appeared in the hall, drawing attention to himself by hurrying over to speak urgently to Lord Metcalf. After listening for a few minutes, Metcalf looked over to Freda. "A sentry has reported that Count Cedric is on his way."

CHAPTER FIFTEEN

Upon hearing the news that Count Cedric was on his way, Justin and Leonardo, as though reading each other's thoughts, both moved quickly toward Metcalf. "What's your plan?" Justin asked the lord of the manor.

Seated at the table, Metcalf looked up at the two tall men in a defensive manner. "I'm not about to conceal my decision. I'll tell the count that I gave permission to Philip to marry Emma. As long as Philip and Emma are safe, and I assume they have gone into hiding by now, there is no sense in trying to hide the fact."

"I admire your honesty, but the count is going to be extremely angry. I fear he may act rashly. As you know, he travels with some of his guards. Perhaps you should retire to your bed and pretend to be unwell. Someone else can give him the news," Justin suggested, figuring Metcalf hadn't minded using that ruse the previous day.

The old warrior scowled, clearly insulted by his suggestion. "There is no need for that. My steward has already alerted everyone in my service. If Cedric tries to seek reprisal for my action, he will find that I am not alone."

Indeed, as Metcalf was speaking several men were silently

entering the hall and settling at the tables. But the men were farm workers and servants, and Justin judged that although they might outnumber Cedric's guards, they were hardly trained for confrontation.

Before Justin could give his opinion, Metcalf continued. "Perhaps you and Sister Gilda should be on your way, Lord Justin. I know you have a mission to finish. There is no need for you to be involved further in this matter."

Listening to this exchange, Gilda was sure of how her husband would reply, and she smiled when she heard Justin's words.

"There is no hurry, Lord Metcalf. Gilda and I will finish our meal and say a last goodbye to Count Cedric."

Not fooled by the casual reply, Metcalf's face softened, and he smiled. "Bring Lord Justin and Sister Gilda more food," he instructed the servant nearest him.

When Count Cedric, a purposeful expression on his face, strode into the hall, he was obviously surprised to see a robust Metcalf seated at the high table. "Greetings, Lord Metcalf. I am pleased to see you are feeling better," the count commented.

"Good morning, Cedric," Metcalf replied. Bishop Gunthar wasn't far behind, and Metcalf stood up and nodded to him. "Make room for the count and bishop," he said to his chief steward, indicating a place at the head table.

Several guards crowded together at the door behind the bishop. "I'm afraid we have a full house this morning. Your men will have to wait outside," Metcalf added. "I will send out some refreshment."

Wrinkling his brow, Cedric looked around at the crowded tables. When he saw that even the space around the room was occupied, he nodded to a soldier who was apparently the leader of his men. As the guards withdrew, he asked, "Is this a special occasion for which your workers are gathered?"

"It is," Metcalf answered, without explaining further.

This brief answer seemed to make Cedric wary, and his eyes traveled about the hall again. Seated at a table just below Metcalf's, Justin and Gilda were busy eating. At the high table Sister Freda, seated beside Metcalf, kept her attention on Cedric, and he nodded to her. Finally, he asked, "Where is Lady Emma this morning?"

Ignoring his question, Metcalf waited until both Cedric and the bishop had taken their places. Then he addressed Cedric. "I have an apology to make to you, Count Cedric. As you know I wished to have my daughter married and settled before I passed from this world. In my hurry to accomplish this, I proposed a match with you, but at the time I did not realize you had recently wed."

Cedric's eyes narrowed. "It was a wise proposal, Lord Metcalf. Married to me, Emma will be a countess. You have already heard from Lord Justin that my marriage was a mistake and that I have requested an annulment that will soon be granted."

Metcalf nodded. "Yes, I have considered that. But in proposing the match between you and Emma I did not pay attention to my daughter's wishes. You will remember that you sent your stepbrother to me to be trained as a warrior. He spent a great deal of time with us, a fact which you approved at the time."

Cedric interrupted Metcalf before he could say more. "I suspect where you are headed. I am aware that Philip has his own wish to marry Emma. But the boy has nothing to offer, and I must tell you that he is not a trustworthy person. I suspect that he made advances to Lady Mariel when he acted as my surrogate."

Unable to ignore this unfair allegation, Gilda stunned everyone by speaking out in a voice loud enough to echo through the hall. "That is not true. Philip befriended Lady Mariel, but that is all that happened between them."

Cedric's red face gave evidence of the anger he felt at being interrupted by Gilda. Her words seemed to unleash his frustration, and he shouted at her. "You know not what you are talking about!"

Turning back to Lord Metcalf, Cedric struggled to control his rage and speak in a normal voice. "Sister Gilda has been interfering in this matter since she arrived at Mainz, my lord. I call her 'sister' as she dresses as a nun, but in fact she is a married woman," he said, clearly attempting to excuse the fact that he shouted at her. "I can't understand why the king chose her to represent him in this matter."

Before Metcalf could react to this outburst, Lord Justin stood up and spoke in a reasonable tone of voice that contrasted with that of the count. "May I speak, Lord Metcalf?"

"Yes, of course."

Determined to ignore the personal attack on Gilda as well as his desire to throttle the count, Justin called upon his experience as a diplomat to remain calm. "Gilda knows more about the marriage of the count and Lady Mariel than anyone. At the Convent of Saint Ives, she interviewed Lady Mariel and heard directly from her what passed between her and Philip. The only reason they were together was because Philip was a surrogate in the count's marriage to Lady Mariel. On the long journey from Bordeaux to Mainz, Philip befriended a frightened young woman. There is no evidence to support Count Cedric's accusation that Philip made advances toward Mariel and much evidence that he was being kind."

Cedric shook his head violently. "When Mariel arrived at Mainz, she claimed to be married to Philip. I think that claim speaks for itself." Then, before Justin or Gilda could speak again, he turned back to Metcalf. "In any case, I think you know I would be a better husband than Philip and that Emma would have a more secure life as my countess, Lord Metcalf."

Growing annoyed by the personal attacks on Philip and Gilda, Metcalf waved his hand in the air as though to banish further words on the subject. "For a time, I did believe that. But Philip is a well-trained soldier and has the ability to make a name for himself by serving the king."

"As a soldier! What kind of life is that?" Cedric burst out, then remembered who he was speaking to and attempted to revise his statement. "What I mean is, he is very young and just starting out."

No longer making an effort to hide his impatience, Metcalf said, "My daughter wishes to marry Philip and with my blessing has no doubt already accomplished that deed."

Leaping to his feet at this news and upsetting his seat in the process, the count glowered at his host. "I will find them, and believe me, Lady Emma will be a widow before the sun sets."

"Sit down!" Metcalf roared at Cedric so loudly that the manor farmers and servants rose to their feet.

"Guards!" Cedric shouted, but his words were lost in the growing chatter in the hall.

"The door is bolted, Count Cedric. I repeat, sit down!" Metcalf demanded, shouting loud enough to be heard over the noise in the hall.

As the room quieted, Justin and Leonardo, surprised by Metcalf's vigor, looked at each other with raised eyebrows. "He seems to have a plan," Leonardo whispered.

"You can't keep me here," Cedric replied, refusing to sit.

"Not forever, but for a while," Metcalf answered smugly.

The force with which Metcalf had spoken to the count showed that he was prepared for trouble. Justin suspected he had ordered the doors locked to gain as much time as possible for Philip and Emma. Since neither Metcalf nor Cedric seemed in the mood to settle things peaceably, Justin feared what would happen when the door was unbolted.

Glancing at the bishop and remembering how he had attempted to keep Cedric calm the day before, Justin wondered if perhaps there was a way to settle the matter without either party resorting to violence. Freda's nephew, Brother Arnulf, had told Justin that the bishop was interested in having the rich farmland of Metcalf's manor come under the control of Mainz, where he and Cedric shared power and ruled pretty much as they wished. While Cedric and Metcalf were still shouting and accusing each other of bad faith, Justin moved to where he could speak to Bishop Gunthar.

Leaning close to his ear in order to be heard, Justin said, "A rift between Lord Metcalf and the count may persuade Metcalf to seek alliance with other protectors. I appeal to you as religious leader of Mainz to persuade Cedric that it is best for all parties to make peace with his brother Philip and accept his marriage to Lady Emma."

Gunthar was watching Cedric and Metcalf as they continued their argument. "If I persuade Cedric to accept the marriage of his stepbrother and Lady Emma, how can I be sure Metcalf will still look to Mainz for an alliance? Metcalf hardly seems a reasonable man, and Philip has no cause to love his brother."

Justin knew a lot depended on his ability to win Gunthar over. "Philip and Emma are headed for court while Sister Freda is staying on to help Lord Metcalf manage his estate. She is a peace-loving woman, and I know she will use her influence to encourage a settlement between Metcalf and Cedric. They are close neighbors, and violence between them will hurt both parties. Mainz is Philip's home, and his marriage will forge closer ties between Mainz and Metcalf's manor. Sister Freda will see that this happens. It would be best if you urged Cedric to celebrate the marriage."

Gunthar looked at Sister Freda with distaste, but Justin's reasoning, as well as the number of men gathered to support Metcalf, must have made an impression as he nodded curtly, then rose to his feet. The bishop pounded his heavy staff on the floor to call for quiet. No one paid him any attention, and the chatter in the hall continued until Justin shouted out, "The bishop has something to say! Let him be heard."

When it was suddenly quiet and all eyes had turned to him, the bishop seemed taken aback. Justin nodded to encourage Gunthar, who frowned, then began to speak. "Lord Metcalf has made his decision and tells us that Lady Emma and Philip are already married. Philip is a Lord of Mainz and by his marriage forges closer ties between Mainz and this manor. Although Count Cedric is disappointed for himself, I'm sure he will want to celebrate the marriage of his brother."

As Gunthar parroted his words, Justin kept a serious face. He watched Cedric and hoped the count, much as he might dislike the idea, would be smart enough to understand why it would be best to accept the marriage. His goal had always been to acquire access to the manor's rich farmland, and marriage had been a means to reach this goal. But the count didn't seem willing to respond to the bishop's urging.

The hall was quiet as everyone anticipated Cedric's next outburst. Gilda knew the result Justin hoped for, and she wanted to urge Cedric to accept his brother's marriage. But since he resented her part in the proceedings, she knew her appeal would only make things worse. Instead she addressed Lord Metcalf, the man she judged to be the most likely to be moved.

"My lord, as a father you have made the decision you think best for Lady Emma, but you had previously made promises to Count Cedric."

Metcalf scowled at her. "I have apologized for my part in those negotiations."

"Yes, you have. As a sign of your good faith, you could now promise to cooperate with the count and the Bishop of Mainz in the future. As close neighbors it will benefit you both to live in harmony."

There was another silence in the hall as Metcalf seemed to consider Gilda's proposal. Clearly, he had been ready for a battle and perhaps even looked forward to it. Gilda held her breath, hoping the old warrior would forego his urge for one last battle. As she watched, she saw something she was sure no one else would notice. Sister Freda give Metcalf's elbow a discreet nudge.

When Metcalf spoke, his words were strong, and if he had any regrets about saying them, they were well under control. "I will apologize to you once again, Count Cedric. I admit I made a mistake." The words must have been difficult to say, as he lifted his goblet and took a long drink. "Now I propose we drink to stronger ties between my manor and Mainz."

Without saying a word, Count Cedric raised his goblet. Neither Metcalf nor Cedric was overjoyed by the compromise, and the mood in the hall was more an easing of tension than a celebration. Still, confrontation had been avoided.

It wasn't long before Count Cedric and Bishop Gunthar said polite, if stilted, farewells. Once they had left the hall, the mood became joyous and several toasts were proposed to the absent newlywed couple. When the peasants left to return to their fields, Metcalf finally spoke directly to Justin and Gilda.

"Charlemagne granted this manor to me. My men and I could have defended it," he said. "But I have to say I admired the way you handled the situation, Lord Justin. The way you managed Bishop Gunthar was truly inspiring."

"Thank you, Lord Metcalf. But we prefer to think of ourselves as nudging parties toward a compromise," Justin replied.

"You do it well and seem to have found the perfect helpmate," Metcalf said, glancing toward Gilda and thus acknowledging her contribution. "Sister Freda tells me that you are wed."

Gilda came to stand close to Justin. Hidden by the folds of her skirt, he took her hand. "Our marriage is still new to us," Justin explained.

"Is that why Gilda continues to wear her habit? Perhaps you'd like to have some of Lady Emma's clothes. I insisted she have some new garments made for her wedding to the count." He paused. "Every time I think of the mistake I was so close to making, I have to shudder. Emma rejected those gowns, and I'm sure she left them here."

Sister Freda spoke up. "I can show you the gowns, and you can make up your mind if you wish to take any of them for your journey to Reims."

Looking down at Gilda, Justin remembered how her habit had mystified him the day before, and then Gilda had undone some fastening and it pooled around her feet. She must have known what he was thinking about, as her face turned the becoming shade of pink that he liked so much. "I rather like the habit," he whispered softly so that only Gilda could hear.

She smiled at him. "But it might be interesting to try something different," she whispered back.

Thinking of the many different things he wished to try with Gilda, Justin's voice was hoarse with emotion when he spoke to Freda. "I'd like to look at the gowns with Gilda." Realizing this was an unusual request, he added, "I wish to help her decide if they are suitable for her introduction at court."

There was friendly laughter in the hall, and Justin suspected that at least some of it was directed at the two of them as they followed Freda to Emma's room.

Once the door was closed behind them, Freda turned to the couple. "I wished to say a few words to you in private before you leave for Reims. When the king chose to pair you for the assignment of investigating Count Cedric's request for an annulment, I'm sure he had no idea how well you would work together. You complemented each other perfectly as you defused the situation out there. I imagine you'll go on to serve the king and do great things together."

Tears flowed down Gilda's cheeks as she listened to her friend's words. "I'm going to miss you so much, Freda," she whispered.

Freda seemed a little startled at Gilda's display of emotion and blinked her eyes several times as she struggled to hold back her own tears. Unable to speak, she patted Gilda's shoulder, then turned and rushed from the room.

As she wiped her tears, Gilda asked, "Do you think she'll be all right here?"

"I do. Sister Freda is a strong woman who knows her own mind, not unlike you, Sister Gilda. Will you miss being a nun?" he asked, a little afraid to hear her answer.

"I'll miss the sisters and Abbess Ermguerrd, but I have discovered that life with you is what I desire, Justin. There is so much for us to do together. I think we have a responsibility to make sure that Philip and Emma are safe. Perhaps I can ask Chetwynd to help Philip form his own army. We should also keep an eye on Freda and Metcalf to see that they hold their own with Count Cedric. And maybe the king will give us more assignments."

Smiling from ear to ear, Justin listened to his wife talk excitedly about their future. "Don't forget having babies so that you'll have children of your own to teach."

"Oh, yes, we can't forget that."

"Since Emma's discarded gowns await your attention, perhaps you'd like to remove your habit?"

They could hear the joyful sounds of celebration from the great hall. "Is the door bolted?" Gilda asked.

Justin moved quickly to push the bolt in place, then he turned back to watch Gilda's habit once again pool around her feet. "I love the way that happens. In the future you can wear the fanciest gowns in the empire, but I'll always have fond memories of your plain black habit."

Gilda rushed into his arms. "Perhaps we could start right away on making those babies," she suggested.

The only bed in the room was piled high with the gowns Emma had left behind. Keeping one arm around Gilda, he leaned down and swept them onto the floor. "You have the best ideas."

ABOUT THE AUTHOR

Ida Curtis was born in 1935 in New Haven, Connecticut. She grew up and went to school in Newington, Connecticut, where at age eighteen she contracted polio. After two years of rehabilitation, she spent two years at St. Joseph's College in West Hartford before marrying her husband, Jared. Following his academic career, they lived in various places, including four years at Indiana University, where Ida finished her BA degree in history. In 2002, after thirty years in Vancouver, British Columbia, they returned to the US to live in Seattle, Washington. Ida has been writing fiction and memoir since she retired in 1996. A member of Pacific Northwest Writers Association, she won first prize for historical fiction at PNWA's annual convention in 2009. Her novel, *Song of Isabel*, grew out of that experience; *The Nun's Betrothal* was developed from characters appearing in *Song of Isabel*. She published *My Polio Memoir: 1953–2016* with Lulu.com in 2016.

Author photo © Emily R. Ashmore

SELECTED TITLES FROM SHE WRITES PRESS

She Writes Press is an independent publishing company founded to serve women writers everywhere. Visit us at www.shewritespress.com.

Song of Isabel by Ida Curtis. $16.95, 978-1631523717. In ninth-century France, a handsome officer in the King's army rescues preteen Isabel from an assault by a passing warrior. When the officer returns to her father's estate several years later, sparks fly and emotions tangle.

Dark Lady by Charlene Ball. $16.95, 978-1-63152-228-4. Emilia Bassano Lanyer—poor, beautiful, and intelligent, born to a family of Court musicians and secret Jews, lover to Shakespeare and mistress to an older nobleman—survives to become a published poet in an era when most women's lives are rigidly circumscribed.

After Midnight by Diane Shute-Sepahpour. $16.95, 978-1-63152-913-9. When horse breeder Alix is forced to temporarily swap places with her estranged twin sister—the wife of an English lord—her forgotten past begins to resurface.

Elmina's Fire by Linda Carleton. $16.95, 978-1-63152-190-4. A story of conflict over such issues as reincarnation and the nature of good and evil that are as relevant today as they were eight centuries ago, Elmina's Fire offers a riveting window into a soul struggling for survival amid the conflict between the Cathars and the Catholic Church.

Conjuring Casanova by Melissa Rea. $16.95, 978-1-63152-056-3. Headstrong ER physician Elizabeth Hillman is a career woman who has sworn off men and believes the idea of love in the twenty-first century is a fairy-tale—but when Giacomo Casanova steps into her life on a rooftop in Italy, her reality and concept of love are forever changed.

Faint Promise of Rain by Anjali Mitter Duva. $16.95, 978-1-938314-97-1. Adhira, a young girl born to a family of Hindu temple dancers, is raised to be dutiful—but ultimately, as the world around her changes, it is her own bold choice that will determine the fate of her family and of their tradition.

CPSIA information can be obtained
at www.ICGtesting.com
Printed in the USA
JSHW020336010720
6433JS00003B/3